# Other Titles by Crystal-Rain Love from ImaJinn books

## Blood Revelation Series

### Blood Curse
*Book One*

### Slayer's Prey
*Book Two*

# Blood Curse

The *Blood Revelation* Series
Book One

by

## Crystal-Rain Love

IMAJINN

ImaJinn Books

This is a work of fiction. Names, characters, places and incidents are either the products of the author's imagination or are used fictitiously. Any resemblance to actual persons (living or dead), events or locations is entirely coincidental.

IMAJINN

ImaJinn Books
PO BOX 300921
Memphis, TN 38130
Print ISBN: 978-1-933417-05-9

ImaJinn Books is an Imprint of BelleBooks, Inc.

ImaJinn Books was founded by Linda Kichline.

We at ImaJinn Books enjoy hearing from readers. Visit our websites
ImaJinnBooks.com
BelleBooks.com
BellBridgeBooks.com

10 9 8 7 6 5 4 3 2 1

Cover design: Deborah Smith
Interior design: Hank Smith
Photo/Art credits:
Man© Viorel Sima | Dreamstime.com
Background © Subbotina | Dreamstime.com

:Lcbv:01:

# Dedication

Dedicated to Miriam Sargent, who "forced" me to quit daydreaming about writing books and actually do it.

# Prologue

HE CAME TO HER at night, when the moon was high and the rest of the world was at sleep. This was when he prowled, as all bad things do. She sensed the darkness immediately, yet she couldn't restrain the carnal hunger surging through her body as he stepped through her balcony doors, entering her bedroom without invitation.

Eyes closed in sleep, she couldn't see him but she felt him, every part of him. The desire that burned deep within him, the taint of darkness lurking in his soul, the pain and longing that cried out to her, obliterating her instinct to run. She could feel his strength, the intoxicating allure of his aura, the raw masculinity that seemed to spill from his pores.

She knew she wanted him without even a glimpse of his physical appearance, even though he wasn't an ordinary man. He was . . . immortal? The word pulsated through her mind as she snapped open her eyes. Immortal? Not possible. She moved her gaze from the ceiling down toward the foot of her bed. There he stood, illuminated by the moonlight like some dark angel. But, he was no angel. There was a coldness about him, a dark beast that lurked inside. She stopped breathing as her body ignited with a desperate craving, an aching need unlike anything she had ever experienced.

He was over six feet of dark-haired, brooding perfection. Dark, stormy eyes stared down at her from within a tanned, chiseled face complete with the most enticing mouth she had ever seen. His bottom lip alone, she could suck between her teeth for days. She ran her tongue over her own lips just thinking about it.

He took a step toward her and her gaze roamed to his broad shoulders. Although sheathed in a loose white silk dress shirt and black pants, she knew every inch of his body was rock hard. Especially the part that bulged beneath the fabric of his pants, she noted, as her gaze fell there.

"Rialto," she breathed as a suffocating heat took over her body, surprising her with the knowledge of his name. She knew the man, or beast, behind it. She remembered the heat of his lips pressed against her stomach, the soft whisper of his breath against her collarbone. She had cried out that name while staring into those tempestuous eyes, emblazoned with passion. She didn't know when, but she knew she had . . . many, many times before. And she would again. Tonight.

"You belong to me," he said, standing over her, his voice a sensual melody of deep, rich tones. "You cannot run from the craving."

And, oh, did she crave. The desire to possess and be possessed gnawed through her like a ravenous beast, intent only on feeding its hunger. She didn't recall moving, but she found herself against him, her legs wrapped around his waist. Then she was lowered back to the bed, the fever inside her body growing as he branded her skin with hot kisses and deftly ripped away her chemise and panties. Fully exposed to him, she felt no shame. The midnight stranger washed away her inhibitions as he laved her body with his tongue.

Once he'd tasted her from toe to neck, he rose to his knees and tore his shirt from his body, baring the hard, sculpted torso she had known was hiding beneath the silk. Impatient and dying to feel him inside, she quickly helped him dispose of the remainder of his clothing before pushing him onto his back.

"No, we can't!" The storm clouds in his eyes parted, replaced with a lightning bolt of fear.

"The hell we can't." She took the opportunity to taste that juicy lip, biting down just hard enough to scratch the skin. A drop of blood touched her tongue and sent an electric shock jolting through her body, causing her to gasp. Her body quaked in response to the jolt of hunger that started furrowing low in her belly.

"No," Rialto pleaded as he looked into her eyes. "We must stop." He pushed up to his elbows and started to scoot backward toward the other side of the bed.

"More," she growled, frightening herself with the guttural sound of her own voice as she impaled herself onto Rialto's erection, stopping him from fleeing. She rocked back and forth on him with a speed she had never known she possessed. The hunger inside her intensified; the world around her ceased to exist as she concentrated only on the friction between her and her midnight lover, the pleasure pulsating through her body, but there was something else she needed to truly go over the edge. She needed the sweet taste of his blood.

"No," he protested, his own voice growing stronger and deeper. Looking down into his eyes, now burning with the same desire she felt, she knew he wanted her as badly as she wanted him. Then her gaze fell to the trickle of blood slipping from his bottom lip.

Without thinking, she sucked at his lip, drinking in the blood, feeling it flow through her body, intensifying her every emotion. She couldn't pull back no matter how much Rialto pleaded. The blood was her drug. She would kill for it.

She heard a deep growl and then she was against the wall. Her legs were wrapped around Rialto's waist and he was thrusting inside her with a force that should have hurt but instead sent her into one orgasm after another, until she experienced a level of ecstasy that left her mind empty. She could only focus on the sensations rolling through her body, knowing the blood had heightened her sensitivity, increasing her pleasure.

She wanted him to feel what she felt, to share the gift he was giving her. As she rode out another orgasm she screamed his name and used her nails to cut through the skin at the base of her own throat, offering the dark creature of the night her own blood as thanks for giving her the ultimate in pleasure.

Rialto froze mid-thrust. His eyes began to glow with his dark need, his nostrils flaring as the smell of her blood reached him. "I'm . . . so . . . sorry." He lowered his head to lick the red droplets from her fresh scratches. Another orgasmic shock hit her body as his tongue licked over the open skin, filling her with a warmth that turned bitter cold as he threw his head back and roared like an animal, giving her a clear shot of the two gleaming white fangs descending from his upper gum.

Impossible. Within the second it took before he tore into her jugular, she blinked, trying to dispel the image, but it was too late. She had become the monster's prey. As her veins flowed with the strong sexual desire that came with sharing blood, she realized this had to be a dream. It was impossible for her to desire this creature. He was a vampire.

She was a vampire hunter.

RIALTO WOKE WITH a start, sitting straight up in the cramped confines of the small cave he had hidden in the night before after failing to beat the sunrise. The dream followed him no matter where he went. It was getting stronger. *She* was getting stronger, whoever *she* was, this woman who'd crept into his dreams over the past two decades, enticing him with her golden skin, long, dark hair and crystal green eyes. She mesmerized him, and how wonderful was that. A vampire hunter!

He rose to his feet, wiping the sweat from his face as he inched his way down the cave's long, narrow tunnel. His inner clock told him the sun had fallen completely. It was safe for him to find her.

As he stepped out of the cave and breathed in the twilight air, he wondered at his own stupidity. He couldn't control anything in the dreams. They were never exactly the same but all very similar. In the more recent ones, he came to her at night while she slept and found her in an aroused state. He was always in her head. He saw himself but he couldn't feel anything, only what she felt. And she felt him. She *knew* him. Right down to his name and what he was. She knew he was immortal before she even opened her eyes, before her eyes adjusted to the moonlight spilling through her balcony doors and allowed her to see him clearly. Sometimes they made sweet love for hours before the bloodlust set in. Other times they pounded into each other like rutting animals, pleasuring themselves with the pain. He tried to escape before the hunger for her blood overtook him, but she managed to overpower him every time. She was too strong, she, a mere mortal. What did it mean?

He never finished the dream, always startling himself awake when he plunged his incisors into her neck, so he didn't know if he killed her or pulled back while she still had enough blood to survive. He didn't know why the thought of killing her devastated him so. The dreams were going to drive him insane if he didn't find her and figure out why she had invaded his mind every night for the past several years.

He stood on the cliff close to where he'd hid his rental, gazing over the state of Maryland. He could feel her more strongly here. It wouldn't be much longer now.

He should have his head examined for going after a vampire hunter who could overpower him so easily in his dreams, but he'd received a direct order from the Dream Teller to find the woman. He couldn't refuse. He was going to find this so-called huntress and discover her secrets.

He was going to finally discover how she knew who he was and how she managed to engulf him with raging lust when he didn't even know her damn name.

# Chapter One

MAKING HER WAY past a group of tourists who had joined together along Cathedral Street, Aria pretended not to notice the elderly woman who waved her hand in her direction, undoubtedly about to ask how to get to Edgar Allan Poe's grave site or one of the many shops which dotted the road along the Inner Harbor.

She didn't really mind the tourists; she herself had been one when she first came to Baltimore. She'd give anything to go back to the days when the artistic little shops, delightful smells, and eccentric characters of Inner Harbor, Little Italy, and the assorted other neighborhoods of the "Charm City" mesmerized her with their beauty. Baltimore had been her haven back then.

She thought she'd escaped all the ugliness of her childhood when she and her mother uprooted from Indiana and flew out to Baltimore, taking up residence in a small downtown apartment. She still lived in that apartment, but her mother would sleep forever in her silk-lined casket beneath the earth. Because of that, she ignored the tourists as she made her way toward the Enoch Pratt Free Library. She didn't want to remember how, like them, she had once been too mesmerized by the city's charm to see the danger lurking in its shadows.

"Aria, I have some more books that might help you with your research!" Curtis, the carrot-topped librarian's aide, called out to her as she stepped through the front doors. Winding her way back to the table in the far corner of the room, she aimed a polite smile his way as he rushed to check out books for a woman standing at the counter. She barely managed to remove her black leather jacket and rest her bottom in the chair before Curtis appeared at her side with a stack of books.

"I've got it now," he said, beaming while he deposited the books on the table in front of her. He had been trying for months to figure out why she was researching vampire lore so heavily.

"Shoot."

"Well, the other day there was a drop of paint on your jeans. You're an artist and you're doing a vampire-themed collection." He rocked restlessly from foot to foot with his arms crossed over his chest, the light of excitement and admiration shining in his pale green eyes.

"Very observant." Aria nodded her head in approval. "But not entirely correct."

"So you are an artist though, right?" He pulled out the chair next to her and sat, planting his elbows on the table so his hands could cradle his chin. Aria almost smiled at the way he watched her in fascination. He obviously had a crush on her, and that dampened her spirits immediately. It wasn't that he wasn't even remotely attractive or that he wasn't at all her type. What disappointed her was the knowledge that once the summer rolled in and its sun darkened her skin, he would no longer want her.

"I'm an artist, yes." She winced at her harsh tone, feeling like a jerk when she saw the hurt flutter through his eyes. She tried to smile sweetly to offset the bitterness that had erupted within her. "But that isn't why I'm researching vampires."

The light slowly left his eyes as they lowered to a book he had taken from the stack. He was holding onto it almost as if he didn't want to part with it.

"What's that?" Aria asked.

A soft redness diffused his cheeks as he glanced up, still holding onto the book. For a second, Aria thought his hands were shaking. "I, um, came across this and thought it was something that might interest you but . . ."

"But what?" Her curiosity grew at his discomfort. Without a word, he slid the book toward her.

Aria looked at the book with unveiled interest. She could tell by the binding and the smell of aged leather that it was incredibly old. As worn as it appeared, the book still retained a noble beauty. There was no title.

She opened it gently to find handwritten pages alternating between an elegant cursive script and printed entries which weren't as neatly made, some in English and some in another language. "This is a diary."

Curtis grinned sheepishly. "It was my great grandfather's. He thought of himself as a great vampire hunter." He circled his index finger around his temple. "Crazy old fool was what he was, but he researched vampires extensively too. I thought you'd like to read his research." His eyes narrowed thoughtfully as he sat back in the chair. "You're not trying to be a vampire hunter yourself, are you? You don't really believe in them?"

"No, of course not," Aria answered a little too quickly. She realized Curtis had picked up on it as his eyes narrowed suspiciously this time. Oh, why not lie? He'd never quit trying to figure out what she was up to if she didn't tell him something, and the truth wasn't an option. Aria purposely lowered her voice to give the illusion she was sharing a very private secret. "Can I trust you, Curtis?"

His head bobbed up and down eagerly.

"All right. My real name is Aria Michaels but I write under a pen name."

"So you're a writer."

"Yes."

"Two weeks ago I asked if you were a writer, and you said you weren't."

"I lied." Aria smiled sweetly and bit back her annoyance. She was about to have some fun. "I write erotica. When you do that for a living, you have to be careful who you tell. There are so many men out there who get all excited over the things I write they try to find me. I have to be very careful. You understand, don't you, Curtis?"

He nodded, and Aria fought the urge to laugh as his fingers flexed awkwardly and little beads of sweat popped out on his forehead. He looked more anxious than a virgin in a strip club. "So you're writing eh-erotic stories about vampires."

"Possibly. That's why I'm doing all this research."

"Oh." He quickly scooted out of his seat and turned in the direction of the checkout counter where someone was waiting. "I hope my great-grandfather's journal gives you some ideas." His face reddened as if just realizing the implication of what he'd said and he nearly ran into the next table.

"Definitely a virgin," Aria said to herself and laughed softly. It was strangely amusing whenever she came across the rare twenty-something male who had yet to get laid.

She took inventory of the stack of books in front of her, but her interest was still captured by the diary. So Curtis's great grand-pops had wanted to be a vampire hunter, eh? It couldn't hurt to learn from the old man, whom she figured wasn't really crazy at all. Or maybe he was, but if so, she was right there with him. For three months she had been obsessed with learning everything she could about vampires, training herself for the battle yet to come. For three months she had seen her mother's lifeless face over and over again in her mind. She couldn't forget the image of those open, glossed-over eyes staring at the ceiling, her pale white body lying on the cold metal slab in the morgue.

Those two perfect round holes in her neck.

Mary Ayers had been killed by a vampire, her body sucked completely dry of blood. The police could convince themselves there was some other explanation yet to be found, but Aria knew what she'd seen. There had been fang marks on her mother's neck, and she was going to catch the killer. She was going to learn everything there was to know about his kind, and when the time was right, she would hunt down the vampire who'd killed her mother and left her body sprawled across the lawn at Druid Hill Park. Then she would send the monster right back to hell where he belonged.

She just didn't know how she was going to do it yet, so she continued to research. She read encyclopedias, magazine articles, and books. It didn't bother her that most of her research was comprised of fictional material. Aria had always believed there was some truth to fiction.

She found that all writers of vampire lore believed in very similar ideas. Vampires did have weaknesses. Fire, sunlight, holy water, and bleeding-out seemed to be the most widely believed causes of death. Some authors also favored crosses and garlic. It was highly debatable whether or not a vampire could morph into a bat or another type of animal, and while some believed they could fly, others just believed they could jump incredibly high and far, giving the illusion of flight.

But of all she read, one fact remained consistent: They were incredibly pale, gaunt, fanged creatures with an insatiable thirst for human blood, and they possibly possessed the ability to read minds. It would be hard to bring one down, but she was sure it could be done.

Aria read the pages of the journal Curtis had given her, discovering a great deal about his great-grandfather. According to the diary, a vampire by the name of Eron had crept into Alfred Dunn's bedroom at night and forewarned him he was going to execute his son for his sins. The following morning, Alfred's twenty-year-old son Patrick was found dead in an alley. That was when Alfred Dunn became a vampire hunter. He searched all of Ireland for the vampire named Eron, but he couldn't find him. He found others, but he didn't kill them. He wanted Eron.

He studied, researched and hunted night and day. The search led him to America, and eventually Maryland.

Aria found the diary portions harder to understand once Alfred reached Baltimore in 1969. His beautiful script had turned into rash scribbles, his once elegant words and phrasing turned into an erratic scrawl, as though his mind were racing faster than he could find words to describe his thoughts and observations.

He made several notes about vampires, listing their known hangouts, names of vampires he'd interviewed or heard of, dates of sightings. Lists of names were long and scattered throughout the pages, not in any logical order. Aria scanned a page of them.

Addison, Bethany, Gregario, Jonathan Deville, Olden, Katerina, Palo, Lionel, Demarcus, Niles, Robert Savant, Seta, Carson, Rialto . . .

Rialto.

Aria halted at the name as images plowed into her. She and a large, golden-skinned man with dark, wavy hair cascading down to his shoulder blades wrapped around each other amid a tangle of white cotton sheets. Her sheets, from her very own bed in her downtown apartment. The window to the balcony was open, and she could feel the wind blowing through it, cooling the droplets of sweat clinging to her naked body as the man moved in and out of her. She could smell nighttime air, fresh linen, and the man's spicy scent. Their sweat fused together and produced a scent of its own, coconut and spicy earth. It was the most delicious scent she had ever breathed in. And the pleasure she felt as he slid in and out of her was more intense and gratifying than anything she had ever experienced. She could barely contain herself as he continued the sweet torture, changing his rhythm from fast to slow, teasing her over and over again, prolonging her ecstasy until she screamed out his name.

Rialto.

Aria wiped away the sheen of sweat which had spread across her forehead and willed her heart to quit racing. "And I thought Curtis needed to get laid," she murmured to herself, surprised by the intensity of her daydream. She could still smell the man's lingering scent, and she was wet from the desire surging through her.

She'd been having dreams of the same man for months, though she struggled to remember everything that happened in them. All she could remember was making love to him. Sometimes it was slow and sweet, sometimes fast and wild . . . but she couldn't shake the nagging feeling that there was something vital she was forgetting.

A sick thought crept into her mind, and she stared at the name in horror. If it was written in Alfred Dunn's journal, it was because the name belonged to a vampire. But surely she wasn't dreaming about having sex with *that* Rialto. The man in her dreams was too dark and muscular to be a vampire, and never, not even in a dream, could she defile her mother's memory by sleeping with the same kind of monster that killed her.

*PAINT SPLATTERS across canvas. Red. Black. Gray mixed with blue. A little girl with dark, flowing hair and pale golden skin stands in the middle of a circle of children, crying as they taunt her. Zebra girl. Half-breed. The words pelt her like stones.*

*The girl now kisses a blond, tanned man, both of them young, barely seventeen. She believes his vows of love and surrenders her body to him willingly. Pink and yellow paint on canvas, the strokes light and airy.*

*Crimson slashes splatter across the pink, and the young man's face now appears red and angry as he hurls the same words from her childhood at her, striking at her with the back of his hand. Her skin has darkened with the summer sun, beautiful and exotic. Mocha cream.*

*Another slosh of red paint. A cross burns in a yard. The young woman cries in front of it. Her emerald eyes shine through her tears. Beyond the burning cross, a body is removed from a small blue house. A white sheet covers its face, but a dark brown hand hangs off the*

*side of the stretcher. Her father's hand. Black paint on canvas. The brush strokes are hard
and angry.*

*Baltimore. The brush strokes soften, but still only the dark colors adorn the canvas.
Black, gray, the darkest of blues and purples. A pale blond woman lies on a metal slab,
her blank eyes staring at the ceiling. Two holes lie in her neck. The vampire hunter stares
at them, balling her fists in anger, vowing to find the one who did this to her mother.*

*Red paint splatters across the canvas. The vampire hunter sits in a library, her head
bowed over a leather book, a diary of sorts. She reads his name and she remembers his
touch . . .*

*The world turns dark and cold, blue twilight creeps through the branches hanging
overhead as he finds himself standing in the silvery forest he's come to know as the dream
realm. The blind witch is there before him. "Protect her," she says to him, "for you will die
without her and so will this world."*

Rialto jolted awake, his heart pounding furiously. She was close. He
knew this now more than ever. She was right here in Baltimore, most likely
still sitting at the library reading that journal.

He crossed the hotel room and entered the bathroom, stepping into
the shower to clean away the sweat drenching his body. Even with the water
streaming over his face, he could still smell her sweet scent. Coconut. Sweet
and tropical. Perfection.

Snap out of it, he cautioned himself. She was trying to avenge a loved
one's death by becoming a vampire hunter, going by the so-called evidence
she'd found in the morgue and information written in a diary. She believed
vampires to be cruel killers, yet she made love to him in her dreams. The
dichotomy didn't matter. She could prove to be very dangerous.

And she had a journal with information about him and possibly more
of his kind. It simply could not be allowed. Vampires survived by remaining
beneath the radar, never allowing their pictures to be taken, changing their
names each decade or moving often. They never allowed documentation of
their existence. Rialto had to know what was in the journal and how the
woman had come to possess it.

He turned off the water and stepped out of the stall. A vampire did not
kill the woman's mother, but she would get herself killed trying to find a
murdering vampire who didn't even exist. And according to the old witch in
his dream, he couldn't allow that to happen.

Although common sense told him to stay far away from this vengeful
woman, he feared the old witch's predictions far more than he feared the
huntress. The witch had come to him with warnings before, and he'd found
that not listening to her caused great suffering.

With a cold shiver, one last remnant from his dream, crawling up his
spine, he quickly dressed in black and left his hotel room to find the
woman.

# Chapter Two

ARIA JUMPED AS a hand landed on her shoulder. She whirled around and grabbed the owner's wrist by reflex, preparing to perform a move she'd learned in a women's defense class.

"Oh! I'm sorry!" she blurted when she realized she had grabbed hold of Curtis, startling him in the process.

"Um, I have to lock up now, Aria. The announcement was made over the intercom a little while ago, and the computer systems have all been shut down. I can save these books for you behind the counter if you'd like. You can check them out tomorrow."

Aria turned her head and noticed the time on the large clock hanging from the wall in front of her. She had been so wrapped up in Alfred Dunn's journal she hadn't heard the announcement about the library closing, much less noticed it emptying out. It appeared she and Curtis were the only two people remaining in the building. "Oh, that's okay," she said finally, realizing Curtis was staring down at her, an odd expression on his face. She closed the journal she had been immersed in, but couldn't quite hand it over. She found herself holding it protectively to her chest. "Actually, would you mind if I kept this for a while? There's a lot of useful information in here, and I've really just begun reading it."

"Oh, uh, well . . ."

"Please." She gave him her best persuasive smile.

Curtis's forehead wrinkled as he looked uneasily from the book to her face. "I guess you can. You know there isn't any truth to what's in there, right?"

"Of course, silly!" Aria forced herself to laugh, hoping it didn't sound fake. "What your great-grandfather wrote about is just so interesting, really clever."

"Really?" Curtis seemed to radiate pride for a short moment before something else stole the sparkle from his eyes. "People said he was a mad man."

"Oh, well, he had an interesting mind. Very imaginative. The journal has given me quite a few ideas. This could be my chance to make it into horror fiction!"

"So you think you might be the next Anne Rice?"

"Maybe."

"Yeah, sure. You can keep it for a while. I don't have any use for it anymore." Curtis shrugged as he grabbed a stack of books from the table and carried them toward the counter. Aria pulled on her jacket, swung her backpack over her shoulder and grabbed the remaining books, following behind. "Oh, thanks. I could have gotten those books for you, though."

Curtis took the remaining books from her with an awkward smile and put them beneath the counter with the others. "I'll have these ready for you when you stop by tomorrow." He straightened and shuffled his feet nervously. "It's, uh, pretty late. Can I give you a ride?"

"Oh, no thanks. I'd prefer to walk."

"This late at night? There are a lot of unsavory characters out there, Aria."

"I'll be fine. I have my Mace with me." And a backpack filled with other goodies. Besides, she didn't need witnesses for what she was about to do. The journal listed several addresses of known vampire hangouts right there in Baltimore, and some of those places were still around. Now it was time to see if the vampires themselves were still around.

She let Curtis walk her out of the library, but waited until he got into his car and drove away before she turned opposite the direction of her home and started walking toward The Lair. She had never been a club person herself so The Lair was not familiar to her, but she knew the club sat in the same spot The Serpent's Tooth used to occupy. The Serpent's Tooth was one of the vampire hideouts listed in the journal.

Suddenly, Aria froze as she felt a set of eyes boring into her back, but the feeling that came over her was more than one of just being watched. She felt as though someone was listening to her, hearing the very thoughts which ran through her mind, searching those thoughts for information. She turned and looked back toward the library. Nothing was there but shadows. Yet, she still felt it—the alarming yet oddly comforting feeling that someone was there listening. Slowly, the feeling dissolved and she turned back in the direction of The Lair.

Immediately after her mother's death, she'd started gathering items for her vampire arsenal. The backpack she now carried contained matches, lighters, wooden stakes and squirt guns filled with holy water. She fingered one of the three crosses hanging from her neck for extra reassurance as she neared the vicinity of the club. If The Lair was still a vampire hot spot, she needed to be ready. Although her original idea was to kill her mother's murderer, she wouldn't hesitate to take out anyone who got in her way. If she'd learned anything from Dunn's diary, it was that vampires protected their own. If she had to go through several of them to get to the one who took her mother's life, so be it. They were all bloodsucking killers anyway.

She repeated that to herself as she continued her trek.

A block away from the club, the feeling of being watched crept down her spine again. She turned in a circle, scanning the dark streets for the cause of it, but found nothing out of the ordinary. Empty buildings, mostly businesses which were closed for the night, lined both sides of the street. Nothing moved but the shadows. The only sound was that of the gentle wind.

"Get it together, girl," she told herself, dismissing the strange feeling as a by-product of fear. She walked past vacant stores and narrow alleys, summoning the painful image of her mother's dead body for motivation. She would not hide in fear. She would not back down. She would spare no mercy. Any vampire who got in her way would die tonight. For her mother.

As The Lair loomed before her, her anger mounted. She paused momentarily to study the building. Sitting at the end of a dead-end street with no nearby street lights, the dark gray brick monstrosity seemed befitting a vampire hangout. The windows were dark, but she could see the flashing of red and purple strobe lights inside. Large red lightbulbs glared from around the black vinyl door, as the beat of eerie techno music wafted through the air. There was a steady stream of young Goth and punk partygoers entering the building, laughing and hanging upon one another in various stages of drunkenness. How nice it would be to feel young and carefree, but that life was not for Aria. That life had been stolen from her a long time ago.

She couldn't help wondering if the young partygoers were just people like her . . . or vampires. Realization finally slammed into Aria. How was she supposed to know until it was too late? She couldn't very well just approach an unusually pale person and stab him, could she?

"What the hell am I doing?" she muttered beneath her breath, swaying under a sudden dizzy spell. Doubt and trepidation battled with her need for revenge while she tried to decide on a plan of action. She had studied vampires for months. She couldn't let another parent's death go unavenged. "I have to do this."

Aria studied the club for a few minutes longer. If the place really was filled with vampires, it wouldn't be wise to walk right into the middle of them. She would rather take them down one at a time, if she had to, especially if they really did have superhuman strength. There had to be a back door. Maybe there was a back window she could peek into without being seen. Then, after having a better idea of the club's internal layout, she could devise a plan of attack. At the least, she would have knowledge of what actually happened in the club.

She turned right and walked down the alley which would take her to the rear of the building. Just as she'd suspected, there was a back door and two small, barred windows on either side. She headed toward them.

Two feet away from the door, a dark shadow emerged from behind a Dumpster in front of her.

"Well, well, well. Lookie what we gots here, June Bug," the figure said as he swaggered in her direction. Not a drunken swagger, but the cocky walk of an average street punk who thought he was about to get his jollies.

"Looks yummy," another male voice, which Aria assumed belonged to June Bug, responded from four feet behind her.

Aria quickly took in her surroundings. She was stuck between the back of The Lair and another large building. The Dumpster the first man had been hiding behind sat in front of a seven foot tall wire fence which prevented any escape from that direction, even if she were able to get past the man.

As the first man neared, she made out his features. He was Latino with a sharp nose, narrow dark eyes, and a scar which ran from the corner of his left eye down to his chin. His jeans were ripped and loose fitting, his white T-shirt smeared with grime. The red bandanna wrapped around his head hid his hair and brought attention to the gold hoop in his right ear. He couldn't have been any older than nineteen.

"What do you want with me?" she demanded.

The scar-faced man laughed. "Well, for starters, *chica*, we're going to take all your money and those crosses hanging around your neck." He reached out and lifted the large gold nugget ring, which also hung from her neck on a gold chain, as June Bug closed in on her from behind, his erection pressing against her buttocks. "We're gonna pawn those, but I think I'll keep this for myself."

"Then we're going to screw you," June Bug added, his hot breath crawling across her neck. "At the same time."

"Too bad for you guys that you just made one crucial mistake," Aria growled as she repositioned her feet and subtly positioned her hands for attack.

"Yeah?" Scar Face laughed again. "What's that?"

"Nobody takes my daddy's ring." Aria slammed the heel of her right hand into the scarred man's nose, breaking it instantly while she reached behind her with the left and grabbed hold of June Bug's testicles, yanking them hard enough to make the man scream. As Scar Face howled in pain and backed away with his hands covering his broken nose, Aria took the opportunity to spin and use her backpack to hit June Bug in the head, knocking him down. He landed face down on the ground, his hands covering his crotch while he wailed in pain.

Aria slung her backpack over her shoulder and started to run, but Scar Face grabbed her by her long hair and spun her around, hard enough to send her flying into the back wall of The Lair. Her head rammed into the brick and pain ricocheted through her skull. Before she could sink to the ground, Scar Face placed his forearm beneath her chin, pinning her to the wall and making it harder for her to breathe. He reached behind him with his other hand, pulling a gun from the back of his waistband.

"You wanna do this the hard way, bitch?" He cocked the gun and pointed it in her face. "We'll still do ya after you're dead. Don't make us no damn difference."

Aria stared down the barrel of the gun but refused to cry. Unbelievably, she almost laughed at the absurdity. She had come to the club prepared to kill and was now about to be killed herself. Her father had been killed by a racist, her mother by a vampire, and now she was about to be taken out by a teenaged, grammatically-challenged punk and his friend who had yet to quit crying over his nuts.

She lifted her gaze from the gun barrel and aimed it straight into the punk's eyes. "Screw yourself, you little uneducated twerp."

Scar Face's eyes flared in surprise and then fury, as he raised the gun up, as if to smack her with it. Before he could, Aria saw a blur of motion plow into him, and she was dropped to the ground. She gasped in fresh breaths of air and massaged her sore throat, barely aware of the sound of scuffling around her. Realizing her backpack was no longer on her shoulder, she searched the ground for it, a feat which wouldn't have been so hard if not for the way her head seemed to be spinning. Finally, she saw the bag a foot away and crawled to it, still not ready to stand. She closed her hand around it, only to have it jerked away.

Aria looked up and gasped. The man she had dreamed of for months stood before her, his profile illuminated by moonlight as he unzipped her backpack. He was real . . . and he had just come to her rescue.

The shock of seeing the man quickly transformed into anger as she realized he was going through her property.

"What do you think you're doing?" Aria grabbed for her backpack but the man quickly grabbed her by her throat and held her back. She looked into his dark eyes and gulped. She'd thought his eyes were stormy in her dreams. Now they were typhoons. Hostile typhoons.

Then reality slammed into her. If this was the man she had been dreaming about, the man whose name was in Alfred Dunn's diary, then he wasn't a man. He was a vampire, and he had her by the throat. He could kill her at any second.

She opened her mouth to scream, but his large hand left her throat and clamped over it before she could get out a sound. "Be quiet, woman. We're in a dark alley with two dead bodies. This is not the time to draw a crowd."

Aria looked around the alley for her attackers and found them lying on the ground, motionless. Scar Face's head lay at an awkward angle. The one called June Bug, a heftier version of Scarface, stared toward the sky, his eyes frozen in horror. "What did you do to them?" she asked as the man released his grip on her throat.

"I broke their necks," the man, the *vampire,* said as calmly as if the fact he'd just taken two lives meant nothing. He continued rummaging through her backpack, chuckling as he pulled out the wooden stakes and tossed them aside. "What?" He stopped his perusal to look at her in annoyance, obviously feeling the glare of her accusing eyes and reading the thought behind them. "It was either kill them or watch them kill you. Personally, if I were you I'd be happy with the choice I made."

"They were just teenagers!"

"They were murderers and rapists. Besides, breaking a man's neck isn't half as cruel as dislocating his testicles." He looked at her pointedly, then continued his search, his eyes gleaming as he pulled out the diary and let the backpack drop to the ground. He opened the book and perused the pages. "Where did you get this?"

"None of your damn business," Aria growled. "What's it to you?"

"Do you know my name?"

Rialto. The name echoed through Aria's mind as she stared into the man's eyes. He watched her intently, curiously. She knew his name. She knew his body and the way he tasted. The wild, spicy smell that enveloped him now was even a remnant from her dreams. She knew him, and she didn't. The thought terrified her.

"Should I?"

"No."

"Then why did you ask if I did?"

"Because you do."

If he truly was a vampire, he wouldn't want anyone to know. But he knew that she knew who he was. Aria looked at her backpack. It was too far away and he stood between her and it. The crosses around her neck hadn't stopped him from grabbing her by the throat. She was defenseless against him, so she did the only thing she could think of. She turned and ran.

Running as if her life depended on it, and she was sure it did, Aria ignored the tight feeling in her chest and the throbbing pain ricocheting through her body as she reached the end of the alley . . . and ran right into a hard chest.

"Rialto!" She spoke the name in a confused daze as she looked up into his angry face. "How did you . . ." Her voice trailed off as fear silenced her. He had been right behind her. How could he have just stepped out from around the corner at the end of the alley? Nobody was that fast, and he wasn't even sweating.

"So you do know my name. How?"

"I don't know." Aria started to inch her way backward, but was stopped as Rialto clamped one of his hands on her arm, squeezing just hard enough to make her flinch. "I swear I didn't know that was your name, not for sure."

His eyes narrowed. "Then why did you just say it as if you were sure it was my name?" He shook her when he didn't get a response. "Where did you hear it?"

"In my dreams," Aria blurted as she fought back tears. Oh God, he was going to kill her. He was going to suck her blood until she was completely dry and leave her behind just like her mother.

Just like her mother.

"You killed my mother, didn't you?"

"No." He released her arm and closed his eyes, his jaw set tightly. She saw the vein in his temple bulge before he reopened his eyes and looked at her, a strange combination of hatred and sympathy coating his gaze. "I would never kill an innocent, as I'm sure she was."

"Well, one of you bloodsuckers did. You are a vampire, aren't you?"

The side of his mouth, his too luscious not to notice mouth, turned up as he handed her backpack to her. "And you're a vampire huntress, I assume. I'd guess that you're still in training, hmm?"

"Don't mock me, you bastard," Aria spat, instantly regretting it when his eyes blackened in anger. Her mouth went dry as she watched the muscle in his jaw clench, wondering if he would soon show her his fangs. She suddenly realized she hadn't seen any.

"You're right," he said tightly. "I am a bastard, and you, my dear, are a pathetic vampire hunter. Take your little bag of goodies and let's get out of here before someone exits the back of that club and finds those bodies."

"I'm not going anywhere with you!"

"Yes, you are. You've already tried to outrun me, and you've seen what a waste of time and energy that was. You have no choice in the matter."

"Are you going to kill me?" she asked, hating the way her voice trembled.

"That's up to you. Let's go."

Aria thought over her options. Staying in a dark alley with a man who might or might not be a vampire wasn't exactly safe. Maybe following him would buy her the time she needed to come up with a plan.

"I know you don't trust me, but think about it," he said, again seeming to read her mind. "Why would I save your life if I wanted you dead?"

He had a point, Aria conceded. Still, she was reluctant to move.

"I gave you back your weapons. I wouldn't do that if I intended to attack you. You play nice and I'll play nice." He waited for a response, his eyes displaying his growing irritation as she remained silent. "Look, lady, if I wanted to kill you I would just do it. I wouldn't be standing here discussing it with you!"

Aria gave in and nodded in surrender. If he wanted to kill her, he could do it right here. And he *had* saved her life. She shifted the backpack on her shoulder and followed him out of the alley. He was right. Running from him was pointless. "Where are we going?"

"Someplace where we can talk." He didn't glance back, and Aria found herself admiring the way his broad shoulders filled out his black shirt as she walked behind him. She mentally scolded herself as her eyes, of their own volition, traveled the length of his back. What was wrong with her? The man, or *vampire*, could very well be leading her to her own death and she was checking him out?

"What do we have to discuss?" she asked.

He stopped abruptly, nearly causing Aria to run into him, before he turned and gazed down at her. Way down. He had to be six-four at least. "How old are you?"

"Twenty-six. Why?" Aria couldn't define the look he gave her, but it made her shiver.

"Because you know my name, although we've never met, but I don't know yours." He glared at her, the look hard and assessing. "And apparently I've been dreaming about you since you were just a baby. It's time I find out who the hell you are and what danger we pose to one another."

# Chapter Three

STUPID! STUPID! Stupid! Aria inwardly cursed as she led Rialto up the staircase leading to her third-floor apartment. When she'd set out looking for vampires she hadn't intended to bring one home with her. Not that he'd admitted to being a vampire. He had barely spoken a word to her during their walk back to the library—obviously he'd been the one she'd felt watching her when she'd left there—and once they were both seated in his black sedan he remained silent, except to ask for directions.

And here I am leading him right into my home, Aria thought as she slid her key into the lock and opened her apartment door. For all she knew, he could be a serial killer instead of a vampire. She hadn't seen any fangs; the crosses around her neck hadn't worked, and he'd killed two men without drinking their blood. Why would a vampire waste perfectly good available blood? But she had dreamed about him, and he did admit to dreaming about her. Of course, she could be going insane and he'd just seen a chance to trick a crazy woman and took it.

That would be the logical explanation but deep inside she knew they were meant to meet. Whether the reason for their meeting was good or bad she didn't know yet, but she'd dreamed of him for too long not to find out.

She started to drop her backpack to the floor but thought better of it, hoisting it more securely onto her shoulder instead. "Have a seat if you'd like," she muttered as she strolled through the cluttered living space to get to the kitchen. "I'm thirsty. Do you want anything?" Anything but my blood, that is, she thought to herself.

"Water would be great," Rialto answered in his rich textured voice as he stood before a painting propped on one of the many easels scattered about the room. Aria tried to ignore the shiver snaking its way down her core as the deep throaty tone of his voice seemed to reach out and caress her. Vampire or not, he was incredibly sexy.

"What a damn shame," she whispered to herself as she checked to make sure he was out of sight, then reached into her backpack for one of the water guns.

RIALTO STOOD BEFORE the painting, fixated by the emotion spent on each brush stroke. Through her art, he could see her. Aria. A befitting name, he mused to himself. Beautiful. Strong. Mesmerizing. She painted with vivid colors, bold strokes. Her very heart seemed to bleed right onto the canvas. He touched the painting before him, and for a moment it seemed as though he were touching her skin, feeling the teardrops which often dampened her cheeks.

He pulled his hand away, knowing it would not serve him well to let down his defenses against the beautiful stranger, and shifted his focus to studying the apartment. The building itself had seen better days, but her apartment was kept nice, even though it was cluttered. He found art everywhere he looked. Paints and brushes were strewn on tables and easels, canvases were stacked or mounted in all directions. The furniture was simple, consisting of a light blue sofa and chair and a wooden coffee table. A small dinette set occupied the far corner of the room. The decor consisted of several paintings and a few framed pictures of a couple who, he realized, were Aria's parents.

Who was she and why was he so drawn in by her art, by her pain? By those damned green eyes that seemed to pull him under a spell every time he connected with them. His dreams hadn't prepared him for meeting her. She was beautiful on levels he couldn't begin to fully comprehend. Never in nearly two centuries of existence had he been so enamored by a female face, a soul. She must be some sort of powerful witch, he mused, for never had a woman frightened him so badly either.

"Here you go."

Rialto nearly jumped, so lost in thought he hadn't heard her approach, a sloppy mistake which could easily get him killed. He had no doubt the woman was a danger to him. Beauty be damned, she was the enemy.

He turned to see her standing before him, a glass of water held out in a trembling hand, her other hand tightly fisted around a silver knife.

"What are you planning to do with that?" he asked with a pointed glance at the knife before taking the glass from her, careful their fingers didn't touch. He had the strangest feeling doing so could burn them both.

"That all depends on you. Don't think for one second that I trust you."

"Likewise," he responded, struggling not to grin. The woman had guts, he admitted, even though it was that same foolish bravado which would most likely end up getting her killed. And according to the old witch in his dreams, her death would cause his own.


ARIA WIPED A sweaty palm along her pant leg as she watched Rialto sip from the glass, the action drawing her attention to the long, tanned column of his throat. She'd never realized that watching a man drink water could be so sensual. *Drinking holy water*, she reminded herself, waiting for him to disintegrate. He didn't.

"Thank you, Aria." He placed the glass on the table and turned to survey her apartment.

Aria didn't know which bothered her more: The fact that the holy water had done nothing to him, him being in her apartment, or that she couldn't take her eyes off him. Snatches of dreams played through her mind, despite her efforts to shove them away. She shouldn't be visualizing him naked, not when she knew deep down what he truly was. As crazy as it seemed, she knew deep in her core that the man she'd been dreaming about, the man standing in her apartment, wasn't a man at all. He was a monster, a killer. Even if he had saved her life and was unaffected by the holy water, she couldn't allow herself to forget what he was.

"You are an incredible artist," Rialto commented as he walked through the room, studying each canvas. "I can feel your pain through your work."

Aria rolled her eyes, earning an arched eyebrow and a smug grin from him.

"You don't believe me?"

"I find that men make comments like that only in an effort to try and con me into bed," Aria answered candidly, a little surprised a man blessed with his physical attributes would resort to a line at all. Then again, maybe he was doing some sort of Jedi mind trick, making himself appear drop-dead gorgeous to her.

His grin widened as he stopped before an easel and gestured toward the painting perched on it. "The dark colors . . . the purples . . . the blacks . . . are your anger and hatred. The bold strokes of crimson are your vengeance, your lust to see justice rendered. And this small line of bluish white which seems to be encircling the darkness is the goodness that still remains, holding your dark desires in check."

Aria's mouth fell open as he described exactly what she'd felt while painting the piece.

"And for the record," he said as he stepped closer to her, "I wouldn't have to resort to false flattery to get you into bed."

Any response Aria would have made was cut short as he pointed to a canvas sitting against the wall. "That one represents your father's death, the one next to it represents those who made fun of you during your childhood." His gaze fell back to the painting on the easel. "This is all about the person who killed your mother and the way it's tearing you to pieces inside, bringing out your own darkness."

"The *vampire* who killed my mother," Aria corrected him, "and how do you know all this?" She crossed her arms over her breasts, suddenly feeling naked and vulnerable.

"I saw these things."

"You saw them? How?"

"In my dreams. I have dreamed of you for years, but recently . . ."

"Recently, what?" Aria fought to control her body before she succumbed to a fit of shivers. She didn't want him to see her shaken. He had to be manipulating her somehow.

"I've dreamed of you since you were just a baby. At that time my dreams were mostly just that. A baby crying. As you grew I caught glimpses. Then for the past several years, I only saw your adult face. These last ten years I've had more graphic dreams of you, but now I also dream in flashbacks. I see what hurts you."

"Just what is it you see?" she asked cautiously.

"I saw your father being removed from his house after he was murdered. I saw you being ridiculed by your childhood peers, degraded by your first lover, and I saw your mother in the morgue."

Aria winced as the images appeared before her. She was pained by the memories and furious that someone she didn't even know had access to her own private hell. "How *dare* you."

"It is not of my choice," he answered coolly. "I just close my eyes and there you are. You've been doing the same thing, correct?"

"I don't violate your privacy by dreaming about your personal business! I only dream that . . ." Aria broke off abruptly, turning her face to hide the flow of color she felt rising there.

Obviously, he didn't suffer the same embarrassment. "I come to you at night while you lay in your bed, and we make love."

"Yes." Aria squared her shoulders and forced herself to look him in the eye, willing herself not to get lost in their black depths. "But it's just a dream, not a fantasy, and definitely not a premonition."

"Good."

The clipped manner in which he spoke raised Aria's hackles. If her dreams were any indication, he'd give anything to bed her. Wait. What was she thinking? The man was a vampire, and she was irked because he didn't want to make love to her? *Get a grip, girl.* "That's right. Your loss. So what do you want from me?"

He looked at her, appearing to study her , then he walked over to the table and picked up the glass of holy water, draining the last of its contents before slamming the glass back down on the table.

"What is it you're not telling me?" Aria asked, getting as close to him as she dared. "Besides the fact that you're a vampire. I know you are, even if it seems insane."

"Yes, I drink blood." He slowly turned his head to meet her gaze, igniting both a fear and a hunger inside her. Her limbs began to tremble. "I was born a little over two centuries ago and I have yet to die. In that sense, I am a vampire. I don't wear a cape and I never rose from the grave. Crosses and garlic have no effect on me, nor does the holy water I suspect you poured into my glass, but I guess you figured that much out when I didn't explode."

Aria could feel her cheeks redden under his mocking gaze. "Well, you can't blame a girl for trying to defend herself," she said, self-consciously rubbing her neck.

"I suppose not," Rialto said dryly as he used his index finger to tip her chin up, leaning in uncomfortably close. "However, movie and storybook nonsense will get you nowhere."

"Some of it must work," Aria managed to say despite the fact that her terrified, quivering little heart was lodged in her throat. "What if I rammed a stake through your heart?"

"I'd break your pretty little neck before you could get it in deep enough. Same as I would if you cut me with that little knife of yours."

"Go to hell."

"If I do, I'm taking you with me."

"I've already been."

"I know." Rialto released Aria's chin and turned toward the sofa, finding a seat among the blue cushions. "I know you've been through hell. I've witnessed it all, and I'm not here to hurt you any further, not unless you make me."

"What is that supposed to mean?"

"I was given an order to protect you."

Aria stood still, blinking at him, sure she'd heard him wrong. "You were sent to protect me?"

"Yes."

"By whom?"

"The Dream Teller."

"The what?"

"The who," he said, correcting her. "The Dream Teller is a very old witch, a prophet for my kind. She forewarns us of imminent danger, and to date she has never been wrong."

"And this witch sent you to protect me, an ordinary woman?"

"How do I know you're an ordinary woman? You could be a very clever witch. None of that matters though. I was sent to protect you, so here I am. That's all you need to know."

"I don't believe you," Aria said, tightening her hold on the knife. "One of you bloodsucking leeches killed my mother, and you've been playing with my head, sending me these dreams."

"That's impossible. I don't have the power to invade dreams."

"And I'm supposed to take your word for that?"

"You're going to have to because I'm here to protect you whether you like it or not, whether *I* like it or not."

"A monster is supposed to protect me," Aria spat in disgust, as the rage inside her intensified. The man had confirmed her deepest fear. Vampires were real, and her mother had been murdered because the disgusting creatures lived off of human blood. Now he was spinning a story about a witch sending him to protect her. "How stupid do you think I am? You're probably the same sick bastard who drank my mother to death, and you're here now just to toy with me!"

She made a lunge for the cocky vampire sitting on her couch, jumping onto the coffee table with the knife raised over her head, fully intending to plunge it deep into the monster's heart. But in a flash of movement, he pinned her to a wall on the opposite side of the room, his hand squeezing her wrist with brutal force until she dropped the knife to the floor.

"If you ever do something that stupid again," he growled as two fangs lowered from his gums, "I'll kill you without hesitation, regardless of my orders. Do you understand?"

Too terrified to speak, Aria nodded meekly and was dropped to the floor as Rialto stepped back and took a deep breath as his fangs receded.

"I'd actually thought you might be a witch," he said as he bent down to retrieve the knife Aria had brandished against him, "but there's no way a witch would be stupid enough to pull a knife on a vampire without disabling him in some way first."

He shook his head as he walked into the kitchen, coming out seconds later with the wood block containing every knife Aria owned. She watched helplessly as he opened a window and threw out the knives before lowering the window pane back in place. "This will go a lot more smoothly if I don't have to worry about you stabbing me while I sleep."

"You're sleeping here?" A tremor of fear snaked its way down Aria's spine as she wondered how she was supposed to sleep with him nearby.

"If it comes to that. I have yet to discover what the threat against you is, although judging by that little display of poor restraint, I can imagine how easy it would be for you to get yourself into a great deal of trouble."

"Don't mock me. There's nothing wrong with wanting to avenge a loved one's death!"

"There is when you get yourself killed trying to do it, which is exactly what's going to happen to you if you don't slow down long enough to think rationally. And you won't be avenging anyone's death if you kill someone who had nothing to do with it. I didn't kill your mother, and the fact that I'm a vampire doesn't make me a blood-crazed, murdering psychopath."

"You kill people, drinking their blood to prolong your existence."

"I don't *have* to kill in order to feed. The fact that I am a vampire doesn't make me a monster. I'm a person just like you, and just like all life forms there are good and there are bad, but don't you dare insinuate I'm some evil devil-spawn because I happen to have lived decades longer than most. You of all people should know what it's like to be prejudged, to be an outcast."

Aria looked away, shame making her want to hide her face. "That's not fair."

"Very little in life is fair," he muttered as he stepped past her, leaving the room.

After several minutes had passed and he didn't return, she rose from the floor and followed him, instinctively knowing where he'd went. As suspected, she found him standing before the open doors of her balcony, moonlight highlighting the hard planes of his face as he stared at her bed.

"This is it," he said, almost more to himself than to her. "This is the place I always find you in my dreams."

"Why are we dreaming of each other?" She folded her arms across her chest and watched his back as he turned to stare out past the balcony.

"I have no idea. Two centuries of existence, and I've never experienced anything like it."

She waited a few minutes longer, but sensing he wasn't going to further elaborate on the thought, she changed the subject back to business. "I can't let my mother's death go unavenged. How do I find the vampire who killed her?"

The sigh he emitted was highly audible, even over the sounds wafting up from the street below. She waited as he turned back into the room, locking the balcony doors behind him, checking the locks to make sure they were secure. An odd gesture to be made by someone who had threatened to kill her a few moments earlier, she thought, but didn't comment on it. Hell, the whole situation was odd. A frigging vampire was in her bedroom, and she was carrying on a conversation with him as if it were the most normal thing in the world!

"There is no vampire," Rialto said carefully, slowly, as if he were speaking to a traumatized child. "No vampire attacked your mother and left her body behind."

"Bullshit!" Aria's body shook with anger. "You just can't admit it, can you? It would kill you to own up to—"

Rialto's finger was pressed against her lips before she even saw him cross the room. Before she had a chance to ask how he had gotten that close so fast, he spoke harshly. "I'm not screwing you over, Aria, and I'm not protecting anyone. A vampire didn't kill your mother. I saw your mother's body through your eyes. I saw those puncture wounds."

"And you know her body was completely drained of blood," Aria snapped. "How can you deny a vampire did that?"

Rialto's eyebrows furrowed. "Actually, I didn't know her body was drained of blood, but despite that, a vampire didn't leave those marks." Rialto paced across the room, turning back toward Aria once he reached the opposite wall. "*Completely* drained?"

"Completely drained," she responded. "Who else could have done that?"

"I don't know." Rialto shook his head, continuing to pace. "I just know it couldn't be a vampire that drained her."

"You keep saying that. Why? The proof was right there!"

"The proof, as you call it, was a sham. Vampires don't leave puncture wounds. If we did, don't you think the entire world would know about us, not just a few people?"

Aria considered that. If vampires wanted to remain undetected, they couldn't just leave bodies lying around with fang marks, could they? "How do you bite into people and not leave marks?"

"Our saliva has healing properties in it. It's virtually impossible for a vampire to bite a person and leave a mark."

"No matter how deep the wound?"

"No matter how deep."

"That's impossible."

"Some would say it would be impossible for you to be standing in your bedroom talking to a vampire," he responded with a mocking grin. "The world is not as black and white as you mortals tend to think."

"I don't believe you. You may not have killed my mother, but one of you did."

"Oh, so you believe I'm innocent now?" One dark eyebrow arched as he folded his arms, grinning down at her. "That's noble of you."

"Look, I know you could have killed me in the alley, and you could have drank the blood of those punks who jumped me, but you didn't. You could have just killed me in the living room a little while ago, but again, you didn't. You do have restraint, but I'm betting not all of your kind do."

"The same could be said of your kind."

"Let's not make this a debate. I may be just an angry, foolish little mortal to you, but I'm not stupid. My mother was murdered, her blood completely drained from her body, and the only damage done to her were two small holes, two perfect fang marks. Next thing you know I'm dreaming about some sexy vampire—"

"Sexy, huh?"

She glared at him. "I'm not complimenting you, I'm just stating the facts. I started having erotic dreams about a vampire, the most repulsive creature I can think of by the way, and lo and behold if that same vampire doesn't pop up out of the blue and save my life, claiming he was sent by some old witch to protect me. Obviously my mother's death is connected to whatever is going on between us."

"That may be," Rialto conceded, "but that doesn't mean a vampire actually killed her. I'm telling you the truth about our saliva. There would be no fang marks left on her body if she'd been bitten by a vampire. The broken flesh would have completely healed."

"Sure it would. I'll believe that when I see it."

"Fine with me," he said, clamping his hand around her wrist. "Let's go."

"What? Where are we going?" Aria asked in alarm as she was pulled down the hall behind the angry vampire. He walked with purpose in his step and didn't slow down, not even when she began punching him in the back of his head and back in fear.

"And to think you actually thought you could take out a club full of vampires," he taunted as he pulled her toward the front door. "You can't even hurt one."

"How'd you know I was going into that club to kill vampires?"

"What else were you planning to do with that bag of stakes?" he asked but she didn't miss his frown and knew there was something more about his knowledge of her intentions.

"What are you doing?" she asked as he tugged her out the front door.

"You don't believe our saliva heals, so I'm going to show you it does."

"How are you going to do that?" she asked, gulping hard as he started down the interior hallway of her apartment building. "Where are we going?"

Rialto chuckled, the mischievous sound bordering on evil as he gazed down into her eyes and smiled.

"To feed."

# Chapter Four

I MUST BE OUT OF my mind, Rialto thought, as he pulled Aria down the narrow alley bisecting Fat Kracker's from one of West Baltimore's most notorious apartment complexes. Both the bar-slash-grease pit and residential building were crawling with criminals and addicts. The scents of greed, desperation and various drugs hung heavy in the air. Beneath his fingers, Rialto could feel Aria's pulse beating rapidly in her wrist and wondered whether it was he or the neighborhood she feared. More than that, he wondered why he gave a damn.

"Rialto, do you know how dangerous this neighborhood is?" Aria asked, her voice quivering as her eyes darted side to side. "And at this time of night?"

"Trust me, I'm the most dangerous thing out here tonight," he replied, grinning as he felt her pulse spike.

They continued down the alley, stepping over discarded bottles and piles of rotting waste, and again Rialto wondered what was wrong with him. He'd confirmed the woman's suspicions that he was indeed a vampire, a dangerous and sometimes fatal mistake to make with a mortal, and now he was bringing her with him to feed. Why? Because she'd pissed him off, he conceded, thinking back to her earlier remarks. He'd been called a monster thousands of times, but repulsive? It shouldn't bother him what the mortal thought about him or his kind, but for some reason it did, and that pissed him off even more.

She thinks I'm a repulsive monster? I'll show her a repulsive monster, Rialto thought, as he ducked under a rickety set of fire escape stairs, positioning Aria with him among the shadows so they could see the alley without being seen themselves.

"What are we doing here?"

"Hunting," he answered irritably, and again asked himself why. He wasn't in dire need of blood. He could go another night or two if need be, but here he was, hiding among the shadows with the woman he'd dreamed about for over two decades yet was still a stranger. So why hunt at all tonight?

*Because you saw the desire in her eyes,* he reminded himself. She'd tried to chase it away, but not before he'd seen the heat of it blazing in those eyes of pure green. It was the same look he saw in her eyes when he dreamed of her, right before she scratched her own throat to offer him her blood.

He would not allow the dream to become real.

She tensed before him, and he realized he was squeezing her wrist too tight. He released his grip and brought his other arm around her waist, holding her so that her back was firmly pressed against his chest. She let out a soft, barely audible whimper, reminding him of a kitten trapped by a pit bull, and her fear spiked another degree. He could sense it rolling off her in fervent waves as blood pumped harder through her veins, calling to him like a siren's song. He dipped his head, smelling the skin of her neck peeking out from the collar of her jacket. Coconut and leather fused together, combining with the fragrant aroma of blood and fear, begging him to taste the droplets of sweat glistening along her collarbone.

"Try it and die," Aria warned, and he felt the unmistakable point of a sharpened stake pushing against his throat.

Rialto blinked rapidly, drawing himself out of the fog he'd been under, and realized he had nosed her jacket aside and was only seconds away from plunging his fangs into the delicate skin of her neck. He pulled his head away which only gave Aria better access to his jugular. He cursed himself for allowing bloodlust to set in so deeply and for being careless. He'd never thought to check inside the woman's jacket. He'd assumed she carried all of her weapons in her backpack.

"Staking me in the neck won't bring an instant death," he warned as his fangs receded. His own heart raced now, pumping valuable blood through his system, wasting precious power. He was suddenly ravenous.

"No, but it'll make it damned hard for you to drink me before I get a chance to finish you off."

"You're not a killer, Aria." *But I am,* he thought grimly, as hunger rolled through his system. Even with the stake at his throat he had a good chance of beating her. He could easily push her away from his body, knocking her off balance and buying himself the time he needed to sink fangs into her flesh before she could recoup and shove in the stake. But he couldn't do it. He was far too hungry now. He couldn't trust himself to leave her enough blood, especially when he could sense just how damn good her blood would taste. "Forgive me. I was thirsty and you smelled really good. I won't let it happen again."

"Why should I believe you?"

"I've saved your life once already." *Please lower the stake so I can spare it once more,* he pleaded silently as his self-control wavered. Damn it. He was two centuries old. His control had been impenetrable for more than one of them. What was it about this woman that weakened it? "I'll allow you to keep the stake," he said, deciding it might actually be for the best. He doubted the Dream Teller would consider draining the woman to be protection, and in his current state he just didn't know how well he could uphold his vow to keep his fangs out of her flesh. "Just lower it."

He sensed the fear and indecision swirling inside her mind as she remembered their first meeting in the alley behind the nightclub. In her heart she knew he was trustworthy, but her mind wouldn't let go of the fact he was a creature of the night, a monster . . . a vampire who'd came too close to tasting her.

Rialto nearly gasped as realization slammed into him. He was picking up on her thoughts and they hadn't even shared blood. Before that moment he would have sworn such a thing was impossible.

It was his ability to pick up on her thoughts which told him the frightened woman had no intention of lowering the stake. Instead she kept him there, close enough to lick her skin while the hunger inside him grew. He didn't want to fight her, much less drink from her, but his hunger wasn't giving him very many options.

Salvation came in the form of an obese, sweaty pimp. The back door of Fat Kracker's swung open, and a large round man and a young, scantily clad blonde, who was too drugged out of her mind to manage the simple act of walking, came out. The man shoved the girl to the ground and reached into his jacket.

"I'll teach you to steal from me, you filthy crack whore," he said, pulling out a handgun.

Rialto shoved Aria to the ground and plowed into the man with lightning speed, tackling him before he could get off a shot and knocking the gun from his grasp in the process. The man was too dumbfounded to scream, but he fumbled to defend himself, scratching Rialto's skin with his watch as he tried to get a grip on his throat.

Too hungry to waste time playing with his meal, Rialto sank his fangs into the wet, salty skin covering the man's jugular and drank his fill, ripping his way across the man's neck, making sure he would leave a gaping wound for Aria to watch heal. The man smelled of sweat, smoke and fear, but his blood was rich and quenching, just what Rialto needed.

It didn't take long until he'd satisfied his thirst but the images which assaulted his mind while he drained the man forced him to keep going until he took the last sip of blood the man could spare. It wasn't until the man's heart beat its last beat that he dropped him to the ground like the pile of waste he was and stepped away.

He reached into his back pocket for a moist towelette packet, but stopped short of opening it. Aria needed to see him this way, with his victim's blood dripping from his chin. She needed to see him at his worst in order to chase away any lingering remnants of desire she still held.

"Come here," he said gruffly, turning to face her, unprepared for what he found.

She had crept a few feet away from the fire escape, positioned as though her initial intention was to run away, but her gaze had apparently locked onto him during the attack. He'd expected terror and disgust, maybe even sympathy for the victim, in her gaze, but instead he found her looking at the scene in rapt fascination, her eyes warmed with hunger.

"Aria!"

She shook her head as though coming out of a trance and looked once more at the scene. The hunger and fascination in her eyes was replaced with fear before she turned and made a run for it.

Rialto bit out a curse and ran with the speed of light, capturing her quickly. He held her with one arm wrapped around her waist, the other clasped over her mouth, and lifted her off the ground. He carried her toward the man as she kicked her legs and tried to bite through his hand, ignoring the pain and the frustration she evoked.

"Look at him," he ordered, lowering her so she stood firmly on the ground before the dead man's body.

Right before their eyes, the huge gashes he'd made in the man's neck healed. "He is not completely drained," he explained as she gazed down at the man's body in disbelief. "To kill someone, you drink until the heart ceases to beat and then you let go. Considering the man is an obvious lowlife, there probably won't be much of an investigation into his death. If there is, it'll be determined that he died due to heart failure." He sensed her fear ebbing and removed his hand from her mouth.

"You didn't have to kill him to prove your point," she said in a low voice, thick with fury and a touch of guilt. Rialto could touch her mind well enough to realize she thought he'd killed the man for the sole purpose of showing her how the healing properties in vampire saliva worked.

"My initial intention wasn't to kill tonight. Look at her," he said softly.

Aria shifted her gaze to the blonde lying unconscious on the ground and gasped, finally seeing what he'd known all along. "I thought she was a woman. She's just a girl!"

"I'd say about fifteen." Rialto's stomach churned in disgust. "This man was her pimp. He made her sell her body and her pay was cocaine, a drug which possessed her and made her do whatever he wanted until he was through with her. He was about to kill her when I intervened. If I hadn't killed him, he would have merely gotten up, dusted himself off, and repeated the process with another unfortunate little girl . . . or boy."

"How do you know he was her pimp?"

"I can see inside people's minds when I drink their blood." He let her go so he could wipe away the blood starting to dry on his face and waited for a response. After receiving none he took his gaze away from the young girl and turned it toward Aria. His breath caught in his throat as he felt the heat of her desire. He followed her hungry gaze, realizing he hadn't wiped the blood away from his neck where the man's watch had scraped him. She was staring at the scratch and, to his horror, she licked her lips.

"Aria!"

She jumped at his harsh tone as he quickly wiped away the trickle of blood that had escaped the small scratch. It was just like in his dream. She saw his blood and became instantly addicted. He wouldn't let her taste it. She would be lost then.

"I, uh—" she stammered as the longing daze in her eyes subsided. She looked around in confusion and, if he was correct, embarrassment. "The girl. We can't just leave her here, can we?"

"I suppose not," Rialto murmured. He bent down and hoisted the unconscious girl onto his shoulder. "There's a church nearby. The pastor there is a night owl. He'll watch over her."

"A pastor?"

Rialto grinned as the irony struck her. "Yes, Aria, although you've seen about the worst of me, I still do associate with men of God on occasion. So far I haven't been struck by lightning while crossing over a church's threshold."

Fifteen minutes later, Rialto and Christian, the church's leader and fellow vampire, stood over the young girl's body and prayed. Though he focused his concentration on asking God to save this unfortunate girl from her addiction, he could feel the weight of Aria's disbelieving stare. How sad it made him to know she never would have suspected he prayed, that he believed in God and goodness. He chose not to tell her that Christian was a vampire. She'd had enough surprises for one night.

"Amen." The vampires ended the prayer in unison.

"Take care of her," Rialto said, extending his hand to his old friend, a man who was older than him by far but looked younger. His dark hair was cut into a short, boyish style and his flawless, golden skin added to his youthful appearance.

"You know I will," Christian said solemnly, shaking Rialto's hand before casting a glance to where Aria sat in a nearby pew, her normally bright eyes darkened by a mix of anger, confusion and sorrow as she stared at the young girl's unconscious form. "Who's the woman?"

"Her name is Aria. The Dream Teller sent me to protect her," Rialto answered, his voice low.

"She's mortal," Christian stated.

"I know."

"Why would the Dream Teller send you to protect a mortal?"

"I have no clue."

"Well, what are you protecting her from?"

"Again, not a clue. Her mother was murdered not that long ago, left in a park with supposed fang marks in her neck. That probably has something to do with it."

Christian studied Aria for a moment. "Does she have any brothers or sisters?"

"I'm pretty sure she doesn't, why?"

"Because the mother of one of my parishioners, a young man, met the same fate a few weeks ago."

A cold chill ran through Rialto's body. "The killer has struck more than once and is leaving fang marks on the bodies?"

"This is not good."

"That's an understatement. The Dream Teller must have known and sent me here to stop it."

"Maybe the woman is supposed to be the next victim."

Rialto clenched his fists tight, knowing if anyone dared lay a finger on Aria he would rip them limb from limb. He blinked, wondering where his rage came from. Despite the years of dreams, the woman was still a stranger to him.

"Rialto?"

He turned to look at his old friend and noticed the odd look he got in return.

"Rialto, does this woman know what we are?"

He looked away before answering, feeling ten kinds of fool. "She knows what I am, but in my defense, she knew it before we met."

"How could she know? Who is she? Is she a hunter?"

"No," he answered, grinning at the memory of her in the alley with her little bag of stakes and holy water. "She's just a murdered woman's daughter."

"Murdered women's daughters make vengeful acquaintances. Does she believe a vampire truly killed her mother?"

"She did, but now she knows a vampire couldn't have left fang marks."

"She knows this because you told her and she took your word for it?" Christian asked, but by the way he looked at the teenager's body Rialto could tell he was putting the pieces of the evening together.

"She knows because she watched me kill this young girl's pimp."

"Oh, Rialto, what have you done?"

"I saved a young girl's life and showed a woman hell-bent on revenge that vampires aren't to blame for what happened to her mother," Rialto answered defensively, already on edge enough from the night's events. He didn't need to be reprimanded by his friend on top of everything else.

"How do you know she doesn't still blame us? She could just be waiting for the right moment to attack."

"I know because I've touched her thoughts," Rialto admitted, struck again by the enormity of that fact.

"She allowed you to drink from her?"

"I haven't taken a single sip of her blood."

Christian stared at him in confusion. "I thought you could only touch the thoughts of a mortal while you drank from one."

"So did I."

They both focused a curious gaze upon Aria who chose that moment to look up at them. She looked so lost that Rialto's heart constricted just looking at her. He'd give anything to put a smile on her lovely face. Frowning, he wondered where the hell that thought had come from and quickly pushed it aside.

"I need to get this girl situated before my morning rush of parishioners hits," Christian said, scooping the teenager up in his arms. "Be careful, Rialto. Something strange seems to be going on here. You might want to contact Seta."

"Good idea," he said in agreement before leveling narrowed eyes on Aria. "And don't worry about me being careful. It takes more than a pretty face to get me to let my guard down." He might not have to worry about the woman trying to kill him, but he knew she was still dangerous. Witch or not, she was working some kind of magic on him, and for that reason alone, he knew better than to turn his back on her.

He said goodbye to his friend and walked over to Aria. "Ready to go home?"

The look she gave him was spiked so heavily with uncertainty he didn't have to touch her thoughts to know he still frightened her.

"You still have your stake, Aria, and I promise not to touch you. I've already drunk my fill of blood."

"Am I expected to believe you?"

"I'm a lot of things but a liar is not one of them," he murmured, holding out his hand. "You trusted me enough to bring you here. Nothing about me has changed since then, so trust me enough to see you home."


"ARE YOU SURE you're all right?"

"Yes," Aria answered for the tenth time since their departure from the church, although she didn't know if she would ever be all right again. The very world she had always known no longer existed.

*I just witnessed a vampire slaying a man.*

She should be frightened, horrified, repulsed, *something* other than what she was feeling. And what was she feeling? Whatever it was, it wasn't normal. But what about her life *was* normal?

Her parents had decided to have a biracial child in tiny little Pickahoe, Indiana, knowing such a thing was not condoned there.

Not normal.

Her father was murdered by white supremacists.

Not normal.

Her skin color changed dramatically from warm seasons to cold, causing her to appear either white or black depending on the time of year.

Not normal.

Her mother was murdered by a vampire, only it wasn't a real vampire because they don't leave marks, so it must have been someone pretending to be a vampire.

*So* not normal.

And now she was sitting in her apartment with a real vampire, a sexy as hell vampire who repeatedly seduced her in her dreams, no less. A vampire who had just killed a man in front of her, and rather than be disgusted, she had felt herself wanting to . . . what? Reach out with her tongue and lick that small trace of blood which had seeped out of the scrape on his neck, that small trickle she had smelled from eight feet away?

*Way not normal.* In fact, it was down right demented, and that made her one sick puppy.

"Maybe I shouldn't have fed in front of you."

*No, you shouldn't have,* she thought as she looked at Rialto, who sat on her sofa, his long legs stretched out before him as he leaned back against the cushions, each arm stretched out over the back. It worried her how natural he looked lounging on her sofa, in her apartment, in her life.

"Well, for what it's worth, I believe you now," she conceded.

"Then at least it worked." His eyes were full of concern, odd as that was.

She found herself wanting to cross the floor, wanting to get closer, but instead opted to remain seated at the dinette table. Her mind was tired and making her see things that weren't there. This man was not a protector, despite having saved her life. He was a vampire, and she couldn't overlook that little fact.

"So, the question is, who killed my mother and made it look like a vampire had done it? And what was the motive?" she asked, needing to get her mind off him and what he'd done.

He seemed to think about that. "Any number of enemies. Anyone who knew for a fact of our existence and wanted to bring us out into the open, some twisted vampire wannabe, a psychopath . . . or some wacko who just thought it would be fun to see what would happen once her body was found like that. I don't know."

Aria nearly smiled, so thankful he hadn't referred to her mother as "The Body" like the jerks at Baltimore Homicide did. To them, once a person died, they became just another body. They failed to think of that person as someone who meant a great deal to those who were left behind, someone who had been filled with so much life. An errant tear escaped before she could blink it back.

"Aria."

"I'm fine," she choked as raw emotion filled her throat, more tears threatening to fall, but he was already kneeling before her.

"We'll find her killer."

"*We'll* find her killer? Why are you being so helpful now? It wasn't so long ago you threatened to kill me."

"It wasn't so long ago *you* tried to kill *me*," he responded with a hint of a smile. "The Dream Teller sent me to you for a reason, and so far your mother's murder is the only reason I can see."

"You were sent to help me find my mother's murderer?"

"I think so. For whatever reason, this murderer branded your mother with fang marks. My kind can't take the risk of mortals discovering our existence."

"I take it you won't be calling the police if you find the killer?"

"We have our own way of meting out justice," he answered, his eyes darkening with the promise of retribution.

"Maybe it's wrong of me, but I'm glad to hear that," Aria admitted. "Anyone evil enough to kill a woman as kind as my mother deserves no mercy."

She thought back to the alley behind Fat Kracker's and imagined him delivering the same justice to her mother's killer. The image stirred something inside her, some dark part of her struggling to get out, and she recalled the scent of Rialto's blood so strongly he may as well have been bleeding before her now. Her mouth watered with anticipation as she wondered how rich and flavorful his blood would taste coating her tongue.

Shocked by her own thought, Aria bolted straight up in her chair, her mouth gaping as she looked into Rialto's narrowed eyes.

"What is it?" he asked.

"N-nothing," she stammered trying to still her heart before it lurched out of her chest. What the hell was wrong with her? "I'm just trying to piece together why someone would kill my mother and make it look as if she were a vampire victim."

"Are you sure that's all?" He seemed to study every inch of her face, his stare cutting right through her, straight inside her mind. And suddenly she knew that he knew. Just like he knew it when he saw her staring at that small trickle of blood on his neck, licking her lips, thinking of what it would taste like. He *knew*.

"Of course."

He didn't believe her. Any idiot could see the proof of that etched into every line of his gorgeous, bronzed face.

"Aria, what you saw tonight, what you've been through, would be hard for anyone to understand. I know it must be confusing, and you're probably unsure about what exactly it is you're feeling right now . . ." He broke off, letting his gaze fall to the floor, as if he might find the rest of what he wanted to say scattered there.

"I'm fine," Aria said a bit too defiantly, and wondered if she was trying to convince herself instead of him.

He shrugged as if giving up on the argument—if it could even be classified as an argument—and walked back over to the sofa. He snagged Alfred Dunn's journal from the coffee table before sinking back onto the blue cushions. He leafed through the pages and let out a grunt of derision. "How did you come to gain possession of this?"

"I got it at the library. The librarian's aide knew that I was studying vampires—"

"Studying ways to kill us, you mean."

"I thought one of you had killed my mother."

Rialto shrugged, his body language seeming to say it was all water under the bridge. "I can't believe you came across this at a library. I knew this man."

"You knew Alfred Dunn?"

"How else do you think he knew my name? He was a rather odd fellow. He saw dead people. He communicated with them."

"Really?" Aria tried to recall what she'd read in the journal earlier. "He doesn't mention that in the diary."

"Actually, he does. Many of his "sources" listed in here are actually apparitions. To him, seeing dead people was normal. What actually fascinated him was the vampire race. I think that's what drove him crazy. He wanted to hate us, but instead he was in awe of us."

"Why?"

"I have no idea. I only met him once, when he was searching for Eron."

"Did you know Eron?"

"Yes. We were part of The Order, a group of vampires who made it our mission to bring true justice upon the evil who walked among us. We only drank from truly horrid people, killing them in the process. Murderers, rapists, and the worst of all—child abusers."

"Why did Eron kill Alfred Dunn's son?"

"He was a child molester. He never touched his own, but there were plenty of other small victims. Eron never warned Alfred, though. Alfred had a vision, saw Eron feeding on his son. I'm afraid by the time that incident had happened, Alfred's special gifts had already started to drive him mad."

"Alfred Dunn was a psychic?" Aria turned toward Rialto, intrigued by the story.

"Yes, his main gift being the ability to see and converse with the dead. When he had the vision of Eron killing his son, he started hunting us, but he never really posed a threat. He was too intrigued by us to harm us, and we were too intrigued by him. The ability to speak to the dead is something we envy, especially since we have lost so many lives dear to us."

She'd never thought of that. Her own soul was weighed down with grief after losing two parents. How many loved ones had Rialto loved and lost? And why did she feel jealous over the thought of Rialto possibly having loved other women?

"Anyway, some of the stuff in this journal is accurate, like the lists of names and known hangouts, even if it's outdated. Most of what's in here, though, are just the bitter rantings of an old man who loved his son dearly and refused to see the evil inside him."

"An old man who insisted on blaming the real evil on your kind."

"Yes, and it sickened him that he was intrigued by us. Many are intrigued by us. It's not a crime."

Aria cringed under his gaze, knowing exactly what he was referring to. Unfortunately, what she felt while watching him feed was more than intrigue. It was the same thing that coursed through her blood in those fragments of dreams she remembered. Pure, undiluted lust.

"What's the reality, Rialto? What's it like being a vampire?"

He sighed heavily, seeming to mull over the thought. "We're just like everyone else, only we're harder to kill and we do need to drink blood to live, just not as often as people would assume. Unless of course we want to remain powerful. As I said earlier, there are good and bad in all life forms. That's true for us, too. But the good ones—we try to destroy the bad before they can do any harm." His eyes closed for a second and Aria saw a slight flinch as his skin pulled taut. She wondered what awful memory he was reliving but didn't dare to ask.

Then he opened his eyes and continued, "Bottom line, we're stronger than you and we're immune to disease. Some may think it's great to live nearly forever but it's a lonely existence and I wouldn't change over anyone."

"Change over?" Aria couldn't hold back the awe that escaped into her

Blood Curse

voice but immediately wished she had when Rialto's hard, burning eyes torched through her. "Not that I want to be changed over. I was just curious. I mean, can anyone be turned? How exactly does it work?"

"None of your damn business." Rialto rose abruptly and moved across the room, stopping in front of a piece of artwork hanging on the wall. He pretended to study it, but the effort was a thin disguise. He was avoiding her curiosity, clear and simple.

Aria wrung her hands, unsure what she'd done to offend him. Had she even offended him or was something else wrong? She wished she could see his face. Maybe it held a clue as to what was going through his mind, but he kept his back to her.

Turning her head to gaze out the window, she was instantly filled with alarm. The first pale golden hues were rising in the sky, indicating the coming of dawn, and there was a vampire standing in her living room.

"The sun is starting to come up," she said, an edge of panic in her voice. "Shouldn't you be locked in a coffin or secured in a dark cave by now?"

His back shook with laughter. "You have been watching way too many movies," he said, turning to face her. She took in the laugh lines splayed around his eyes and wondered how old he'd been when he'd been turned. Late twenties to early thirties, she assumed. "Ironically," he said, his mouth twisting into a grin, "I did hide in a cave just a few days ago as I entered Maryland, but only because I could sense you so strongly and my stubbornness wouldn't allow me to take time to rent a room. I don't need a coffin, Aria. A dark room will suffice."

"But I thought the slightest bit of daylight—"

He cut her off with a shake of his head. "Only direct rays from the sun can harm us, not daylight itself, and I'm old enough that I've built up some immunity. I can't tolerate it for long, but I won't instantly burst into flame."

"But you'll still burn before you can get back to where you're staying?"

"Yes."

Aria bit her lip, her gut instincts warring with common sense. He was a vampire, a strong, incredibly fast predator who drank human blood and had nearly lost control with her once. Yet he was also a protector, a man who'd saved her from two street punks and had rescued a young girl from a brutal pimp. He was also her best chance of seeing justice rendered. If the police caught her mother's killer they'd put him in a prison and he might be released years later. If Rialto caught him, he'd ensure the killer never hurt anyone again.

"You can stay here," she said quickly, before she could change her mind. "I'll sleep in my mother's room, you take mine, but I warn you that

I'm a light sleeper, and if you so much as poke your head through the bedroom door, I'll separate it from your neck. Vampire or not, that would kill *anybody.*"

# Chapter Five

*A COLD WIND BREEZED over her body, waking her gently from sleep. She opened her eyes, her gaze following a trail of white fog which entered the bedroom from beneath the door. The cold chill left her body, replaced by warmth and a sense of familiarity as the fog swirled upwards at the side of her bed, taking human shape.*

*She pushed the sheets aside and sat up in bed, her heart beating rapidly as the person emerging from the mist became increasingly more familiar.*

*Warm tears trickled down her cheek as she blinked, emotion clogging her throat to the point she couldn't speak. Her mother stood before her, a vision of beauty in a long, white gossamer gown. Her pale blond hair shimmered, as though backlit by the sun, and her smile was pure radiance.*

*"You're dead," Aria managed to whisper as fresh tears slid down her face. "You can't be here."*

*"I am always with you," her mother said, her smile fading. "Even in death I will watch over you."*

*"What's wrong?" Aria asked, watching fear seep into her mother's eyes as cold air once more stirred through the room.*

*"Danger comes your way."*

*"What danger?"*

*"I should have warned you earlier, taught you to be stronger."*

*Her mother's image shimmered, blinking in and out. Aria reached for her, but her hand found no purchase. Her mother was only there in spirit, a spirit which was quickly fading.*

*"Warned me of what? The killer? Mama, who killed you? Tell me his name!"*

*"I don't know the name, only the face." She was fading faster now, mist swirling up from the floor to cocoon her again.*

*"Mom!"*

*"Watch out for the vampire," her mother said as the fog engulfed her and she vanished.*

ARIA WOKE TO find her hand had gone stiff from clutching the crosses around her neck during the night. Her skin was pebbled with goosebumps and dried tears were sticky on her cheeks, but she was alone in the room. No chilled air or tendrils of mist remained.

"It was just a dream," she whispered, not the least bit surprised. It was the first time since her mother's death that she'd set foot in the room. Her mother's scent was everywhere. Between it and her apprehension about Rialto being so near it was a wonder she'd been able to sleep at all.

Rialto.

She threw back the covers and swung her feet to the floor. She'd slept fully clothed, wanting to be ready if she had to wake up to fight off a vampire attack. Despite her gut's insistence that Rialto wasn't a complete monster, she'd decided to follow common sense and keep her guard up. Then there was the dream.

*Watch out for the vampire.*

It was a bit of advice she definitely planned to heed. Glancing at the clock on her mother's nightstand she saw she'd slept until well past noon. "I must have been more tired than I thought," she murmured as she looked around the room, her heart aching as the familiar smell of her mother's belongings overwhelmed her.

She straightened the rose-colored bedding and lovingly ran her finger down the lacy sham which had once rested under her mother's golden head. "I miss you, Mom," she whispered and walked across the room to the closet. She opened the door and the dam holding back her tears broke free as she looked at her mother's beautiful dresses and abundant supply of shoes. "So many beautiful things but none as beautiful as you," she said on a gasp as the pain overtook her. "I'll find your killer, Mom. I'll make sure he pays."

She stood there until she could bring her emotions under control. There were boxes in the closet that she knew she should probably go through, but she couldn't do it yet. She never would have gone through her mother's things were she still living, so to do so now would only solidify the brutal reality that her mother was gone forever.

The phone rang from the living room, grabbing her attention. She closed the closet door, removed the chair she'd propped before the bedroom door and exited into the living area. She answered the phone and smiled as Trevaris's sweet voice filtered through the receiver. The building's maintenance man had become like a family member during her years residing here, and he had been extremely watchful over her since her mother's death.

"Hey there, Sweets. Thought I'd check up on ya. I saw that you had a visitor late last night."

"Those old eyes of yours sure don't miss a thing," she responded with a smile.

"Somebody has to watch out for you, young'un. Did these old eyes see wrong or was your visitor a gentleman caller?"

"He's just a friend."

"Uh-huh," Trevaris said, his tone indicating he wasn't buying her explanation. "It'd do you some good to have a man in your life. You just make sure he treats you like the treasure you are, Sweets. I may be getting up there, but I can still swing a mean bat. Don't make me have to break no legs off of somebody, ya hear?"

"You are crazy," Aria said through a chuckle, not bothering to mention the bat probably wouldn't work against Rialto unless it was sharpened to a point and rammed straight through his heart. "And my guest is nothing more than a friend." Oddly, a wave of disappointment rolled over her as she made the firm statement, and she found herself longing for something more than friendship. Maybe Trevaris was right. Maybe it had been too long since she'd had a romantic interest, since she'd put her fear aside and allowed herself to take the chance.

"Whatever you say, Sweets. Just be careful. A lot of these young men nowadays just don't know how to act around a decent lady like yourself."

"I'll remember," she promised before ending the call.

She walked down the small hall toward her bedroom and stared at the closed door. There was a vampire in there, she cautioned herself as she gripped the door handle, wondering if he were lying in wait for her. Her hand grew sweaty, slipping away from the knob. This is ridiculous, she thought as she wiped her damp hand on her pant leg. She'd sweat buckets last night, and without a shower she knew she was a pungent mess. Her clothes were beyond the door and she'd need to get them before stepping into the shower, unless she wanted to walk around in nothing but a towel until the vampire rose. No, she thought, that wouldn't be a good idea, not when she could still recall the images from the dreams she'd had, and he had apparently had some interesting dreams himself. She didn't want to give him such a broad expanse of skin to notice. And if what she'd read was true, the vampire's lust for sex could quickly give way to other forms of lust, forms which could lead to her death.

She took a deep breath and slowly, quietly, turned the knob and pushed the door open.

He lay on his back in the middle of her bed, the thin white sheets pulled up to his waist, leaving his chest bare. She couldn't help staring at his torso's muscled perfection, wondering why so many books described vampires as being pale and gaunt. That description couldn't be any further from the truth.

Tilting her head, she studied his sleeping form and noticed his chest didn't rise and fall like a person's should. It was as if he was . . . dead.

She walked over to the nightstand and took out one of the stakes she'd started keeping there since her mother's death. Holding it carefully in one hand, she cautiously approached the vampire in her bed. He made no sound or movement. He wasn't breathing at all.

Slowly, with the fear of him popping up at any moment, Aria placed her free hand over his heart and, after a long moment, felt the barest of flutters.

"Rialto." She spoke his name sharply and waited for him to open his eyes. When he didn't, her own heart skipped a beat. "Rialto!"

*I'm all right. Do not worry.*

Aria sucked in a breath of surprise. She'd heard his voice clearly, although his lips had never moved. "Rialto?"

He didn't speak again, if speaking was befitting a term for what she had just experienced. Was it telepathy? she wondered as she placed her fingertip to the corner of his mouth and traced the smooth lines of his lips. She studied his face and tried to guess his ancestry. He could be a deeply tanned white man, but she also picked up a bit of Hispanic in his features.

"How hard life must have been for you back then," she wondered aloud, speaking more to herself as images of her youth flashed through her mind. She'd faced her fair share of ridicule growing up biracial, and she'd been born in the late seventies, when such a thing was more accepted. When was he born? And where? She found herself longing to know everything about his past, all two centuries or so of it.

Sensing no danger from him, she lowered the stake she'd kept poised over his chest and walked to her dresser to pull out clothes for the day, opting for a dark gray T-shirt and worn jeans.

After showering and dressing, Aria emerged from the bathroom to hear her phone ringing. She continued towel drying her hair as she quickly walked into the living room and grabbed the handset.

"Hello?"

"Ms. Michaels? It's Detective Porter, Baltimore Homicide."

Great. Aria felt a ball of nausea start to roll around in her belly and quickly sat on the edge of her coffee table. "Yes?"

"Ms. Michaels, I thought I should prepare you for the latest development before you catch anything on the news."

"Latest development? This has something to do with my mother's murder?"

"We think so. We'll be right over. Please stay where you are."

Aria held the phone in her hand after she heard the click indicating the connection had been broken. She could tell by the man's tone that the news wasn't good. What was so bad that they had to tell her in person?

RIALTO OPENED HIS eyes as he came out of the deep sleep and immediately smelled the presence of strangers. He was on his feet in half a second, pulling on his shirt as he crept barefoot down the hallway toward the sound of voices. He didn't sense physical danger, but something had upset Aria terribly. He paused for a moment to wonder how he knew that without seeing her, then quickly shook off his wonderment. It was irrelevant how he knew.

He entered the living room to find Aria sitting on the coffee table with her back to him, a strange man and woman standing before her. The woman, a stocky brunette with a bun pulled back so tight she couldn't physically blink, noticed him first.

"Who are you?" she asked.

The man, a tall dark-haired Caucasian with a lean build, jerked to attention. His hand quickly reached under his jacket, but just as quickly halted as confusion filtered through his eyes. "Where did you come from?" His tone clearly indicated he wasn't happy with Rialto's presence.

"Are you going to shoot me?" Rialto asked, his mood bordering between amused and annoyed. The way the woman carried herself all but screamed cop. As for the man, well, he screamed cop too. Nervous cop. What did he see in Rialto that would make him instantly go for his weapon?

"This is my friend," Aria explained, her voice shaking with emotion. "He's been staying with me."

"Rialto Renaldi," he introduced himself as the male detective lowered his hand, no longer seeming to need his gun. The woman eyed him curiously, but Rialto ignored her, his attention stolen by Aria's distraught expression. Her eyes were glossy and red, soon to lose their battle with the tears threatening to fall. "What is it, Aria?"

"They think my mother was killed by a serial killer."

"You found another victim?"

Rialto directed the question toward the male officer, but it was the woman who took a step in his direction. "We can't discuss—"

"You can discuss anything in front of him," Aria snapped, turning her head to face the pair. "He's my fiancé."

The two detectives looked at each other, silently conferring, before the woman spoke again. "I'm Detective Reilly, this is Detective Porter. There was a second body found last month, and we found another woman's body in Leakin Park late last night. Both bodies were drained of blood and there were two small holes in their necks. We never released that bit of information to anyone outside the department, so we know this isn't a copycat killer. We have officers searching parks as we speak, seeing if we can turn up any other bodies, but so far it seems as though the killer doesn't have a preference for one specific park. Who knows what might turn up where."

"Who," Aria corrected the woman, her face devoid of expression but her tone firm. "Not 'what.' They may be dead bodies to you but they're someone's loved ones. They're people."

Rialto squeezed Aria's shoulder and glared at the insensitive woman as she muttered a small and meaningless apology. Reilly appeared older than Porter and had undoubtedly already witnessed enough cruelty in her profession to rob her of compassion. Rialto understood completely. Many a vampire had been turned bad by witnessing evil in abundance. Rialto hoped it would never happen to him, no matter how badly it sometimes hurt to care.

"We just wanted you to know before it's out in the open," Porter said. "We have to release a warning to the citizens of Baltimore since it appears we may have a serial killer on our hands. You realize this means there may be reporters wanting to speak with you?"

Rialto felt Aria cringe beneath his palm. He wouldn't allow the press to get to her, no matter what it took.

"I'm sorry for your loss, Ms. Michaels," Porter added. "I wanted to make sure you were aware of the progress of the case and prepared for the possibility of being approached by the media. It's important that if you are questioned you don't give out any information, especially the fact that holes were found in your mother's neck."

The man's voice was compassionate, as though he truly cared about Aria's feelings. However, the look he gave Rialto was anything but warm. "We'll leave you now, if you're sure you're all right." He stared at Rialto, his eyes full of accusation. Why?

He had his answer a moment later when Aria reassured the detectives that she was fine and saw them to the door. He watched as the male detective took Aria's hand and squeezed it, assuring her he would do everything possible to catch the killer. With sudden fury, he realized that the detective had a romantic interest in her. He balled his fists in response and felt the pressure of his fangs pressing through his gums, but he quickly schooled himself.

He had no claim on the woman and no intention of staking one. He'd learned the hard way that vampires and mortals did not mix. Once he found the killer and destroyed him, he was out of Maryland, and Aria could do as she pleased with whomever she pleased. Even if thinking about it made him want to kill.

"You can rise during the day?" Aria asked, keeping a cautious eye on him as she sat on the couch.

"Most of the day," he answered. "Unlike the stories you've probably heard, we do not die at dawn each day, although new vampires are extremely weak during daylight hours."

"What happened earlier? I went into my room to get a change of clothes and you were lying there, barely breathing. I checked for a heartbeat and all of a sudden you were speaking to me, but your lips never moved. How is that possible?"

Rialto recalled sensing her come into the room just after he'd entered the deep stage of sleep. "I remember feeling your fear and hearing you say that I was dying."

"I never spoke aloud. I thought you may have been . . ." Her voice trailed off as she stared at him, her eyes wide in disbelief.

"I heard you thinking," Rialto said, "and you heard me."

She visibly shook before standing and crossing over to the wall that separated the living room from the kitchen. She wrapped her arms around herself. "Do you read people's minds all the time? Can you speak like that to anyone?"

"No. I can only glimpse a person's mind when I'm feeding from them, and except with other vampires, I've never communicated through telepathy before."

"So what happened? You weren't feeding from and I'm no vampire."

"No, Aria, you're not, and I don't know what this connection is between us." He began pacing around the living area, careful not to bump into any easels. What *was* happening between them? He had heard stories before of . . . No. It couldn't be that.

"Why was your heart barely beating while you slept?"

"When vampires sleep, we reach a deep state where we are still conscious of what happens around us, but we are unable to move," Rialto answered, surprising himself by giving away one of a vampire's biggest secrets. Maybe the woman had a little witch blood in her after all. She certainly seemed able to get past his barriers and obtain information he normally wouldn't dare give a mortal. "It only lasts a short while, twenty minutes to a few hours, depending on our physical state. Our heartbeat and speed all decrease as our energy replenishes, but our ability to heal goes into overdrive. This is how we go on living for centuries. This not only replenishes the energy we use every night, but if we've been injured our wounds will be healed once we complete this stage of sleep. I was going through that stage when you entered the room."

Aria was silent, her expression saying she was mulling over this new information, and Rialto took the opportunity to think about a plan of action. "We need to find this killer, Aria. I don't know why, but it feels personal. I don't think this is just some deranged vampire wannabe. I think this is some type of revenge."

"Why do you say that?"

"I don't know. Gut feeling, I suppose. If I could see one of the bodies, maybe I could pick up something."

"Like a psychic?"

"Something like that. Actually, I was thinking I'd get some assistance."

"Assistance? More vampires?"

"A vampire-witch, actually." Rialto angled his head to the side and took in the confusion he saw in her eyes. "What is it?"

She shook her head slowly, as if the motion took all her strength. "I don't think I'm ever going to be surprised again. Vampires, witches, a combination of both . . . What other beings are out there that I don't know about?"

Rialto thought about it, wondering how much information he should give her. "Shapeshifters are the most common after vampires."

Her mouth dropped open and her eyes widened before she lowered her head into her hands and shook it. Rialto could tell this was all too much for her and felt himself wanting to smooth away the frown lines on her forehead. The intimate thought caused his heart to slam in his chest. What was wrong with him? He didn't belong in her world. As much as the thought angered him, she belonged with someone like the detective, a normal human, someone who wouldn't accidentally kill her.

"I must rest," he said, needing to get away from her so he could think clearly. "I just came out here because I felt your distress, but if you're all right now . . ."

"I'm fine. I guess vampires do tend to sleep all day long, huh?"

"We are creatures of the night," he responded, "and if I'm going to stake out the parks tonight I need to be well-rested."

She frowned at him. "Stake out the parks?"

"The killer is dumping bodies in Baltimore's parks. I have a better sense of smell and far better night vision than the police. The best way to catch the killer is while he's dumping the body of a victim," he explained, instantly regretting his choice of words as a shadow fell across her eyes.

"He dumped my mother like a pile of trash."

"I know. I'm sorry."

"When you catch him, destroy him. Promise me that."

He looked into her eyes and was stunned by the hunger for spilled blood he saw there. He'd felt such a need for vengeance more than a century ago, and he was sure he'd had the same look of rage in his eyes as he'd stared down at his father's battered body moments before killing him. Yes, he knew all too well how Aria felt.

"I promise you," he vowed, "your mother will have not died in vain. I will destroy her killer." *And I'll do whatever else is necessary to take that look out of your eyes,* he added silently.

# Chapter Six

THE SUN WAS STILL out, but Aria could feel the approach of night in the cool wind as she walked down West Baltimore Street, and she zipped the fleece jacket she'd donned before leaving her apartment. She had no real destination in mind, just a need to get out of the apartment, away from the vampire haunting her mind.

After Rialto had gone back to sleep, she'd received an onslaught of vivid flashbacks, scenes from dreams she'd apparently been having for a while but for some reason had suppressed. All featuring Rialto . . . and her. But they weren't all sex dreams which was what had really disturbed her.

Though most of the dreams were of them intimately entwined, there were a few that had really set her heart to racing. Images of them together, walking hand in hand through the snow, laughing and genuinely enjoying each other's company; the two of them sitting by a fire, Rialto brushing her hair as she read to him from a book; both of them prowling darkened alleys . . . hunting for blood.

Sex dreams she could understand. Vampire or not, the man was sexy as hell and what normal woman wouldn't fantasize about him to some extent? But the other ones made no sense. Was her subconscious trying to tell her something? That he was The One?

She laughed out loud. No way. The man was a killer, not that his particular skills didn't come in handy when saving her life and for meting out justice when her mother's killer was found. But she knew better than to entertain thoughts of anything more. He was one of the undead, for crying out loud.

No, her subconscious was just telling her it was time to get over old betrayals and brave a new relationship like her mother had been telling her for years. But where could she find a guy? Even before her mother's death she'd been a recluse, never leaving the apartment unless it was to take her finished pieces down to the little shop that sold her work. She thought of the detective, Jonah Porter. He'd seemed interested and was a good-looking man with a nice personality. Yet, she doubted he'd fill her with the heat Rialto sparked in her in all those dreams . . . and when he looked at her with those dark, stormy eyes.

It was a damn shame the man wasn't even human.

"Aria!"

Aria looked toward the direction from which her name had come and saw a tall, thin redheaded man waving from outside one of the buildings belonging to the University Of Maryland School of Medicine. As he jogged closer to her, she made out his face.

"Curtis? You're a medical student?"

"Yeah," he answered as he repositioned his backpack over his shoulder and caught his breath. "Feels like I've sold my soul to science sometimes, but it'll pay off one day. What are you doing in this area? Live around here?"

"Yeah, downtown close to Inner Harbor," Aria answered vaguely. One of the things her mother had always drilled into her head was that you didn't let anybody know where you lived unless you knew them well, which made it all the more surprising she'd so easily led Rialto to her apartment. "I was just out for a walk."

"You look like you have something on your mind."

*Just the fact that I'm fantasizing about a blood-drinking killing machine. Oh, and the serial killer that murdered my mother is still on the loose which I find just a bit upsetting.*

"I'm fine, just out walking. Helps me to get ideas for my writing, you know."

"How is that going?"

Aria started to answer, then gazed back at the building Curtis had just exited, an idea hitting her. "Actually, I'm stuck on something. Tell me, medical student, do you know much about hermatology?"

"You mean hematology?" Curtis grinned at her.

"Yeah, that's it, I think. The study of blood, right?"

"Yeah, and I know a bit about it, I guess. Why?"

Aria smiled. "I'm writing about vampires, remember? I need to know something about blood, don't I?"

"I suppose," Curtis answered as he shifted his backpack which appeared to be overstuffed with books. "Tell you what, I'm done with classes for the day, so let's discuss it over dinner, my treat."

Aria looked into his hopeful face, sensing his invitation was more than just a friendly one, and tried to figure out the nicest way to turn him down without hurting his feelings. Although her subconscious was insisting she could use a little romance in her life, there was just something about Curtis that seemed all wrong for the part. But she needed as much information as she could get from him, and she didn't know anyone else who might have studied hematology.

"Come on, Aria. It's not a date, just two buddies hanging out, discussing the gross subject of blood over dinner." He bobbed his eyebrows up and down in such a pathetic attempt at humor that Aria felt inclined to say yes out of sheer pity.

"Okay, but let's make it quick. I should get home before dark"

An hour and a half later, Aria was more confused than ever. If a body couldn't possibly be completely drained of blood, then why were the victims being left without a drop? Of course, Curtis was only a medical student. Someone who'd studied hematology exclusively for several years could possibly figure out a way. In fact, someone obviously had.

"I insist on seeing you home," Curtis stated firmly as Aria turned to tell him goodbye.

"I've been walking these streets for years, Curtis, and you've already paid for my dinner, which was more than kind of you."

"Aria—"

"Hush, now. You go on home and study or whatever it is you need to do. I'll be fine, I promise."

He cocked his head to the side, a strange look passing through his eyes as his body tensed, and Aria wondered if she'd somehow offended him.

"All right," he finally said, then added with a smile, "but the next time I see you, you'd better be safe and all in one piece."

"I will be."

"Be careful," he added, his expression serious. "Be aware of your surroundings. You don't know what all walks these streets at night."

*Oh, I have an idea,* she thought, wondering if Rialto was out prowling yet. "I'll be careful," she promised and shooed him away before turning to walk home.

The sun had set, and now the streets were illuminated by the glow of lamps and the pale blue moon. Looking up at the sky, Aria gazed past the eerily tinted moon and wondered if her mother was up there gazing down at her.

Suddenly, a tremor of fear snaked its way down her spine, distracting her from her thoughts. Someone was watching her. The feeling was similar to the one she'd had the night before when Rialto had followed her, but this time there was something different. Whoever was watching her now was furious, mad enough to kill.

Aria started to run down the sidewalk, but the angry presence didn't leave her. After a couple of blocks, she felt the emotion engulf her and knew that whoever was radiating this fury was dangerously close. She panicked, running into the street, not realizing her mistake until she heard the screech of tires and was blinded by the headlights of an oncoming car. She started to scream, but was silenced as she felt her body being propelled backward.

She landed on the concrete with a thud, but luckily something broke her fall. Or some*one,* she realized, as she turned her head to find that she was sprawled atop Rialto's body. The barely contained anger burning deep in his eyes stunned her, rendering her oblivious to her surroundings. She didn't notice the crowd forming around them or the barrage of questions being tossed at them. She remained speechless as Rialto ran his hands down her arms and legs, as if checking for fractures. Apparently satisfied that she was okay, he maneuvered out from under her and stood to grab her hands, slowly pulling her up from the sidewalk.

"She's fine," he announced to the crowd as he gripped her arm and led her down the street, forcing her to nearly sprint in order to keep up with his long strides. It was then that Aria realized the angry presence she'd felt had been him after all.

"What the hell were you doing?" He nearly spat the words at her once they were out of the crowd's eyesight. "Who were you with? Why the hell did you run out into the street like that?"

"I was running from you," Aria snapped. "I felt someone watching me, someone mad enough to kill me. What in the world is wrong with you?"

"My fury wasn't aimed at you. I felt that you were in danger and came looking for you, ready to kill anyone who might've hurt you. Now, I'll ask you again. What were you doing, and who were you with?"

Aria looked at Rialto in disbelief as she struggled to keep up with him. "I was having dinner with a friend. I wasn't in any danger until you scared the bejesus out of me."

"Who's this friend?"

She started to tell him none of his business, but then she thought better of it. He obviously wasn't in a mood to be put in his place. "The librarian aide from Enoch-Pratt. He's a medical student, and he told me that a body can't be completely drained of blood. How do you suppose my mother's body was drained?"

"Somebody obviously figured out a way to do it. Was the librarian aide the only person close to you tonight?"

"As far as I know." Aria shrugged in aggravation. "He's harmless. I wasn't in any danger."

"Yeah, well, you're not going out by yourself at night anymore. Baltimore is a dangerous city."

"And just what am I supposed to do? Stay locked in my apartment every night?"

"Sounds like a good plan to me," Rialto responded with a narrow-eyed glare as he led her through the main doors of a hotel. "We're stopping by my room so I can shower and change clothes."

Aria was ushered into his room without further comment. He locked the hotel room door behind them before going into the bathroom to shower. Aria looked about the room, but she didn't find any personal items that might give her some insight into Rialto's life. The curtains were drawn, so instead of looking out the window, she passed the time by pacing, trying not to imagine the water from the showerhead sluicing down the contours of Rialto's naked body.

Her attempts were futile as the sound of the running water reminded her of another dream. In this particular dream, she and Rialto were in the shower. Her back was pressed against the tiled wall as he held her by her waist and glided her onto his shaft as the water rained down over them. They moved together for what seemed an eternity until she felt him nip at her neck and . . .

The image shattered as she heard Rialto turn off the water and push aside the shower curtain. With the dream purged from her mind, she clearly recalled the way he'd so rudely dragged her down the street, as if she were a petulant child. Who did he think he was anyway? She turned to ask him just that as she heard the bathroom door open, but went mute at the sight of him.

He stood in the doorway with his damp hair hanging down to his shoulders, sending little droplets of water on varying paths down his muscled torso, eventually disappearing into the towel which hung low on his hips. Extremely low. Aria held her breath, afraid that one little exhalation was all that was needed to send that white scrap of terrycloth falling to the floor.

"Sit down, Aria."

She nodded obediently as she took in the sight of him, then anger surged as she realized what she was doing. "I'll sit when I damn well please, *master!*"

Rialto's eyebrow shot up and he held up his hands in mock surrender as he crossed the room, brushing past Aria to get to the dresser. His slight touch sent a shiver of awareness through her entire body. Damn, the man looked good for a dead guy.

"I'm not, nor have I ever been, a dead guy," he said angrily as he pulled a dark pair of pants and a matching shirt from the dresser.

"Don't do that!"

"Do what?"

"Read my mind!"

"It's not my fault you can't block your thoughts worth a damn."

"That doesn't give you the right to eavesdrop."

"You don't have the right to judge me, but you keep doing it anyway," Rialto snapped as he threw the clothes onto the bed.

"What are you talking about?"

"Monster, killer, walking dead . . . Any of those names ring a bell?"

"You're a vampire. You *are* the walking dead."

He grabbed her arm, pulling her so tight against him that she had no choice but to feel the hardness of him against her stomach. "Does that feel dead to you?"

She gasped, too close to him to think straight, too close to think at all. As her body flushed with heat, any fear she had of him quickly fled. All she knew was that he was a man and she was a woman, and she'd already had enough dreams to know they'd fit together perfectly. If the hunger in his eyes as he dipped his head was anything to go by, he knew it too. She let her eyelids lower and her lips part as she awaited his kiss, gasping in surprise when she was thrust away instead.

"Stay away from me, Aria, and for chrissakes, guard your mind when you're fantasizing about me!"

Aria gasped and sputtered as heat crept into her face. "You arrogant ass!"

"I'm doing you a favor," Rialto replied, his voice completely emotion-less. "Despite these dreams we've both had, the two of us can never be intimate."

"Then don't play games with me if you don't want me."

"I'm not."

"Then what the hell was that? Pretending you were going to kiss me only to shove me away and make me feel like an idiot? Is that the way you get your kicks?"

"I *was* going to kiss you—and a whole lot more than that—but fortu-nately my brain caught up to the other parts of my body. Once you get your hormones under control and can think clearly, you'll see that I did the right thing."

Aria huffed. "Believe me, vampire, I do not have my panties in a twist over you, so don't speak to me as if I'm some hormonal teenager throwing myself at you!"

"You're not? Those fantasies you're having are so strong I can pick up on the actual images. The heat in your eyes while you look at me can damn near burn my flesh. You're not angry right now because I've said something to offend you. You're angry because despite the fact that I'm a vampire and a killer you want me anyway."

"Oh really? So why are you so mad right now? Maybe because you want me but aren't man enough to—"

Aria found herself pressed against his chest, his mouth ravishing hers with passionate force, effectively cutting off the rest of her barb. The kiss softened, but it remained just as intense as it had begun, and Aria had to agree with Rialto on one thing—a dead man certainly couldn't kiss like *this*. She felt the kiss all the way down to her toes which were curling from the overwhelming sensations coursing through her body. Images from her dreams slammed into her mind, and she had to find out if the live version of the man could compete with the dream version. She lowered her hands to the towel at his waist, but a sound at the door jerked them to a halt.

The bolt Rialto had set slid to the side and the door swung open to reveal a young Spanish beauty with deeply tanned skin, raven-black hair and full, ruby red lips.

"I came as quickly as I could, darling," she announced as she entered the room and snapped her fingers, causing the door to close by itself. She came to an abrupt stop, her brow arching in surprise, then grinned while taking in the scene before her. "Am I interrupting something, sweetheart? You appear to be entertaining."

Aria stared at the buxom woman in the tight fitting black pants and turtleneck and seethed. No wonder he'd shoved her away. How in the hell could she compete with *that*?

*You don't have to compete with her.*

Although Rialto's mind-voice held a touch of amusement, there was an undercurrent of annoyance simmering beneath his words.

Aria looked between the two, noticed the way the smug grin on the woman's face filled Rialto's eyes with irritation and wondered what she'd gotten herself caught in the middle of.

*Well, whatever sick fantasies you have running through your mind, I won't be a part of them. I'm not into the whole threesome scene.* She directed the thought at him, along with a few choice names for not telling her he was involved with someone, figuring he'd pick it up like he'd picked up her other thoughts.

"Well, I think I'd best be on my way home," she said, struggling to keep the hurt from her voice. True, she'd barely known the man, but for some reason she felt as if her heart was breaking. *It's not him,* she thought, *I'm just so tired of being betrayed and rejected.*

"You can't leave, Aria. Someone was watching you earlier."

"Yeah, you," she reminded him as she crossed the room, averting her eyes from the woman. So far things hadn't gotten catty and she hoped they didn't. If the woman could close a door with the snap of her fingers, Aria didn't want to think about what she could do to her. She certainly wasn't going to stick around and find out. Going up against a vampire was one thing, but a woman who could move objects without touching them? She was not that stupid.

"No, you felt my anger after I sensed you being watched," Rialto explained. "You can't leave."

*This woman isn't who you think!* he added, his mind-voice beseeching her.

"Goodbye, Rialto," she stated firmly, ignoring him as she wrapped her hand around the door knob. If the woman wasn't his lover then why couldn't he speak to her out loud?

"Aria, this is my mother."

She froze, letting his statement sink in before allowing her hand to fall away from the knob. Slowly, she turned and looked at the two of them. The woman had moved to where Rialto stood and placed her hand on his arm. Aria hadn't noticed it before, but they did have the same dark ebony hair, the same full lips, and the same shaped eyes. But she looked younger than him, and not just because she would barely come up to his chest in bare feet.

"You're both vampires?"

Rialto nodded as his mother looked between them, her eyes full of questions and glowing, as if she saw something amazing.

"How can that be?"

"It just is," Rialto snapped as he grabbed his clothes from the bed and stomped into the bathroom, slamming the door behind him.

"Oh, my, I believe I gave the wrong impression when I entered," Rialto's mother finally said, a subtle pink coloring her cheeks. "My name is Seta, and I take it you're Aria?"

"Yes." The word came out as a low mumble, humiliation finding its way into her voice. "I'm sorry, I . . ." She paused. What was she supposed to say? *I met your son yesterday, but we've been having erotic dreams about each other since long before then, so please excuse my initial reaction to you, but I want nothing more than to find out if the real man can live up to his imaginary counterpart?* It didn't exactly seem like the appropriate thing to say to a man's mother upon their first meeting.

Seta smiled. "You're very beautiful. No wonder my Rialto is so taken with you."

"Taken with me?" Aria couldn't help snorting. "Hardly."

"I know these things, young one," Seta said with a knowing smile. "I'm not just a vampire but a witch as well."

"How is that possible? And how can you be Rialto's mother when you're obviously younger than him?"

Seta laughed. "My child, I am over two centuries old, and for that matter, older than my son by eighteen years."

"You gave birth to him before you were . . . changed into a vampire?"

"Yes." A dark shadow fell over Seta's face, and she looked away briefly before producing a strained smile. "I was born a witch, as all true witches are, but I wasn't aware that I was, in fact, a witch. I saw things before they happened, but I had no control over the gift before I was changed over. If I had, I would have foreseen my destiny, and well, I probably wouldn't be living as I am now. Nor would my son."

"You wouldn't be vampires?"

"No."

"You changed him over?"

"I did what any mother would do when she saw her child dying. I saved him."

# Chapter Seven

RIALTO EXITED THE bathroom and frowned. The shock of hearing his mother, a woman who valued her privacy more than most, disclosing such personal information to a stranger faded the anger he'd felt just seconds before.

"Mother." He greeted Seta, planting a warm kiss on her cheek. "I'm sorry I did not welcome you immediately upon your arrival. I was deeply engaged in conversation and didn't feel your presence until you had already thrown the door. You could have knocked though," he teased.

"My apologies, sweetheart. I wanted to surprise you, and strangely enough, I didn't feel your guest's presence. Your auras are so similar I thought it was only you in the room."

For a moment Rialto wondered over her last comment, then shrugged off the strange feeling it gave him. So what if his and Aria's auras were similar? They were both mixed race outcasts who had suffered much. It stood to reason that there would be some similarity. "And I see you have become acquainted with my guest, Aria Michaels."

"Yes, a very beautiful young lady," Seta responded before turning to address Aria directly. "I am sorry to hear of the loss of your mother and in such a heinous manner as well."

Aria looked truly baffled as she looked between the two. "How did you know about my mother?"

"I called upon her," Rialto answered, speaking directly to her for the first time since dressing. Then, turning to his mother, "I'm glad you heard me. I was afraid that you might be too far away."

"Darling, we could be at opposite ends of the earth and I would still feel when you need me." She walked gracefully to the bed and settled at the end. "I could feel the presence of evil as I neared the city, but I can't feel it anymore. It's as if whoever has done these evil things has put up a shield. I get the sense it is a male, but that's the only knowledge I have for now."

"Do you think you'll be able to find him?" Aria asked.

The look of pure, desperate hope glowing from within Aria's deep green eyes caused Rialto's chest to constrict. He couldn't allow himself to give into the desire drowning them, but he would find her mother's killer and at least give her that much peace.

"My mother and I will not rest until he is found," he promised, knowing his mother surely felt just how badly he needed to do this and would agree.

"Rialto speaks the truth," his mother added. "We will hunt down this monster and destroy him. If I can just lay my hands on a victim's body, I might be able to see him, or at least get a sense of who he is and why he is killing these women."

"We'll search the parks tonight and every night," he explained to Aria. "Eventually we'll happen upon a body he has left behind. My mother has the ability to sense images and emotions from bodies. These clues could tell us who the killer is."

"I want to go with you," Aria pleaded.

"No, that's not a good idea. You're a liability. Police will be searching the park. We can't take a chance of them seeing you. Mother and I move too fast for them to see us, and besides, I don't think you could handle what we might happen upon. You're not used to seeing the things we've seen."

Aria visibly sulked as she walked over to the bed and sat on the mattress. Rialto glanced at his mother, telling her with a look that it was time for them to go. "Stay here, Aria. Lock yourself in and rest. You could use a good night's sleep."

He looked back at her as he pulled the door shut behind him, fighting off the need to comfort her.

"SO, WHAT EXACTLY did I intrude upon?" Seta asked several minutes later.

Rialto's mother had been silent as they'd raced toward Leakin Park, but once they were inside the large park, scouring over an area which hadn't yet been reached by the police, she'd finally asked the question he'd known was coming. "It wasn't as it appeared, Mother."

"Really, because it appeared that you were nearly naked and holding a woman in your arms."

"I had just stepped out of the shower. We were talking, nothing more. Nothing was going to happen."

"And why not?" Seta paused to plant her fists on her hips. "Don't try to fool me. The lust shared between the two of you when you look at each other is thick enough to cut with a knife. There's pain there, too. What's going on?"

"Mother, please, we have a killer to find."

"And I have a son to take care of. Your auras weren't similar, Rialto. They were identical. Standing together in that room, both of you were wrapped inside the same exact aura. Do you know what this means?"

Rialto shrugged as he continued to open his senses to the land around him, continuing his search for a body, or better, the killer, although he doubted the man was crazy enough to enter the park while it was being searched by the police, no matter how easy it was to hide in such a large area.

"She's your soul mate, Rialto."

"My soul mate?" Rialto laughed. "Have you taken to reading romance novels?"

"Don't mock me, son. I know what I'm talking about. I can see inside your mind, remember? I already know how passionate you are to protect her. I know you dream of her. When did it begin?"

Rialto cursed beneath his breath as they continued to move through the park. From the moment she'd changed him over she'd been able to read his mind like a book. "Twenty-six years ago, when she was born."

Seta's eyes widened. "That was fate telling you your mate had arrived."

"That's ridiculous, Mother."

"Then why else would you dream of a complete stranger? You're already in love with her. You're just too scared to admit it aloud."

"And I have reason to be scared," Rialto snapped. "I still haven't forgotten what happened to the last innocent woman I loved."

"What happened to Antonia was awful, but you can't let her death stop you from loving again. Antonia wasn't who you were meant to be with. Maybe that's why she didn't take to the change."

"So it was fated that I had to kill her?"

"I'm afraid so," Seta answered, lowering her gaze to the ground.

"Well, then, fate can go to hell!" Rialto stomped away, cursing vehemently as he tried to purge images of Antonia out of his mind.

"Rialto, I don't think you fully realize what this all means!"

"What does it mean?" Rialto stopped and glared at his mother. "Why don't you explain clearly what fate has in store for me."

"Do you recall The Blood Revelation?"

"That fairy tale about predestined mates saving the world from Satan's wrath?"

"Three sets of vampires who can reproduce, creating warriors, one of which will save the world from eternal darkness."

"Yes, what about it?"

"The dreams the two of you share are erotic, are they not? You wanted her before you ever laid eyes on her, and you've told her things about our kind that you normally wouldn't even think of telling a mortal."

"What happens in our dreams is none of your business, Mother."

"It's every vampire's business. She is your soul mate, and the two of you are destined to create a child who just may grow up to save the world from destruction. Wouldn't it be wonderful to have a baby, Rialto? Haven't you ever wondered what it would feel like to be a father?"

Rialto frowned at her. "I believe your magic has driven you insane. I couldn't possibly father a child."

"You could if you were one of the prophesied three couples, and you are, Rialto. Two people who dream of each other, as you have, and share the same aura are predestined. You and Aria together make one of the three sets!"

"It's impossible."

"I could argue that it's impossible for you to read her mind when she's not one of us, but I know you can, Rialto, so don't deny it."

He shook his head adamantly and started walking again. "There must be some other explanation."

"There isn't. Although you've inherited enough magical ability from me to read the minds of mortals while you feed from them, that's the extent of your telepathic abilities. You know as well as I do that vampires can only read the minds of other vampires. She's a vampire waiting to happen, Rialto. It is your destiny to change her over and take her to your bed where you will create a child, a warrior."

He shook his head even more adamantly. "Then my destiny shall remain unfulfilled. I vowed long ago never to change over another innocent person, especially not someone I care for. I can't risk the chance of losing another woman the way I lost Antonia."

"If you don't change her over, you will lose her anyway. She'll grow old and die."

"Yes, and she'll go to the Lord as she should. Why should I do anything to prevent that?"

"To save—" Seta stopped mid-sentence, her eyes widening as her body stilled. Rialto could tell she was picking up on something, so he opened all his senses, pushing them to their limits, until he smelled the decay.

"This way," Seta instructed, quickly walking north.

Rialto followed her until they reached the body. They found it lying halfway under a patch of vines, the body of a brunette Caucasian woman, complete with two small rotting holes in the neck. What was left of her body was a shriveled husk. There was no doubt she'd been drained dry. Rialto used his hypersensitive hearing to locate the positions of the police. They were still far enough away to allow them time to examine the body.

Seta kneeled beside the corpse and placed her hands over the jeans clad legs, careful not to move the body. The police would need to find it just as it had been left. Rialto watched as, with her eyes closed, Seta flinched. Her body went stiff with the onslaught of images and emotions that were being pulled from what was left of the woman's aura. From the degree of decay Rialto could see and smell, he knew she wouldn't get much. Whoever the woman was, she had been dead too long.

A moment later, Seta broke contact with the body, quickly backing away and wiping her hands on her pants as if to get rid of residue left by the woman's aura.

"What did you see?"

Seta shook her head. "The woman wasn't scared, not at first. She thought he was a nice young man, well-educated and mannerly. I saw a needle. Something was in it, something clear. I saw blood, lots of blood. And I saw Eron."

"Eron? Are you sure?"

"Yes, I'm positive it was him."

"Eron couldn't be the killer."

"Of course not!" Seta looked back down at the body, her brow furrowed. "I couldn't see the killer. I can't get anything off of this body that will lead me to him, and I think he has me partially blocked."

"The body is too old. Maybe if we find one that hasn't been dead as long."

"Maybe," she said but he could see the doubt in her eyes. "Do you smell what I smell?"

Rialto kneeled next to the body and sniffed. What he discovered caused his blood to chill. Mixed in with the scent of rot and decay was an unmistakable odor. It wasn't as strong as it should be, as if it were diluted with some other substance, but it was there. "The scent of a vampire, but not quite vampire."

"I know. It's barely there, and whoever he is, he's blocked me. Only a vampire, another witch, or someone knowledgeable of black magic would make sure they couldn't be tracked by a witch. He actually cleansed her aura of all traces of himself."

"But you know she wasn't scared of him."

"Yes, but I can't get a face or a name."

"Why did you see Eron?"

"I don't know, but it worries me. He's missing."

Rialto stared at her in surprise. "Missing?"

She nodded. "I haven't heard from him in a while, and his Keeper hasn't seen him."

Rialto examined the holes in the corpse's neck, trying to shake off his feelings of unease. "The bite marks look real, Mother. Why wouldn't they heal?"

"I don't know. And all of the blood has been taken. You can tell by how shriveled she is. Maybe that has something to do with them being unhealed."

"What exactly happens if you continue drinking after death has set in?"

She shrugged. "We get our strength from the blood that still has life flowing through it. As you know, Christian drinks bagged blood. It merely sustains his life, but it has no power to it."

"Could the killer be a new vampire? Someone too ignorant to know that you're supposed to stop feeding when the heart ceases to beat?" Rialto could feel the dread creeping into his voice. How was he going to tell Aria that one of his kind had, in fact, killed her mother?

"No." Seta shook her head. "No single vampire could stomach that much blood, even if a pack of them feasted on this woman they wouldn't have taken every single drop. Once the heart stops pumping blood, it's hard to extract. Whatever evil being did this, it was not a vampire."

"But, the scent—"

"That doesn't matter. It isn't the right scent for a vampire. I have no idea what kind of creature is doing this, but we will find out."


ARIA SLEPT FITFULLY, waking repeatedly throughout the night. The sixth time she awoke, a shadow loomed over her bed. She gasped, jolting upright.

"It's me," Rialto said as he sat beside her, easing her back down against the pillows. "Relax."

"Did you find anything?"

"We found a body but I'm afraid my mother wasn't able to get enough off it to identify the killer. We're not through yet, Aria. Not by a long shot."

Aria tried to bank down her disappointment. At least they were trying. She shook her head in wonder, still a little surprised that the vampires were turning out to be the good guys. More surprising was the fact they still wanted to help her after the way she'd reacted when Seta had entered the room. The woman must have thought she was unbalanced. "I'm sorry about earlier. I saw a beautiful young woman and I thought that . . ."

"I know," he said, smiling knowingly, and Aria knew he could sense her confusion as she tried to sort out the jumble of emotions coursing through her. "She looks much younger than I do. I have to remind myself of that when we're out in public. If I call her Mother, we get quite a few odd looks."

"I can imagine. I hope I didn't offend her. Where is she now?" She hoped the woman wasn't staying away because of her earlier behavior.

"Actually, she likes you a lot, but reading auras off the deceased takes a lot of energy. She needed to feed." Rialto grinned again. "Now go to sleep."

"I can't. I keep waking up."

"Bad dreams?"

"Incredibly good ones." She could tell by the way his eyes dilated that he knew exactly what she'd been dreaming of. He was leaning over her, his mouth close to hers, and Aria threw caution to the wind, grabbing him by the back of the neck and pulling him closer, giving in to the attraction she'd been trying to fight.

"Aria—"

She stopped his protest by covering his mouth with hers, quickly dipping her tongue inside to discover the depths she had so recently explored in her dreams. Rialto started to pull back, but she quickly wrapped her leg around his and rolled, landing on top of him in the big bed.

"Aria, you're coming out of sleep, out of a dream."

She shook her head as she stared down into his gorgeous face. "I'm not asleep. I want this. If I'm going to be honest, I've wanted this all along, despite knowing what you are."

And that was no lie. The longer she was with him, the more dreams she remembered and dreamed anew, the less she thought of him as a creature. He was a man, a sexy as hell man who would continue to haunt her dreams until she finally discovered what he was able to do to her body in reality. If it was half as good as what he delivered in her dreams, she'd be a fool to deny herself that pleasure.

"Aria, I don't want to hurt you."

"You won't."

"I could."

"You won't."

She kissed him until she felt him respond, matching and surpassing her own intense passion. Clothes were strewn across the room as they continued their foreplay, kissing, touching, and licking every body part they could find. She wasn't a virgin, but she felt as though she had never been touched by a man before this night. No other man had ever mattered. This man, this vampire, was who she belonged to. It might seem insane, but it was a fact she knew in her heart.

She gasped as his fingers sought entrance to her throbbing body, mimicking the same action his tongue played inside her mouth. She tightened her fingers over his shoulders, trying not to come apart. Not yet. She wanted him with her when she went over the edge.

"Rialto, please—"

"Not yet," he groaned as he bent his head to take one hardened nipple into his mouth, swirling his tongue over the tip.

"Ri-ahl-to!"

"Not yet." He continued suckling at her breast, stroking her with his fingers as though playing a piano, hitting each note just right. Aria felt the first sweet tickle starting from that very spot, then spreading through her body until she shook from the enormity of it.

"Rialto!" she gasped, breathing heavier now as her body was racked with a pleasure she had never thought possible. Would it always be like this with him? She knew sadly that it wouldn't. He would either leave her or else stay only to watch her grow old and feeble, unable to satisfy him in this way.

*You can go with him, be like him.*

She stilled as the whispered voice invaded her thoughts, and Rialto cupped her cheek. "Are you all right?"

She nodded, unable to find words to explain what had just happened. She shrugged off the odd feeling that she was being guided and gripped his narrow hips. "Your turn," she breathed, raising her own hips to meet his, sliding him deep inside her body and sighing with pleasure as she felt every hardened inch of him slide against her slickened walls until she was completely filled.

He groaned low in his throat and started to move, gliding in and out, alternately fast and slow, his hands over her breasts as his mouth mated with hers, stifling her cries. She moved with him, riding out one orgasm after another as he continued to find that magic spot and stroke it just right. Oh, how to make this last? Whatever she had to do, it would be worth it.

*You can be with him like this forever.*

How? Aria asked silently, hoping whoever was guiding her could give her the answer that would make Rialto hers for eternity.

*Share his blood.*

The thought should have disgusted her. Instead, she found the concept highly erotic, remembering when he had taken her to the alley to watch him feed. He had looked so powerful, so strong, and she remembered the smell of his blood as his neck was scratched, the delicious aroma that had whet her appetite.

Growing hungry with the thought of it, she bit down into Rialto's lip and suckled at the juicy flesh. Her body screamed with pleasure as the first tangy droplets touched her tongue, electrifying her instantly.

Rialto pounded inside her until he groaned, his body shaking as his own orgasm hit him fast and hard. Aria continued to drink from the tiny spout she'd created in his lip until he pulled away to dip his head against the hollow of her neck. She felt something scraping across the skin at the side of her throat and cried out in ecstasy as she was hit with another bone jarring orgasm.

Then something changed. Rialto pulled away, his face etched in horror, his eyes glowing. She could see blood on his lips, hers and his. The hunger inside her sent her flying for his mouth but he grabbed her before she could reach it, pinning her to the bed with her hands raised over her head. She struggled against his grasp. Although she felt a new and powerful surge of strength inside herself, she was no match for him.

"No, Aria," he growled. "No . . . no . . . NO!!!" His shout was as mighty as a lion's roar before he disappeared from the room in a blur of motion, leaving her in his bed, naked and burning with shame, although she didn't know why she felt ashamed.

She loved him, she realized suddenly, as pain held her fragile heart in a vice. He was a vampire and she knew very little about him, but she loved him. Her brain could scream at her all it wanted about how stupid she was to even consider loving him, but she couldn't deny what she felt inside. She wanted this man, and the voice in her head had told her sharing his blood was the way to be with him forever. But, obviously, he didn't want to share the rest of his life with her.

Aria buried herself under the sheets and cried into the pillows, her heart aching for Rialto's love and her body aching for his blood.

# Chapter Eight

ARIA WOKE TO find herself still naked, wrapped up in the sheets from Rialto's bed. She didn't have to peek out from beneath the covers to know she was alone. Groaning, she sat up in bed and willed herself not to cry. The pillowcases were still slightly damp with the tears she'd shed the night before after Rialto practically vanished right before her eyes.

"I never could pick them right," she mumbled to herself while finger-combing her mass of unruly hair.

As the events of the previous two days came rushing back, she shook her head in disbelief. "I slept with a vampire," she said to herself, needing to speak the words aloud in order to emphasize just how serious an action she'd taken the night before. When she was with Rialto, he was just a man, nothing mystical or supernatural. But when she was away from him, she was able to look at the situation from a different perspective and she instantly realized her mistake. She couldn't have a relationship with a vampire. It couldn't possibly work, so why were her feelings for a stranger so strong?

Because he wasn't a stranger, she conceded. He'd dreamt about her since her birth, and for whatever reason she'd had her fair share of dreams about him. They were linked somehow.

*Watch out for the vampire.*

Her mother's words rang through her , reminding her how reckless she'd been. Her mother had always had a way of knowing things . . . which made it all the more surprising she'd been murdered. She should have seen her killer coming from a mile away. Mary Ayers had been an excellent judge of character and had the uncanny knack for sensing trouble brewing. She'd even woken in the night screaming the moment Aria's father had been murdered. If her mother had managed to come back in a dream to warn her about the vampire, she'd do well to listen.

Still, his rejection hurt. Aria looked at the clock sitting on the nightstand and saw it was nearly noon. She wondered where Rialto had escaped to. He was probably sleeping now, possibly in another room at the same hotel or maybe he'd needed to get completely away from her.

She walked over to the small bathroom, trying to ignore the dull throbbing between her legs which served as a reminder of the passion the night before, a reminder of just how long it had been since she'd trusted anyone enough to allow them inside. And no, it wasn't just her body that Rialto had entered, but her heart and soul as well.

"Leave it to me to fall for a frigging vampire who I barely even know," Aria grumbled to herself before she looked into the bathroom mirror and gasped, shocked by her own reflection. She raised her hand to her face and ran her fingers over the newly darkened skin. It looked as though she had been in a tanning bed, her skin now slightly darker than it reached in mid-summer. "What in the world?"

She continued to stare at herself in wonder, trying to figure out how she'd darkened so dramatically overnight. All she had done was sleep and have sex with Rialto. And . . . she had tasted his blood. She gasped, recalling that part of the evening. Heat grew inside her as she remembered its taste as it spilled over her tongue, the way it seemed to empower her more with every sip.

She ran her fingers over her neck while she looked at it in the mirror, but if Rialto had bitten her, there was no evidence to be found there. The healing properties in Rialto's saliva would have erased any punctures. But she remembered the feel of his teeth scraping over her neck before he'd fled. She'd drunk from him, and he had quite possibly drunk from her. Was that why her skin was darker?

*Oh, dear god, had Rialto turned her into a vampire?*

Aria ran back into the room and pulled on her clothes, then paused just as she started to run outside. If she was a vampire, could she handle the sun? Rialto said the UV rays would destroy them. She thought about sticking her hand out a window just to see, but fear stopped her. She didn't feel any different except, maybe, a bit stronger, and that wasn't by any large degree. She ran back to the bathroom mirror and checked her teeth. No fangs. Of course, Rialto didn't have visible fangs most of the time either.

"So you drank his blood, hmm?"

Aria jumped at the sound of Seta's voice and whirled around to find the elegant beauty standing just beyond the bathroom's entrance, a knowing smile plastered to her face. Realization slowly dawned. "It was you I heard last night!"

"Yes."

"Why?"

"It is your destiny to be one of us, to be with my son." Seta walked to where Aria stood and held her chin with the tips of her long fingers. "This is the real you, Aria. The blood has revealed the way you are meant to be seen by the world. You are so beautiful when you don't try to hide from what you are."

"I'm not hiding."

"I'm a witch, Aria. You may lie to yourself, but I see the truth. I have seen images of your past. I know your mother encouraged you to stay out of the sun and cover yourself in excessive amounts of sunscreen in order to appear white."

"I had to," Aria explained, coming to her mother's defense. "In the town we lived in, racism was so bad it was easier to pretend we were both white."

"And why didn't that change when you came to Baltimore? You should not be ashamed of what you are."

"I'm not ashamed," Aria stated as she exited the bathroom to sit on the bed. "It's just that, well, the areas I've lived in haven't been ideal for someone like me. Passing myself off as white was just easier than dealing with the scorn of being biracial."

Seta gently shook her head. "But it was wrong. I don't blame you. I have already seen your past, and I know you were taught to hide this very special part of yourself. In fact, it probably saved your life while you lived in that dreadful little town. Now, however, it is time to accept who and what you are. Your destiny is beckoning."

Aria eyed her skeptically. "And just what is my destiny?"

"You are to join with my son and save the world."

Aria started to laugh, then bit her tongue to stop the sound from emerging when she saw the seriousness in Seta's eyes. "How could I help save the world, and what would I be saving it from?"

Seta flinched and turned her head toward the door. She muttered something too low for Aria to hear and wrung her hands nervously.

"What is it, Seta?" Aria asked in concern.

Seta frowned as she returned her attention to Aria. "It's Rialto. The stubborn fool knows I'm talking to you, and he is rushing over here right now, in broad daylight."

"In daylight!" Aria's chest contracted, and her heart felt as if it would burst with panic. "Won't daylight kill him?"

"It could, but he's moving quickly and he's protected himself. He stayed at your apartment last night instead of renting another room here."

"Why would he risk being out in daylight?" Aria asked, too concerned with his safety to care that he'd stayed in her home without her permission.

"Because he doesn't want you to know the things I want to tell you, so I must be quick. He's almost here." She spoke rapidly. "Aria, Rialto feels strongly for you and wants to protect you from your destiny, but it isn't necessary. You were meant to be one of—"

The door slammed open before Seta could finish her sentence. Rialto appeared in the doorway, wearing the same clothes he'd worn the day before, and his head was bowed down like a bull about to charge. "That's enough, Mother."

He looked awful, yet Aria couldn't help the rush of heat that overtook her as she watched him enter the room and shut the door. His clothes were wrinkled, his body rigid, and his dark, angry eyes were red-rimmed as if he hadn't rested in days. And he smelled overwhelmingly of coconut.

"I see you found Aria's supply of sunscreen," Seta commented. Then, to Aria's mortification, she said, "Did I not teach you better manners than to run out on a woman after sleeping with her?"

The tense silence that filled the room fueled Aria's anxiety. She wanted to run to Rialto, despite the tactless way he'd left her before, but as he glared at his mother, the burning fury in his eyes warned her to stay back. He had yet to even acknowledge her presence and she had the feeling he didn't intend to.

"What I do and who I do it with doesn't concern you, Mother."

"In this case it concerns all of us."

He snorted. "Says an old story."

"It's true, Rialto. Stop fighting your fate."

"I will not be with her in that way!" Rialto accentuated his declaration by pointing a finger straight at Aria. "Once we find her mother's killer, I'll make sure I never see her again."

Aria gasped at the same time Seta's face reddened in anger. Rialto still wouldn't look at her, as though she were too unworthy for that much of a gesture. If he didn't want her, he could have said so, but to dismiss her so thoughtlessly in front of another person was a complete humiliation. She searched her mind for some response, something that would let Rialto know that she didn't need him anyway, but she couldn't think of a lie. Her entire body shook with the pain of his confession. He'd only wanted her for one night of sex, and he'd even had to be coaxed into that. In that moment he made her feel lower than any man from her past had ever managed because her ancestry had nothing to do with his behavior. He'd known all along what she was. He simply didn't want *her*.

Aria stormed from the room before she did something she'd regret the rest of her life, like cry in front of the bastard.


"ARE YOU SATISFIED now?" Rialto asked his mother as the door slammed shut. Aria's pain washed over him, but he resisted the urge to chase after her.

"*Satisfied?* How dare you hurt her like that! Have I not raised you better?"

"You didn't start raising me until I was twenty-nine years old," he stated, knowing the comment would hurt his mother deeply. It was unfair and despicable for him to purposely hurt her, and maybe even childish, but she'd forced him to hurt Aria without a second thought. He couldn't stop himself from lashing out. "I'm sorry if I haven't been a good little vampire."

"How could you say such a hurtful thing? You know I was always there watching over you." Her face fell and her eyes were haunted with pain. Rialto almost apologized. Almost. His own pain was still too raw to forgive so quickly.

"How could you force me to do what I just did?"

"I didn't—"

"You would have told her that crap about fate and gotten her hopes up that we could be together. She's in love with me. Damn it to hell, she's tasted my blood!"

"I know."

He studied her through narrowed eyes. "How do you know what happened between us? I know she wouldn't tell you. Dammit! You were listening in, weren't you?"

"Don't make it sound as if I'm some kind of voyeur. It's not like I was watching the two of you."

Rialto roared a string of obscenities and stormed past his mother, slamming the bathroom door closed behind him. He bent over the sink and turned on the taps, then stared at his youthful reflection in the mirror. What he wouldn't give to be normal. Or dead. Physically, he had been twenty-nine years old for more than a century and a half. Inside, he didn't know what he was, but he was definitely too old to worry about his mother catching him in the sack with a woman. Unfortunately, his mother, the vampire witch, was always in his damn head, feeling what he felt. Privacy was a word unknown by the woman. Had she felt the intensity of the sensations which had steamrolled through him the night before? He cringed at the thought.

He grabbed a rag and began washing the sunscreen off his face and hands. The tropical coconut smell tormented him, reminding him of the way Aria had smelled as she writhed beneath him not that many hours ago. He never should have given in to his desire, never should have allowed himself to be in a position to hurt her.

She was perfection. Her smell, the silky smoothness of her unblemished skin, the passion that blazed in her eyes. The pure, intoxicating flavor of her blood.

He'd only suckled a few precious drops before her essence slammed into him, overwhelming him with its strength. He had been tempted to sate his appetite by plunging his teeth deep into her flesh, drinking from her until she ran dry, but thankfully, an image of Antonia flashed through his mind, reminding him of why he couldn't take all her blood. He cared too much for her to let her die, so if he'd taken too much blood he would have attempted to change her over, and that in itself would be her destruction.

So he'd run. He had been dressed and out of the room before he could process what he was doing, fear taking over his body and sending him fleeing into the night. But, he hadn't had many night hours left, and hunger had gnawed at his insides, sending his body into violent tremors. He'd physically ached for another taste of Aria's blood, but he hadn't allowed himself to go back to her. The hunger had grown until he couldn't think of anything but fulfilling his thirst, so he'd run to an area of town known for its abundant supply of prostitutes.

He'd grabbed one without looking and took her behind a Dumpster in a nearby alley. For a moment he'd been tempted to sate his other desires with her, but he'd known she wouldn't satisfy him. In nearly two centuries of living he had bedded many women, but he'd never felt anything as earth shattering and explosive as what he'd felt with Aria. So he'd only drunk from the prostitute, hoping to ease the hunger inside him that had become a deafening roar in his ears, blocking out everything else around him. But the hunger hadn't gone away.

He'd backed away from the woman's limp body, satisfied that he'd left her with enough blood to survive, and pressed his hand to his stomach as it started to protest. He hadn't been able to remember the last time he'd felt nauseous, but it was before he'd become a vampire. Before he'd had time to analyze what his nausea meant, he'd found himself on his knees, throwing up the blood he'd just drank. And he'd still been craving another taste of Aria.

"Rialto! Darling, are you all right in there? You can't avoid me forever."

Rialto shook his head in an effort to obliterate the previous night's memories. Daytime or not, Seta would wait for him until he emerged from the bathroom, and he was too damned tired to delay their argument's inevitable continuance. He turned off the water and dried his face with a towel, wishing for what seemed like the millionth time that this could all be a dream, that he could wake up on the cliffs outside his father's home to find that he'd never been turned into a vampire and it was just a terrible nightmare.

But it wasn't a terrible nightmare, and he couldn't pretend it was.

"I know avoiding you is futile," Rialto told his mother as he reentered the room, "but could we finish this argument later? I'm more tired than I've ever been in my life, both mortal and immortal."

Without waiting for his mother's answer, he stretched out on the bed, feeling a sharp pang of longing as Aria's scent wafted up from the sheets, teasing his nose and heating his groin. *Damn it to hell and back!*

Seta looked at him and frowned, then walked to the bed and laid the back of her hand against his forehead.

He heaved an impatient sigh. "I'm not sick, Mother. I'm a vampire for crying out loud. It's not as if we can catch the common cold."

"You're sick in love and feverish with desire, sweetheart." She took her hand away and wiped the sweat that came with it on her pant leg. "You drank from her, didn't you?"

"I may have taken a little sip."

"Is that why you ran away?"

Rialto squirmed and closed his eyes, wishing she would disappear. He may have been raised by another woman, but this was still his mother, having given him life more than once, and he still felt awkward discussing such matters with her. It wasn't so much the drinking of Aria's blood that scared him as the feeling of completeness when their bodies were joined together. It was too right, and he knew that if he indulged himself in another go-round he'd be compelled to make her his partner for life, no matter the consequence.

"I understand," Seta said cautiously, yet she didn't cringe under Rialto's dark glare. He hated it when she read his mind without his permission. "Hurting her because of your own fear isn't right, not if you really love her. It isn't right to make yourself sick over her, either. Quit fighting it, Rialto. You're already addicted to her, and the feeling is never going to go away. You might as well give in to it."

She walked to the door and, with her hand on the knob, turned back toward him. "I won't tell her anything today. You can rest peacefully knowing that." She watched him with such sorrow in her eyes that it tugged at his heart, making his breath stop for a moment. "Everything I've ever done I've done out of love for you. I hope you will realize that someday."

Rialto stared at the door after it closed behind her, his eyes burning with rage. He knew she loved him, had always known it. He simply didn't deserve that love. Not from her—not from anyone. Not after the way he'd hurt the ones foolish enough to care for him—Antonia, his mother and now Aria.


ARIA VICIOUSLY WIPED away another traitorous tear as it rolled down her cheek. She had spent too many years hardening herself against the blows life kept delivering to let her protective shell be cracked wide open by a bloodsucking asshole. Yet, as she continued her trek down the street leading to her apartment, she knew she was losing the battle. She was all alone against the army of tears threatening to attack.

*Stop. Go the back way.*

Aria froze as Rialto's voice spoke from within her own mind. She whirled around, half expecting to see him. "Rialto?"

*Reporters and photographers are in front of your building. They've been camped out there all night.*

Aria closed her eyes and let herself just feel. He was nearby. She didn't know how she knew that, but she did. Hopefully, he had enough sense to be indoors. After the way he'd treated her earlier, she really shouldn't care if he burnt himself to a crisp, but to her own annoyance, she did.

Per Rialto's instructions, Aria changed course and took a longer path home, weaving through side streets and back alleys until she reached the narrow lane leading to the back of her building. She wasn't surprised to find a tall blond woman and an Hispanic man with a camera lurking on the back stoop. Someone had to realize she might take the back way in once she discovered the crowd in front. Fortunately, she saw them before they had the chance to see her. She quickly changed direction and ran to the side of the building where the maintenance man resided in a small apartment.

The silver-haired black man answered on her first knock.

"Hey, Trevaris."

"Hey, darlin'. How you doing?" The compassion in his voice was as strong as the sympathy in his caramel brown eyes. "I'm 'spectin you wanna cut through here to avoid those damn reporters and camera people. They've been meddlin' around here all day. Bunch of vultures is what they are."

"Would you mind?"

"Course not, young'un." He stepped aside so she could enter his small, humbly decorated apartment. "Say, you sure did darken up since I last saw you. You look kind of Brazilian or something."

Aria nervously ran her hand over the base of her neck. "Yeah, I know. I guess I got too much sun." She ignored Trevaris's speculative glance. They both knew damn well there hadn't been that much sun out since they'd last seen one another.

"Well, you look good." He led her to the door that opened into the building's interior hallway and warned her to stand back while he checked for reporters. "Looks like they're heeding my warning to stay out of the building itself," he said after making sure the hall was clear. "Damned cops must've leaked your name. The story about the killer was on the morning news. Now everybody wants to interview the families of the victims like they actually give a rat's ass. All they want is to sell a damn newspaper." He shook his head in disgust.

Aria smiled, touched by his concern. She'd do anything for Trevaris. He was really the only friend she had. "I suppose my name did get leaked, but it'll all die down soon. I just have to avoid them."

"Take care of yourself, kid, and I'm sorry you're goin' through all this," he added sincerely. "You need anything, anything at all, you just holler. I'll be watchin' out for ya."

"I know you will, Trevaris." Aria hugged the older man before walking out into the hall. "Thanks for having my back."

"Always, Sweets, always."


IT WAS CLOSE TO midnight when the fine hairs along the back of Aria's neck stood on end. She paused, her hand holding the paintbrush freezing just over the canvas. In front of her, Rialto's dark gaze stared straight into her own eyes, daring her to look away. Behind her, the real version stood watching, waiting . . . Craving?

"The balcony doors were locked." She didn't turn. Didn't dare take her eyes off the painting of him. The oil-based version of Rialto was no danger to her. The inspiration for the painting was lethal.

"Locked doors have never stopped me before." His voice was a low rumble, the sound of warning thunder moments before a deafening storm broke loose. The sound of it sent bolts of electricity surging through her veins, igniting an inner storm inside her own body. It caused her stomach to roll over, just as it had been doing for the past three hours, starting with the first hunger pain. At the same time her skin had begun to fade.

"I came to tell you something."

Aria set the brush on the easel tray and stood. Refusing to look at him, she walked out of her bedroom, away from the warm inviting bed that gave her too many bad ideas, knowing he would follow. She stopped in the middle of the living area, her arms folded across her chest, trying to ignore the goosebumps dotted along them and the icy coldness quivering through her. She had been running hot and cold all night, no doubt coming down with a bug of some kind. Just her luck.

"Aria, look at me."

She was tempted to, but she wanted him too badly, even after he'd dismissed her so crudely, that she knew it would be a mistake. She swallowed hard against another bout of nausea. "I'd rather not. I don't feel well, Rialto, and I really don't want to hear what you have to say. I think you summed things up quite well at the hotel earlier."

"I never intended to hurt you."

Was that pain in his voice? Remorse? A flicker of hope ignited in her chest but she quickly doused it with a wave of reality. He had dismissed her carelessly, thoughtlessly. He would do it again.

"You can't hurt someone if they don't care." She shrugged her shoulders, attempting to appear aloof, hoping he couldn't see through her facade. She might not be able to reclaim the pieces of her shattered heart, but at least she could walk away with a little dignity. "We had one great romp. Let's not analyze it to death. You're free to move on. I don't need anything from you."

"You need my help finding your mother's killer." He seemed to growl out those words, almost bitterly. Or was that just her imagination? "And you hardly seem the type who just goes about *romping*."

"Well, I'd like to think I haven't reached slut level, but I enjoy the pleasures of the flesh as much as the next—" She broke off as he stepped in front of her. His face was covered in sweat. His sweat-dampened hair was pulled back into a low ponytail, his face pale. His body . . . It didn't appear nearly as strong and intimidating as it had before. "What's wrong with you?"

"I'm sick."

"I didn't think vampires could get sick."

"I didn't either."

Aria gasped, thinking of the way she had been feeling. Her temperature switched from burning to freezing, she battled with fits of nausea and intense hunger, yet couldn't bring herself to eat anything. She wanted something to fill her, but it wasn't food. It was . . . blood. "You're sick and whatever you have you gave it to me."

"You mean like an STD?" His mouth quirked into a slight grin, an eerie sight against the dullness of his once golden skin. "Impossible. Vampires don't carry diseases, nor do we catch them."

"Then how can you be sick? Why am I sick?"

"Maybe you're coming down with the flu." He shrugged impatiently, almost angrily. "That's not what I came to tell you about. I came here to warn you—"

The sound of his voice faded as Aria caught a glimpse of the throbbing pulse point in his throat. She watched it beat rhythmically under his skin, and like a song, it beckoned her closer. She could imagine the crimson blood pulsating just under the surface of Rialto's skin, could nearly smell its intoxicating aroma, feel the warmth of it, taste it rolling over her tongue. She licked her lips in anticipation, preparing to dive in, when Rialto's hands gripped her shoulders and shook her.

"Aria! Have you heard a word I've just said?"

Aria's stomach rolled as the air in her body was sucked dry and the room went dark. She blinked and realized she was now on the floor, Rialto looming before her.

"Aria! Are you all right?"

"I need to sleep," she managed to croak through her parched lips as her eyelids drooped. They were suddenly very heavy.

"Aria, listen to me—"

"No listen. Just sleep. I need—" Aria's eyes closed by their own volition. "I need a nap."

"Dammit, Aria. Listen to me!" Rialto shook her again, violently this time, until her eyelids cracked open a sliver. "I'm trying to tell you that the killer wants you!"

# Chapter Nine

ARIA'S EYES FLEW wide open. "The killer *what?*"

Rialto helped her to the sofa and then backed away. "Seta had a vision. The killer had you strapped on a metal table and he was about to inject you with something. Poison, no doubt."

"So she saw who he was!" Excitement surged through her body, reenergizing her. Then Rialto's gaze slid to his feet and he shook his head.

"We still don't know who or what the killer is. Seta only saw hands."

"How would she know they belonged to a man if she didn't see him?"

"She saw the hands clearly enough to establish that they were too masculine to be anything but male, and she can feel things. She . . . I can't explain it. We found a body in the park last night and all she got off it was that a male had killed the woman, but she'd sensed that much coming into the city."

"Why are you saying male instead of man?" Aria stepped in front of Rialto as he turned his head away, in an attempt to avoid her eyes. She gripped his chin, forced him to look at her, before letting go. "You said you didn't know who or *what* the killer is, and we both know it's not an animal. What aren't you telling me?"

"It's too early to speculate—"

"Save it, Rialto. You know something. I can see it written all over your face so spill it." She was giving a direct order to a vampire, a being that had undoubtedly killed far stronger men and women than her, but she didn't care. She had to know what he was hiding from her and he definitely *was* hiding something. Whether it had to do with her mother's killer, or what was happening to them, she didn't know; but damned if she wasn't going to get the truth out of him whether he liked it or not.

"Tell me, dammit! What killed my mother? Why are you sick, and why the hell am I sweating buckets?" She emphasized her last question by wiping the sleeve of her pajama top over her brow, mopping up the excess moisture that glistened there. "What did you do to me?"

"I didn't do anything to you," he answered, "not intentionally anyway. And I honestly don't know what killed your mother." He turned away from her scrutinizing gaze and let out a sigh filled with frustration.

"You know something," Aria coaxed, trying not to sound so irritatingly persistent, but her patience was running out. "You have an idea, a theory. Don't you?"

His silence was her answer. The guilt rolled off him in waves, painting a picture for her that she didn't want to see.

"It *was* a vampire, wasn't it? One of you killed her."

"Aria—"

"No!" She extended her arm in the universal sign for stop, palm facing toward Rialto as he turned. "Don't come near me. Don't try to fill my head with more lies."

"I never lied to you."

"Oh really? Then give me an answer. What did you discover last night? What killed my mother?"

As his stormy gaze struggled to hold hers, his expression was pained. Deciding that he would never admit to one of his kind being the monster that took her mother's life, she cursed violently and started toward the door, ordering him out on her way.

"You're not safe, Aria."

She paused to glance over her shoulder. "I'm not safe from what? You? Your kind?"

"My *kind* wouldn't harm you. We damn sure wouldn't kill an innocent woman, and especially not in that way. I already told you we never drain a body."

"Then what drained my mother?" She asked the question, swearing that if he said he didn't know one more time she would throttle him.

"I already told you I don't—"

Aria let out a steady stream of curses as she attacked Rialto, barely registering the fact that he took each blow of her fists as if they were made of air. She hit him repeatedly, pummeling her fists against the unrelenting wall of his chest while he stood there quietly, not saying a word.

Her energy was drained much sooner than it should have been. No surprise to her. She had been feeling lethargic for the better part of the day. With one final, useless blow she slid down Rialto's body until she landed at his feet, a quivering, feverish mass of spent anger.

"I hate you," she sobbed as she felt her body temperature spike. "I hate you for what you are and what you've done to me."

"Join the club," he muttered after a long pause and stepped over her. She wasn't surprised when he left the room, but it still hurt. How could she have been so stupid to have slept with a man who didn't give a damn about her? She waited to hear the front door open and close, but the sound didn't come. Assuming he had left via the balcony doors in her bedroom, she struggled to stand.

"Whoa now," Rialto said from behind her, his arms encircling her waist, catching her before she tumbled back to the floor. "Let's get you into bed." He scooped her up effortlessly, even though he still looked wan and ill.

Aria groaned as his words ignited a flare inside her body. She still ached for him, physically and emotionally. She shuddered as she draped her arm over his shoulder, her face snug against his chest where his masculine scent teased and tormented her. She heard his heart pounding like a base drum, calling out to her. She licked her lips and trailed her fingers down to rest over his heart. If only she could rip through the flesh . . .

"Here we go." Rialto lowered her onto the bed, the sheets already pulled back. His dark eyes smoldered as he withdrew from her. He knew what she was feeling, felt the same desire himself, if his eyes were telling the truth. "We can't," he said breathlessly and pulled the thin cotton sheet over Aria's body.

"We can't or you don't want to?"

"I want to more than you know," he said calmly, but his eyes were full of emotion as they locked onto Aria's. He held her gaze, looking at her as if he were being forced to, as though he couldn't physically tear his gaze away from hers. Something swirled in his eyes, something intense and hungry that begged to be sated. Aria unconsciously grabbed him by the front of his black shirt.

His mouth met hers with an urgency that refuted any notion that he didn't desire her with the same level of intensity she felt. She sank against the mattress as his body fell on top of hers, molding perfectly to her every curve. His hands explored her body quickly, desperately, as if he feared he might not have enough time to find every intimate locale.

Aria let her doubts fade away and slipped her hands beneath his shirt, luxuriating in the feel of silky smooth skin stretched over taut muscles. A feeling of intense longing swept over her. She was as close as she could get to Rialto physically, but that wasn't close enough. She wanted inside him, wanted to be melded with him for eternity. She could have that, she knew, as the memory of Seta's voice echoed in her mind. All she had to do was share his blood. Rialto's lips were on her earlobe, mere inches from her throat.

*Rialto let out a growl as he picked her up and, still inside her, rammed her against the wall. She gasped in pleasure as he repeatedly thrust inside her, sending her into one orgasm after another, but it wasn't enough. She wanted to share blood. As another orgasm engulfed her body, she screamed his name and used her nails to cut through the skin at her own throat, offering this dark creature of the night the same thing he had given her.*

The fragment of dream was so real Aria had to blink. She was still on the bed and although things were definitely progressing in that direction, Rialto wasn't inside her . . . yet. She wanted that badly, but there was something else she wanted even more.

Forever.

With Rialto.

She scraped her long nails against the soft skin of her throat.

Rialto stiffened instantly as the warm droplets of blood slipped from her neck. Although the scratches were small and shallow, the effect was massive. Rialto lifted his head to meet her eyes, his breathing heavy and labored. She trembled with anticipation and a touch of fear as she gazed into those beautiful black depths which were glowing with want. He looked as though he could eat her alive, and when he licked his lips, revealing the tips of elongating fangs, she thought that was exactly what he was going to do. She felt the most intimate parts of her tingle at the thought, and her fear subsided as her own hunger grew to match the intensity she saw etched into the hard lines of his face. With an eager hand, she grasped the back of Rialto's neck and guided his mouth downward.

He froze, his mouth hovering just over her fresh wound, his body trembling against hers.

"Rialto?" Desire made her voice husky. He didn't respond. He didn't move other than to quiver. She could feel his breath on her neck, hear it coming out in strong puffs. She thought he had slipped into some sort of seizure, until he bellowed out a crude curse and lurched from her body. He was out of the room in less than a second, but he returned before Aria even had time to process that he was once again rejecting her.

"Wash away the blood," he ordered viciously as he threw a damp rag on the bed. "All of it! I don't want to see or smell a single drop when you're done!"

Aria gaped at his retreating back as he left her alone in her room, his hard footsteps punishing the floorboards. She sat there for a moment trying to understand what had just happened, almost too scared to move. Never had she seen anyone so angry. Finally, she picked up the rag and wiped away the red droplets of blood welling above her scratches.

When she entered the living area a good fifteen minutes later, she found Rialto pacing the floor, his fists clenched at his sides. His eyes were black as night, not a trace of compassion to be found in them. He marched toward her, and she found herself trying to disappear into the wall at her back.

"Don't you ever tempt me like that again," he warned from between clenched teeth as he stopped before her, so close his breath teased her skin. "You're playing with poison, Aria. Deadly poison."

She cringed under his voice's unmerciful tone, her gaze focused on his chest, too scared of what she would find in his eyes from this close of a vantage point. An aura of fury seemed to hover around him, causing the hair at the back of her neck to rise. "I don't understand," she whispered once she found her voice, too frightened to speak at a normal volume.

"Of course you don't." His voice was less harsh than before, but she still cringed when he raised his hand to cup her cheek. Noticing the reaction, he stopped short and emitted a very hostile-sounding foreign word before spinning away. "Dammit, Aria, I'm not like your first lover. I wouldn't strike you. Come here and sit!"

Aria lifted her eyes to find him sitting on the coffee table, tapping the sofa cushion before him with his hand. She slowly inched her way over to the sofa and sat on the arm. His face fell as he watched her perch on the edge, slightly more than an arm's width away. "Are you really that afraid of me? All I did was yell."

Telling herself she was overreacting, Aria forced herself to take the seat he had indicated and pulled her knees up to her chest, wrapping her arms around them so that she was tucked into a nice little ball. If she thought the position would make her feel more secure she was wrong. She couldn't have felt more vulnerable if she were sitting here stark naked. "I don't understand what's happening. I don't understand why I act the way I do with you—so desperate. And I don't know why you're angry. I thought you wanted me in the same way."

"I do," he said softly as he touched her cheek, caressing the skin there with his thumb, "but you're a luxury I just can't afford." His hand fell away to rest on his thigh. "Don't feel ashamed of your behavior, Aria. You can't help it. Bloodlust is a strong force, not so easily stopped."

"Bloodlust?"

He sighed heavily, running a large tanned hand through his hair which had sprung free from its elastic band sometime during their encounter in the bedroom. "Generally, non-vampires don't experience it. Hell, I've rarely experienced it, considering the amount of time I've been a vamp, and never this intensely. Sometimes the taste of blood fuels other desires, more sexual in nature. As your sexual desire intensifies, it revs up your hunger for blood until you're insatiable both sexually and thirst-wise. The two desires blend together until you can barely control yourself. With you, I'm afraid I could totally lose control."

"What do you mean by that?"

"I've never hungered for anyone like this before. I'm afraid if I let myself . . . indulge, I might not be able to stop until it's too late."

"You're afraid you would kill me."

"That or something worse."

Aria felt chilled down to her bones. What fate could be worse than death? "So you're saying we can never be together even though we both have dreamed of one another for years, and we both feel an insatiable desire for one another?"

"Yes."

It didn't make sense. Something, some force, had led them to each other. There was a reason why she dreamed of him. There had to be. How many people dreamed of a stranger they would one day meet? There was a piece to this puzzle that she was missing and she knew exactly where to find it. Seta. If only she could get to the vampire witch without Rialto knowing.

"Anyway," Rialto said, breaking the silence as he reached out to lay the back of his hand against her forehead, "you seem to have cooled down. Let's get you out of here."

"Why? Where are we going?"

"I'm joining up with Seta to see if we can find any more victims, and I don't feel comfortable leaving you here by yourself."

"You're taking me with you?"

"Not a chance," he answered as he rose from the table and helped her stand. "I'm taking you to Christian. He will watch over you until I come to bring you back home."

"Your preacher friend?"

"Yes."

"I don't need a baby-sitter, and honestly, what could a preacher do to stop a psycho that wanted to hurt me?"

"You'd be surprised," Rialto answered with a devilish gleam in his eye. "Now get out of your pajamas and into some real clothes. It's time to go."

"I'm staying."

"Oh, but you are an insufferable woman!" Aria nearly laughed at the look of exasperation on Rialto's face. "I've just told you that a murderer is after you and you want to stay here by yourself? Are you insane?"

"I want to go with you and Seta."

"You're a liability. I've already told you that."

"So you think I would be in danger with you?"

"Yes."

"But I would be fine in a church in a very seedy neighborhood with God only knows who coming and going, my only protection being a man who believes in turning the other cheek and the golden rule?"

"Just put some damn clothes on before I dress you myself!" Rialto barked.

"That could be fun." Aria regretted her words the moment she saw Rialto's jaw clench. She half expected to see steam puffing out of his ears. "Okay, bad idea. I get it. Don't get your panties in a twist." She raised her hands in mock surrender and headed for the bedroom.

RIALTO MUTTERED out a string of curses in Italian, his native tongue. It was an old habit that came out when he was extremely frustrated. Aria was as infuriating as she was beautiful, and dammit, if that spark to her personality didn't make him want her even more. He was losing it, he knew. The fever and cold chills, the gnawing hunger that had increased when she cut through her own skin . . .

How in the hell was he supposed to protect her when all he wanted to do was ravish her and get this craving for her blood out of his system? He was physically ill with the need to have her. It was imperative that he get her out of harm's way, and then get as far away from her as possible. It would hurt like hell, but he couldn't chance the repercussions of staying with her for much longer.

"So are you ready to take me to my great protector?" Aria asked as she reentered the room.

Rialto grinned at her sarcasm. If only she knew the power of the man who would be protecting her. He turned to see her and groaned. She had poured herself into a pair of body-hugging jeans, soft and faded in all the right places, and a tight, black rib-knit top. "Don't you have any loose clothes?"

"You don't like my outfit?" Her fake pout was his undoing.

Rialto groaned again. "Trust me, that's not the problem." Keep it in your pants, he reminded himself before he did something stupid like lower her to the floor or take her against the wall. "Let's go."

"And just how are you planning on getting me out of here without going through the reporters? They've been out there all day looking for a comment for their damn stories."

"They won't even see you." Rialto laughed at her doubtful expression as he guided her out the front door and locked it behind him.

"We're just going to walk out the front entrance?" Aria shook her head as they headed down the hallway toward the stairs which would take them to the apartment building's front entrance.

"Correction," Rialto said, stopping her with a firm hand. "I'm going to walk right out the front entrance. You're coming along for the ride, just try not to squeal too much if it excites you. I have hypersensitive hearing."

Before Aria could say another word, he scooped her up into his arms and raced down the staircase, out the front doors and through the small group of reporters and photographers at a speed that defied all scientific reasoning. A second later, as he lowered her to the ground six blocks away, his hunger was at a dangerously high level.

He sat on a nearby bench trying to regain some of his spent energy while Aria stood before him turning in a circle, gaping.

"Wow," she finally gasped. "I've read about vampiric speed, but . . . Wow."

Rialto smiled softly, remembering how in awe he'd been of every new feat he'd discovered and mastered as a newly-turned vampire. He wondered if Aria would be as avid as he was to learn all the tricks and skills.

He closed his eyes and shook his head, trying to shake out the image of Aria as a vampiress. That line of thinking was dangerous.

"Rialto, are you all right?" He tensed as he felt her cool fingertips brush his hair back from his brow. "You're burning up."

"I'm all right. Moving that fast drains a lot of energy. I just need to rest a little." He eased his head down against the back of the bench and tried not to jump when he felt Aria press herself close against his side. Damn, he wanted to taste her. His stomach was roiling with the need for fresh blood, and he knew without a doubt hers would energize him like none other. Unfortunately, he didn't think he would be able to handle that strength enough to know when to stop.

"You moved fast after killing those punks in the alley and later behind Fat Kracker's when I tried to run away. You didn't need to rest then."

"That was different."

"How so?"

"I wasn't running for a six-block stretch, and I'd just fed behind Fat Kracker's."

"Rialto, your mother—"

"Is too nosy for her own good," he interjected, cutting her off before she could bring up the topic of soul mates and other such nonsense.

A moment of tense silence passed before she spoke again. "You don't look well, Rialto. I appreciate you promising to find the killer, but I'm making you sick, aren't I?"

*No, not sick. Feverish with desire*, he thought, recalling his mother's words.

"I'm fine, just a little overexerted is all," he said gruffly as he forced himself to stand. His head spun, but he determinedly refused to let that show. "My finding the killer goes beyond the promise I made to you anyway." He helped Aria to her feet. "This has gotten personal."

"Because it's a vampire?"

Damn, she was stubborn. Yet, it was better for her to think that than to know that it was because he cared for her and couldn't bear the thought of her being harmed. She had already offered herself to him twice, and he didn't know how many more times he could control himself when put into that position. If she knew how strongly he really felt . . .

"Seta thinks the killer is a witch or someone who has a strong knowledge of black magic," he informed her. "It is possible—not likely, but possible—that the killer is some type of vampire, but he is definitely not a full-blooded one. We don't know what the hell he is, but yeah, what he's doing has really pissed us off." More than she would ever know, Rialto thought as he remembered the vision Seta had told him about. No man or creature would ever touch his woman, and whether he could have her or not, Aria *was* his woman. "Besides, this is my job."

"Your job?"

Rialto laughed at the way her brow furrowed, as if she was confused by the prospect of him having a job. "Yeah, my job. Vampires need money too, you know. We can't buy cars and houses with our charm."

"So what do you do?" Her brows were still drawn together, her beautiful emerald eyes intense with curiosity.

"I'm a bounty hunter."

Her eyes widened for a moment, then she nodded. "I see, but I never offered you any money to catch this guy. I probably couldn't afford it."

"Some jobs I don't mind doing pro bono. My car is parked up here." He led her two feet up the sidewalk, where his rental was parked at the curb. "I wanted to make sure we weren't followed by any of the press," he explained as he opened the passenger door and helped her inside.

Once in his seat, he started the car and turned his head to look at Aria. "Are you getting by all right? Does your art provide you with enough income?" Her apartment was small and not in the best of neighborhoods, but he knew that could be personal choice.

"I do all right," she answered softly as she gazed out the windshield. "I used to do a lot of pottery and sculpture for this little store near the art district but since my mother died, I've been mostly living off her life insurance. It's not enough to live off of indefinitely, but it'll get me through this period. I just haven't felt like making anything bright and cheerful lately, you know?"

"I understand perfectly," Rialto answered as he put the Sedan in drive and pulled onto the street. He made a silent vow to himself as he navigated the car through the dark streets. As long as Aria Michaels walked the same earth as him, she would never struggle.

SETA GRIMACED AS she watched Rialto's back shudder from the force of his retching. The moment she'd seen him pull his car into the church's small parking lot she'd known he hadn't let fate guide him. He still refused to share his blood with Aria. And now he was paying the price.

A few hours ago, they'd left Aria in Christian's hands and ventured out into the night, intending to search Baltimore's parks for more clues as to what kind of monster they were up against, but Rialto had needed to feed. His stomach had been practically roaring.

Two victims later she stood behind him in a darkened alley as he vomited his last victim's blood. She had told him he needed to drink from Aria, but he was stubborn, a trait he'd inherited from his father.

Seta bristled at the thought of the man who had planted his seed inside her, whispering words of love as he used her body to produce the one thing his wife could never give him: An heir. No matter how long she roamed the earth, she would never recover from the pain she'd felt the day her tiny son was ripped from her arms by his own father. The wealthy and heartless Count Roberto Garibaldi had informed her that Rialto was to be known as the son of he and his lovely wife, the countess. When she'd fought for her son, the count savagely beat her and then tossed her off a cliff. Twenty-eight years later she'd found Rialto bleeding to death on that same cliff and changed him over.

Seta shook off the memories of the events that had happened on those cliffs. They only served to fuel her anger.

"Rialto, you will find only soured blood until you accept fate's plan for you. Can't you see what is happening?"

"I've listened to enough of this nonsense, Mother!"

"It's not nonsense! Look at all the signs."

"If Aria and I were part of the Blood Revelation, she'd have to be an immortal."

"She will be an immortal if she is changed over."

"She would also have to have some sort of special power. In all the stories I've heard, the predestined mates will each have an ability or genetic trait to pass along to their offspring. I would make sense because I am a vampire. My mate, however, would need a different trait to pass along so there you go. Aria doesn't make sense, even if she were turned into a vampire because then we'd be passing along the same trait. You're desperate and seeing what you want to see."

"Well, it seems as though I know a little something about your soul mate that even you haven't discovered," Seta responded, grinning victoriously.

"What did you do?" Rialto growled the question, his eyes narrowed into slits.

"I barely probed her psyche, nothing that would cause her harm. However, I saw enough to know her mother was a born witch."

Rialto shook his head. "No."

Seta nodded. "Yes. Apparently, Mary Ayers was so good at keeping her powers a secret that even Aria didn't know, still doesn't, but that's the genetic trait she'll pass on. You know as well as I do that born witches skip a generation. Therefore, any child of Aria's will be a born witch."

Rialto's mouth dropped open in shock, but then he closed it and gave her a smug smile. "It doesn't matter. Any child *I* have will be a born witch, so again she is canceled out of the equation. We are *not* part of the Blood Revelation."

"Darling, why do you think you can read the minds of mortals while you feed from them? Do you think opening doors and windows with a simple wave of the hand, sensing emotions or levitating yourself to the tops of buildings are normal vampire traits? Shall I go on listing your special abilities?"

"What are you saying?"

"When I turned you, it was like I rebirthed you. Since it wasn't an actual birth, any child you have will not be a born witch because you took their turn. So Aria makes perfect sense. The two of you *are* soul mates and you *are* part of the Blood Revelation. All she needs is to be turned."

"That doesn't make sense. Why would she need to be turned? She already carries the witch gene. There's no reason why she'd have to be a vampire."

Seta huffed out a breath, her patience thin. Why did Rialto struggle so hard against his fate? "The child will be born a vampire. Can you imagine the toll a vampire child would take on its mother's womb? Do you really think a mortal woman could possibly be strong enough to carry to term a child with that much power?"

Rialto shrugged. "I don't know. It's not as if vampires are *born* everyday."

"No, they're not, but if they were I'd bet only a vampire mother could carry and nurse one. Only a vampire mother could protect one." Seta held her breath and hoped Rialto would accept the only explanation she'd been able to come up with. It made sense to her.

"I won't do it," Rialto said as he rose from his knees and wiped the traces of blood from his mouth. "I won't risk Aria's life."

"She's sick too, you stubborn mule. Sharing your blood can ease her pain as well!"

"She's not a vampire. She'll get over this."

She could lie and tell him that Aria wouldn't get over her need for his blood, but he was too smart for that. And whether he admitted it or not, he believed in The Blood Revelation. He was just too scared to accept that he and Aria were part of it.

"You won't get over yours, Rialto. You need blood to survive."

Rialto lowered his eyes to the ground as he walked past her toward the mouth of the alley. "The night's not getting any younger, and obviously I'm not going to get a good meal. Let's try and find this guy, preferably before he kills again."

Seta stared after her only child, fighting back tears. She'd saved his life two times before. She didn't see how she could save him now. He had to change Aria over . . .

If he didn't, he would die.

# Chapter Ten

ARIA OPENED HER eyes and gasped. She was surrounded by tall trees, tinged blue by the moonlight. There was no breeze, but the air was cold and crisp, sending a shiver down her spine. The coldness seemed to swirl around her, but not a single leaf moved in the trees or on the ground. That was when she realized it wasn't the air that was making her shiver but the knowledge . . . the dark and icy sense of foreboding that something horrible was about to happen.

*Aria.*

She whirled around as she heard her name called from somewhere behind her. She couldn't see anything except trees, but somebody was out there, somebody who knew her name.

"Seta?" She called out the vampire witch's name even though the female voice didn't sound like Seta's. The call was more of a whisper, but loud enough to be heard clearly, and there wasn't the slightest trace of a Spanish accent. "Seta? Please be you."

*Aria, come.*

"Oh, hell." She felt the warning shivers quivering up her body, dotting her skin with goosebumps along the way. "I want to go back to the church."

Wait a minute. She *was* at the church. She was sleeping in a pew. Aria laughed as she realized she was having a dream, a completely realistic, frightening dream.

"Okay, all I have to do is wake up." She closed her eyes and focused on waking, yet the coldness seemed to intensify. Then she heard the crunching of leaves in front of her.

"Oh, I am so screwed," she whimpered as the footsteps slowly neared. She kept her eyes closed, too terrified of what she would see if they were open. The louder the footsteps grew the more she shivered. She'd heard that when ghosts appear the temperature dropped to freezing. As cold as she was, it was as if death itself were walking toward her.

Whomever or whatever it was stopped right in front of her, and she felt an icy cold breath blow over her face. *Oh shit. It's right in front of me.*

"Aria. Open your eyes." The voice was deeper now but scratchy. It sounded like the voice of a weak old woman. A hag.

"No," Aria said, struggling not to scream or cry. She had to think. This was a dream. It was all just a dream. "You're a dream, a nightmare. Go away."

"Open your eyes, Aria. You *must* open your eyes."

"Why?"

"In order to have a future you must understand the past."

"Who are you?"

"A very old witch. They call me The Dream Teller. I won't hurt you."

Aria recognized the name and realized this was the witch who'd sent Rialto to her, but still she couldn't open her eyes. It was so cold. She, this strange woman, was so cold. Cold and scary.

"What do you want with me? Why are you so cold?"

"I am not cold. You are sensing what you are about to see in the realm of your dreams and you are frozen with fear. You are right that this is a dream, Aria, but you can't wake yourself from it until you learn the secrets I have come to share with you. I am here to help you and Rialto. He is dying."

Aria gasped, reflexively opening her eyes. Her gaze collided with a pair of platinum white orbs set in an old shriveled face. The woman was covered in a hooded cape, but a trail of long, ratty white hair peeked out from beneath the hood. She looked every inch like an evil old hag. Aria would have screamed and run, but the witch's eyes shocked her motionless.

"You're blind."

"Oh, but I still see clearly," she answered with a crooked smile that looked ghastly against her pale wrinkled face. "Now you must see."

The witch, or The Dream Teller, backed away and crooked a gnarled old finger, indicating that Aria should follow her as she walked back into the trees. Aria started to refuse, but then she felt another presence. Rialto.

She followed the witch at a safe distance until they reached a clearing. They stopped at the edge of the trees and looked out upon a group of people dressed in nineteenth century attire. They were travelers, judging by the wagons sitting on the other side of the clearing. Men and women danced jovially around a bonfire as a small band performed music. They were dressed elegantly for travelers, obviously a rich family moving to new land. One woman stood to the side, leaning against a tree with a dreamy expression on her beautiful porcelain face. *She's remembering the feel of Rialto's lips from the night before.*

Aria felt a pang of jealousy as the thought hit her. She didn't understand how she knew what was going through the ebony-haired beauty's mind, but she did. She heard the thought as if it were spoken aloud. She looked closer at the woman. She was dressed in a long dress made of the finest silk, a beautiful clear blue to match her eyes. Her long black curls were stacked and pinned into a regal style on her head, and her full ruby red lips were delicately arched into the faintest of smiles beneath her pert little nose.

She was exquisite. Rialto loved her.

"Yes," The Dream Teller said, although Aria hadn't spoken aloud. "Her name was Antonia. She was Rialto's first love."

Aria felt the need to scream as the hairs on the back of her neck stood straight up. The coldness grew more intense. "Someone's coming. Something horrible is going to happen to these people." She looked at the witch and somehow could see the agreement in her sightless eyes. Then she looked at the wagons where she instinctively knew children slept. "We have to warn them."

"It has already happened," the witch advised, a trace of sadness in her voice. "You are watching a scene from 1842, and there is nothing you can do to alter it. They can't even see you, much less hear you."

Aria's heart rose in her chest as she heard the sound of hooves pounding on the ground. She wanted to close her eyes, already sensing what was going to happen, but something compelled her to keep them open.

The dancers around the bonfire halted when the men on horseback came into view, swords and axes ready at their sides. The look of terror in the travelers' eyes gripped Aria's heart as they too sensed what was to come next.

"I don't want to watch," she whispered to the witch, turning her back on the scene. She folded her arms across her chest in a futile effort to ward off the cold and the helpless feeling of not being able to do anything to prevent the travelers' doom. She listened against her will as the arguments ensued between the male travelers and the seven men on horseback, trying to block her ears with her hands. The arguing turned into screaming as the raiders robbed the travelers and killed the men who tried to protect their women.

She felt the tears well up in her eyes as the women's agonized screams indicated they were being violated. The tears flowed freely when she felt the moment Antonia was raped by three of the attackers. She felt each stab of pain, each tear of intimate flesh as the woman was repeatedly violated. Mostly, she felt the pain in Antonia's heart as the woman thought Rialto would no longer want her. She would never bear his children. *She didn't know what Rialto was.*

"No, she had no idea he was a vampire," the witch said, reading her mind again.

After what seemed like hours Aria turned and saw the bodies of the male travelers littering the ground. From behind the trees at the other side of the clearing, two women crawled toward the wagons where children's horrified faces peeked out. Aria wanted to scream in outrage, but she couldn't find her voice.

"Come," the witch instructed, leading Aria through the clearing. She cringed as they walked around the bodies of the victims, some dead, some close to it, but she followed behind the witch as if in a trance.

They entered the trees at the other side of the clearing and followed the trail of blood. Antonia's blood. Aria cried out in horror when they came upon her body sprawled beneath a tree, covered in her own blood and half naked. Aria could feel the anger and pain radiating from within Antonia's limp body as the woman wished with her dying breaths that the men who attacked her would suffer. She wished their blood would spill for what they had done.

"She was so full of hate and vengeance after the assault," the witch stated softly as she raised her hand to the sky. It suddenly grew even darker. "Rialto has finished feeding. Now he will come."

The witch had barely finished speaking when Aria felt his presence nearing. He was excited. He'd met with Antonia nightly for weeks, as her family traveled to their new home. He had fallen in love with her quickly, intrigued by her purity and beauty. She was so innocent, such an opposite to the darkness which surrounded him. He knew he would eventually have to tell her what he was, and that frightened him, but he hoped their love could survive her initial shock.

Aria felt her heartbeat quicken as he neared the clearing. She couldn't see him but she felt his terror as he saw the bodies and realized what happened.

"Where's Antonia?" she heard him ask, fear and rage lacing his voice.

Aria blinked when she saw him come into view. He was dressed in the style of the century, but otherwise he looked exactly the same. As he came upon Antonia's dying body, he looked so real Aria reached out to touch him, only to discover that her hand wouldn't go the distance. There seemed to be an invisible shield between them.

"He is not real, just a memory. You can't comfort him here."

Aria didn't respond to the witch's comment. She felt an excruciating pain in her chest. Instinctively, she covered her heart with her hand, knowing Rialto's emotions were surging through her. His heart was breaking.

"Antonia?" His voice trembled with fear, sorrow, and anger. The emotions battled with each other for dominance as he kneeled next to Antonia's weak body. He wanted to scream, to cry, to kill, but mostly he wanted to save Antonia's life. "Antonia, please answer me."

"Rialto?" Antonia's voice was weak, fading like the rest of her. She moved her battered head, and Aria saw the recognition in her eyes as she gazed up into Rialto's face. She saw that recognition turn to shame as Antonia struggled to cover her exposed breasts.

"It's all right, Antonia. I will not let you die. Have no fear. We will be one."

"How?"

"I will fill you with my blood, and after you sleep you will awake in a healthy, mended body."

Antonia's eyes narrowed. "You lie to me so that I do not cross over with regrets and wander the earth instead of going to meet the Maker."

"No, it is true," Rialto said. "You will not die. I will not let you."

Aria watched as Rialto's fangs descended. She could feel the anxiety coursing through his blood as he prayed that he did this right. He'd never changed anyone over, but he remembered how Seta had done it to him. Aria could also feel Antonia's emotions. She was horrified.

"Vampire!" Her eyes widened in terror as she looked into Rialto's face. His fangs were fully descended and his eyes glowed with his dark power. *"Diavolo!"*

"No!" Rialto cried as he felt the contempt and loathing in Antonia's tone, and Aria instinctively knew Antonia had called him *devil*. She felt the pain in Rialto's heart, and once again wanted to comfort him, but she was helpless to do so. "It is a gift, Antonia. My mother saved me from death in the same way."

"No, Rialto. Let me go to God!"

But he didn't. He had walked the earth as a vampire for a decade either by himself or with Seta. He was lonely and craved a mate. "You will see when you awaken," he said firmly, and dipped his head to Antonia's neck, ignoring her pleas to stop.

Aria watched as he drank from Antonia until she just barely hovered over death, then used one of his incisors to pierce through his own wrist. He waited for the blood to form a small bubble over his skin and then brought his wrist to Antonia's lips. She jerked her head away in disgust. "Please . . ." she barely managed to whisper. Whether Rialto didn't realize she was trying to say "Please don't," or if he knew it and just ignored her Aria didn't know, but he held Antonia's head firmly and forced her to drink his blood. After the first three forced swallows, Antonia's survival instinct kicked in and, despite her mind's protests, her body forced her to continue swallowing the lifesaving blood being offered to her.

Rialto eventually jerked his hand away, holding Antonia off as he licked his wounded wrist. As the skin healed, Antonia gave up further attempts to suckle more blood and slumped to the ground.

"It is still several hours before dawn, but we shall rest early tonight," Rialto said softly, as he lifted Antonia from the ground and carried her away.

"Did she survive the night?" Aria asked, watching Rialto leave.

"Unfortunately, yes," the witch answered. "She never should have been changed over. She had been violated, and with her heart and soul full of hatred and contempt, she was in the wrong state of mind. Then Rialto, so desperate in his need for companionship, ignored her pleas to let her die. He meant no harm, but in his own way he too had violated her, and she had trusted him."

"Until she knew what he really was," Aria interjected.

"That's right. She loved Rialto the man, but not the vampire. Her mind could not accept that the two were the same."

"What happened when she awakened?"

"She went mad."

"Why did you show me this?"

"So you can understand."

"Understand what?"

"His greatest fear. You must protect him."

Aria blinked. "Rialto said you'd sent him to protect me."

"Watch out for the vampire," the old witch said.

And then she vanished.


ARIA OPENED HER eyes, vaguely aware of the hard wood beneath her and the warmness which enclosed her.

"Aria?"

She blinked until the room came into focus. She was back in the church, and Christian stood hovering over her, a deep frown marring his golden complexion.

"Are you all right?"

"Yes," she murmured as she slowly straightened herself up, shaking off the last bit of chill that followed her out of her dream. Christian settled into the pew beside her, watching her closely. "What is it?"

"You were talking in your sleep," he answered.

"And?"

"You were speaking in Italian."

"What? That's not possible. I can't speak Italian." Aria thought about her dream. She had understood everything that was said, but when she thought hard . . . "They *were* speaking another language."

"Rialto and Antonia?"

Aria jerked her head to the side so she could look Christian fully in the face. "How did you know that?"

"You said their names. If I'm not mistaken you just dreamed about something that happened a long time ago."

"You know what Rialto is, don't you?"

"Yes."

"And you don't condemn him?"

Christian smiled, but the gesture didn't reach his eyes. "How can I condemn him for being what I am?"

Aria gasped as realization dawned. "But you're ... you're ..." She sputtered, trying unsuccessfully to complete a coherent sentence but her shock was too great. "How can you be a pastor and a ... a ..."

"A vampire?"

She nodded, letting her gaze take him in, wondering why she hadn't seen it before—the power which surged under his calm and peaceful demeanor.

"I served the Lord before I was changed over, and I have continued to serve Him since. I won't let evil that was forced upon me blacken my heart or my soul."

"You must be one conflicted guy," Aria said without thinking, and Christian laughed softly.

"It isn't always easy being me, but we all have our struggles to get through. I am no different from anyone else in that respect. But, I am concerned about you." His expression and tone grew serious again. "That didn't sound like a very nice dream."

"It was disturbing, to say the least." Aria shuddered, remembering the senseless slaughter she'd witnessed. She suppressed the urge to cry as she recalled the pain she had sensed in both Rialto and Antonia. "Did you know Antonia?"

"I know of her," Christian answered gravely. "Did the old witch with the platinum eyes come to you in your dream?"

"You've seen her?"

"Yes." Christian briefly closed his eyes, his jaw clenched. "At first glance you may think she is handicapped but those sightless eyes of hers see more than you could imagine. Did she warn you of anything?"

Aria thought back to her dream, to the moment the old witch approached her and it felt as if death itself were stepping towards her.

"No!" She grabbed Christian's hand and shook her head, denying her memory. "It can't be true."

"What can't be true?" Christian asked, giving her hand a reassuring squeeze. "What did The Dream Teller say?"

"Rialto! She said he's dying!"


RIALTO LEANED AGAINST a tree while Seta gave him the details of her latest vision. He was weaker than he'd felt in decades, since before changing over, and he could feel his heart racing, as though he were a mere mortal just finishing a marathon. The day sleep would restore most of his energy, he knew, but he had a sinking feeling that as soon as he ventured out into the night again it would diminish rapidly. How was he supposed to save Aria like this?

Seta's latest vision was of several rows of books with blood spilling from the pages . . . and Eron. "What do you think?" She asked as she turned to look at him, her brow creased in a frown.

Rialto quickly straightened. "A library, perhaps?" He recalled his own vision of Aria hunched over books at the library. Something niggled at the back of his mind, but he filed that fact away for the moment, too tired to think it through. "This is the second time you've seen Eron. He must have something to do with this."

"Are you suggesting he has committed the murders?"

Rialto felt Seta's hard glare hit him like a physical blow. He'd always suspected there was something more than friendship between her and Eron, something more than the normal bond between a vampire fledgling and her sire. Judging by the icy look in her eyes, he knew he was right.

"Of course I'm not suggesting that, Mother, but he is somehow involved, whether it is with his consent or not. When was the last time you saw him?"

"Too long. I've tried calling out to him, but he doesn't answer."

He saw the doubt shadowing Seta's face and the genuine worry. She didn't want to believe Eron had anything to do with these senseless killings, but Eron had been in both of her visions and he wasn't answering her. Being her sire, he could always sense her whereabouts and hear her when she called. So why was he ignoring her?

"Do you think he's . . ."

"No!" Seta hurled her answer before he could finish the question. "If he was . . . dead, I'd know. I'd feel it."

"What do you feel?"

"Nothing." She shrugged her shoulders in frustration. "Not death, not pain, not . . . anything."

"Is that normal?" Rialto knew Seta could feel him as if he were part of her, could read his mind clearly with or without his consent, but they also shared the bond of mother and son. Rialto had only sired one vampire, but she hadn't lived long enough for him to fully understand how the bond between sire and fledgling worked.

"No, darling, it's not normal. If we're far apart, I might not be able to feel him completely, but I've never lost him altogether. There's always a . . . I don't know . . . a faint buzz, an electricity I can sense."

"How long has it been gone?"

"Months," she answered sadly. "Before these murders started."

Rialto could practically see the wheels turning in her head, but he didn't comment. He knew her too well. If he kept pressing the fact that

Eron definitely had something to do with the killings, she would continue to argue why Eron couldn't possibly be involved. If, however, he let her think it over herself, she would realize how much sense it made. Not that it did make much sense. Eron was a powerful vampire, having lived far longer than Seta. He was a good vampire, too. He wouldn't willingly kill an innocent, but how anyone could overpower or manipulate him was beyond Rialto's scope of imagination.

Together, he and Seta continued to walk the streets of Baltimore, dipping in and out of parks and alleys, opening their senses for any signs of evil. She chanted spells whenever they weren't in earshot of tourists and passersby, and he kept his eyes and ears open, searching for something, anything, that would give them a clue as to who was committing these atrocities. He was a good bounty hunter, but that involved hunting criminals and deadbeat dads. Mortals left trails, and the scent of fear and evil brewed under their skin, seeping out through their pores. Whatever they were searching for now knew how to cover up the smell.

*Books. Blood. Needle. Eron.*

Rialto tried to piece together the images from Seta's visions. What did it all mean?

THE MAN LAUGHED as he pushed the needle into the vampire's flesh and watched the powerful blood fill the tubing which led to a gallon jug. He had enough blood to last him years, but he never stopped stocking his supply, mostly because the vampire never stopped replenishing what was lost each night. The vampire race's healing was amazing. He had studied them for years and now had a real-life vamp to experiment on. He had burned him, cut him, made him endure cruel torture, but each night the ancient vampire's body was healed, showing no signs of previous abuse.

"How are you doing tonight, Eron? Just hanging in there?" He laughed at his joke, watching the shirtless, manacled vampire glare at him from where he hung from the wall, bolted to the hard, cold brick by his wrists and ankles. Ordinarily, a vampire could not be contained in such a way, but every night he took enough blood to weaken the powerful beast until he was barely able to move, let alone attack. He also took blood at regular intervals during the day to make extra sure the vampire couldn't regain his full strength.

He never sank his own teeth into human flesh. He used the stolen blood, injecting it straight into his bloodstream, bypassing the disgusting task of actually tasting it. That was what separated man from beast. He was still a man, a strong, mighty man, whereas the animal on the wall was a parasite.

"Why are you doing this?" The vampire's voice was weak and raspy. It pleased him immensely that he had the power to make the ancient being frail and helpless.

"I told you. Revenge." He leered at the vampire as its blood continued to fill the jug, noting that it seemed to be coming out slower than usual. His brow crinkled in confusion as he noticed a greenish color at the vampire's side, close to his back. Moving in closer he saw that it was a bruise. "What is this?"

"Don't you . . . remember?" The vampire glared down at him, looking as though it took all his strength to do so.

"Why didn't you heal during the day?" He looked at the jug on the floor. It should be full. Why was it only halfway filled?

He tore the needle from the vampire's side, quickly bandaging the small hole that remained and studied his pallor and the wound.

"You're dying!" He sealed the jug for storage and ran his hands through his wild mane of red hair. "How long has this been happening?" He thought of all the jugs of blood he'd collected. If Eron was dying, losing his power, it was possible that most of the blood he had in storage wasn't strong enough, wouldn't last him long enough.

He had mostly been feeding the vampire cow's blood. On the occasions that he killed, he brought that blood to him, but maybe the thinning agent he used to get the blood to pour out the body affected the quality. Obviously, the vampire needed more blood if he was to survive.

"I'll have to kill more women," he said to himself, again studying the vampire. "Or else bring you live bait."

He stored the fresh jug of blood in the freezer and left the laboratory, entering another room in the basement level of his home. This room was dark, carpeted in black and painted the same. Red pentagrams covered the walls, and a large one was painted into the center of the carpet. Before it stood an altar, covered in dozens of candles.

"The master will know what to do," the man said to himself as he began the ritualistic lighting of the candles.

# Chapter Eleven

ARIA TURNED OFF the taps and wiped her hands on the towel hanging on the nearby rack on the small bathroom's wood-paneled wall. She'd vomited twice in the last thirty minutes, but she no longer felt sick and feverish. Her nausea was due to the memory of the images she'd seen in her dream and the remembrance of the smell of blood and death. It was so hauntingly real that when she thought of it, she still felt the prickle of tears behind her eyes. Rialto had lived that nightmare. No wonder he seemed so hardened, so adamant they couldn't be together.

But she wasn't an innocent like Antonia. She knew what Rialto was, yet . . . did she want a vampire's life? She still felt the pain of her parents' deaths. Could she endure the pain for eternity, adding to it the death of new loved ones she would meet? She gazed at her reflection in the mirror hanging over the sink. She was pale again, white-looking. Was Seta right? Was she hiding from what she was?

Pickahoe was an awful little town for a biracial child to be raised in, and her mother's fears had been warranted. They'd left town the night after their car had been blown up, a week after their dog was poisoned. And it was all because of the black blood that flowed through her veins. But was she ashamed?

No.

She loved her father. Jesse Michaels was a warm, loving man. He had loved her mother with all his heart and soul combined, and he would have given her the world if he could. But the pair was doomed from the start. Both were too poor to leave Pickahoe. They never married, but instead had met in secret. Aria hadn't been planned, and if not for the uncanny paleness of her skin, they might have all been killed or driven out of town upon her birth.

Jesse had been murdered in his own home while a white supremacist group was passing through. The local police said they had no leads even though they knew exactly what happened to him. Everyone knew. Word leaked out Jesse was seeing a white woman, but fortunately Mary's identity hadn't been discovered. If it had, she and Aria would have met a cruel fate that night, as well. As it turned out, it was another year before the town put two and two together. It was then she'd realized that her first boyfriend,

Brad, had figured out who her father was and let it slip that Jesse was seeing a white woman. The only reason he hadn't told anyone about her and her mother was because he hadn't wanted anyone to know he'd been fooled by a half black girl . . . until he got drunk at a graduation party and confessed all. One week later her mother had dreamed about them being attacked, and they'd boarded a flight to Baltimore with little money and no definite place to go. Aria Ayers became Aria Michaels, finally free to take her father's name.

Aria ran her fingers over the pale skin of her face. Was she ashamed of what she was? No. She had only been doing what she'd been taught to do: hiding her true self in order to survive. And she was tired of it.

Rialto had been tired of hiding after only a decade. She had felt that clearly as she'd sensed him nearing the clearing in the memory-dream. How had he managed to survive for so long hiding himself? She couldn't do it. Twenty-six years was already starting to take its toll and all she was hiding was her ancestry; Rialto was hiding his entire existence and that of those like him. Yet, the dreams they shared . . .

Something had led them to one another, possibly the same thing that had led her mother to her death. She couldn't ignore that. She'd ignored the common sense that would have prevented her from getting involved with Brad, the man who later led white supremacists to her father's door, the man who'd caused her mother to flee to a city where she was later murdered. It was all Aria's fault. If only she hadn't given in to her pathetic need to be accepted, her parents would still be alive.

She couldn't let Rialto die too. The witch had come to her for a reason, and her gut told her what that reason was. She was somehow linked with him, could somehow prevent his death.

*Watch out for the vampire.*

When her mother had issued the same warning in her dream, she'd assumed she was being told she was in danger from the vampire. Now she realized she was being told to protect him.

And that was exactly what she was going to do, even if it meant dying herself. She couldn't possibly continue to live with another death on her conscience.

Aria tore her gaze away from the mirror and exited the bathroom. The hallway she stepped into was long and narrow. Christian had led her beneath the church via a trap door, which was virtually invisible to the naked eye, under the pulpit. They'd walked down a long set of stairs before coming to a thick metal door which had to be unlocked with the use of ten separate keys and in a precise order.

From there, a long narrow tunnel snaked around the underground, widening in various places where a living area, bathroom, and bedrooms had been built. It appeared to Aria that the tunnels and rooms were dug out with a shovel, then boards were nailed into the earth to form floors and walls. Aria was thankful for the wooden planks, which seemed to be the only thing protecting her from the creepy-crawlies, and the well-built ceilings which kept dirt from tumbling down on top of her . However, the air was stale in the narrow passageway. Christian had apologized for the almost claustrophobic feel of the majority of his home, explaining that he rarely had mortal company and the closed-in space didn't bother him.

She slowly made her way down the narrow corridor, her only illumination coming from the flashlight Christian had given her. He kept lamps in the big rooms but allowed no light in the narrow tunnels, just in case someone ever did discover how to enter his dwelling. If that happened, the darkness would work in his favor. He'd explained that his keen eyes needed no light to see.

Light pooled into the tunnel as Aria neared one of the rooms. She caught the sound of voices, one with the trace of a Spanish accent, as she closed in. Rialto and Seta were back. Maybe now she could go home and rest in her own bed.

But something in her gut warned her she might not be leaving so soon. Aria flicked off the flashlight as she reached the opening to the room. Christian and Seta stood in the center, speaking to one another in worried tones, Seta's beautiful face was marred with a deep frown. When she sensed Aria's presence, her eyes turned dark and cold. Aria gulped, wondering if it was just her imagination that Seta was glaring at her.

"Where's Rialto?" she asked, noting that he didn't stand with them. She caught the look of pity Christian sent her way before she looked around the room and found Rialto lying supine on a chaise in the corner, his hands folded over his abdomen. It looked as if he was resting peacefully, but it was exactly the same way Aria's mother had looked in her casket.

"Rialto!" Aria ran across the room and dropped to her knees beside the chaise, placing her hand over his heart. She felt the slight beat beneath her fingers and let out a breath she hadn't been aware of holding. He was still alive, even if his heartbeat wasn't as steady and strong as it should be and his skin was much too pale, completely devoid of its normally golden glow. "Is he all right?"

"No, thanks to you," Seta snapped, her dark eyes boring into Aria's so accusingly she had to blink, unable to withstand the weight of Seta's punishing glare.

"It's not her fault, Seta." Christian admonished the vampire witch with a quelling glare of his own. "Rialto is fighting against fate."

"I can't just let him die, Christian. He was barely weaned when he was taken from me the first time. Twenty-eight years I had to wait for the truth to come out, for him to know who his real mother was! Then I almost lost him again because of that demon Antonia!"

"Demon?"

Aria wasn't aware she had spoken until Seta's head whipped around, her eyes full of fury. The vampiress lunged for her but Christian's arm shot out and sent her flying across the room, her back hitting the far wall.

"Don't make me hurt you, Seta." The warning look Christian sent the woman was a silent promise that he would. "I have too much respect for you to do it, and you know how I hate to resort to violence. Be respectful of the fact that you are a guest in my home, and while you're at it, you can stop blaming Aria. It's not her fault she was chosen to be Rialto's mate."

"What are you talking about?" Aria directed the question at Christian, no longer sure she could trust Seta. The woman looked as though she wanted to kill her.

"Explain it to her, Seta." Christian crossed over to a set of cabinets built into the wall and pulled out a tall glass, following it with a bag of blood from a small refrigerator. "Care for some?"

"You know I prefer mine fresh," Seta answered, looking at the bag with distaste as she rose from the floor.

Christian shook his head and punctured the bag with his thumbnail. He poured the contents into the glass. "Rialto is too weak to stop you from speaking now. Explain to her what is happening, and what must happen." He turned to face Seta, taking a sip from his glass. "The Dream Teller has already visited her, just a few hours ago."

Seta's head whipped around. "The Dream Teller? What did she show you?"

Aria gulped as the vampire-witch crossed the room to stand over her. "She showed me the night Rialto changed over Antonia."

Seta's eyes smoldered. "Did she show you what happened when Antonia awakened?"

"No, but she said she went mad."

"She was a demon." Seta practically spat out the statement, her fists clenching at her sides. "Something went wrong during the transformation. When you are changed over, you drink from your sire, sleep through the day, awaken at night and feed. The cycle is then complete. The sire wakes before you, but Antonia was already gone when Rialto opened his eyes that night. It was the screaming that woke him."

"Whose screaming?"

"The villagers." Seta perched on the arm of a nearby lounge chair, encircling her arms around her narrow waist, her tanned skin an unusual pale color that sharply contrasted with her dark hair and clothing. "When we feed it is for survival. The blood and day sleep are our sources of strength. The blood empowers us, and the day sleep heals and revitalizes. Antonia wasn't just feeding for strength, as she should have been. She was slaughtering for sport."

"Her attackers," Aria murmured, recalling the pain and humiliation Antonia had endured at the hands of the raiders. She'd wanted revenge more than she'd wanted to live.

"No," Seta said, shaking her head. "She woke up evil. She raced through the night to the nearest village and sank her teeth into every human she saw. It was a massacre."

"She killed innocent people for no reason at all?" Aria looked at Christian for confirmation that Seta was telling the truth. The sorrow she saw in his eyes told her she was. "Why would she do that?"

"She was a demon, touched by the hand of Satan."

"How?"

Seta shrugged. "We don't fully understand our own origins, Aria. Antonia is still a great mystery to us. All we can figure is she was never meant to be one of us. It happens sometimes."

"What happened to her?"

"She was destroyed."

"By you?"

"I wish." Seta gazed at her son for a long moment before she continued. "Rialto couldn't sense her when he awakened, which was odd seeing as how a sire and fledgling share a special bond that enables them to sense each other's whereabouts. He ran toward the screaming and found her laughing and dancing around a bonfire, dead bodies lying all around her, their insides ripped out. She was wearing the dress of one of her victims, not seeming to care that it was covered in the woman's blood."

As Seta continued telling the story, Aria felt herself being pulled away from her body until she stood in the village, watching as Antonia pranced around the fire, the white skirts of her bloodstained dress swirling around her. Her eyes were bright and wide, gleaming with a dark power that chilled Aria to her core. The woman's lips were stained with blood, and when she pulled them into a smile, Aria saw blood caked between her teeth like a red plaque.

"Antonia? What have you done?" Rialto looked at the carnage around him, horrified. There were bodies of old men and women, younger adults, and two children. A woman, barely hanging onto life, crawled toward a baby carriage. The infant's cries were the only sound other than the roaring of the fire. If there were any survivors inside the nearby buildings, they weren't advertising the fact.

"I have feasted, my love." Antonia answered with a wicked gleam in her eyes that would mystify the devil. Her voice was no longer sweet and soft. It had turned hard, deep, more like a man's. "Now that you have finally arrived you can join me."

"No, Antonia. This is not right."

Her eyes flared with anger. "This is what you made me, Rialto. Do you not remember the gift you spoke so highly of? I am now yours forever."

"You are not my Antonia!" Anger rose in Rialto's voice, but in his eyes Aria saw what he was really feeling. Guilt. He had created a monster.

Antonia laughed. "Of course I am. You made me, remember? Now, come. I have saved dessert for you."

Rialto watched as Antonia slinked toward the woman and the carriage, no longer poised with grace and sophistication, but instead moving like a jungle cat. A predator.

"Antonia, don't do it." Rialto's eyes widened in fear as Antonia kicked the young mother aside and reached into the baby carriage. "Antonia, don't! Please!"

"Not my baby!" The woman looked at Rialto, her eyes pleading as Antonia raised the screaming infant into the air.

"Antonia, leave the baby alone!"

Antonia turned her head and stared Rialto in the eye, her own eyes dark with a relentless hunger that refused to go unsated. She laughed at Rialto and opened her mouth, baring her fangs.

Before she could sink them into the baby's soft flesh, Rialto was before her. He ripped the baby from her hands, knocking her out of the way with one arm while he gently placed the infant back into the carriage with the other.

By the time he turned, Antonia was lunging for him, her shriek piercing the still night air. He caught her effortlessly with one hand and held her away from his body.

"La colpa la vostra" *The guilt is yours.* She hissed the words as her gaze bored into his.

"I'm sorry," he whispered, carrying her toward the bonfire with tears in his eyes. Antonia looked into the flames, her eyes widening with sudden realization. Knowing what he was going to do, she shrieked and clawed at him, trying desperately to get out of his grasp, but with a quickness only an immortal could possess, he threw her into the fire and rammed a long stick through her chest, pinning her to the ground.

His tears fell like rain while she screamed and thrashed on the ground, the flames charring her skin. She managed to tear the stick from her body and stand just before the flames swallowed her whole, long enough to give him one last message. Even though it was spoken in Italian, Aria understood clearly.

"I hate you for what you are and what you've made me!"

Those were the words that wounded Rialto because they were spoken in the soft, feminine voice of the woman he had loved. He'd destroyed the demon he'd created, and along with it, he had destroyed Antonia.

She had parted from him with nearly the same words Aria had said to him earlier tonight. The guilt of knowing how badly those poorly chosen words must have hurt him snapped Aria back into the present. She gasped, opening her eyes to see Seta and Christian kneeling before her.

"Are you all right?" Christian asked, helping her to sit up. She rubbed the side of her head as it began to throb.

"What happened?"

"You tell us," Seta answered. "I was telling you about Antonia, and you just fell over. Did the Dream Teller come back?"

"No. She wasn't there."

"She wasn't where?"

Aria shook her aching head, trying to clear it. "I was at the village. I saw what Antonia did, and I saw what Rialto had to do." And she'd felt him, felt every trace of guilt and suffering which surged through him. He didn't even stop to acknowledge that he had saved a baby's life. All he knew was he'd killed Antonia and she'd hated him for it. The words she'd spoken upon her death might as well have been daggers, they'd cut him so deeply. Why had Aria used those same words?

She gazed at Rialto where he lay on the chaise, looking at peace while he rested. But she knew peace was the last thing he felt. He believed he had turned someone he cared about into an evil being, and then he'd killed her. He'd lived with that for hundreds of years, and now he was dying because he refused to follow his fate, a fate that somehow involved her.

"What were you talking about earlier when you said Rialto was fighting his fate? What's wrong with him?"

Seta and Christian helped her into a chair before Seta knelt on the floor in front of her. "First, Aria, I want to say I'm not really angry with *you*. I'm just . . . *angry*." Christian nodded his approval before crossing over to the sofa, watching them while he drank from his glass of blood. "If I ever lost my son . . ." Seta's voice trailed off as she gazed mournfully where Rialto lay.

"I understand, Seta." The vampiress may have looked like a teenager, but her eyes, when cast upon her son, were old and heart-wrenchingly sad. She was a mother, and from what Aria could tell, a very loving, protective one. "You said he was stolen from you?"

"Yes." Seta's eyes closed briefly and she let out a sigh. "His father was Count Roberto Garibaldi, a very sophisticated, rich Italian nobleman. I was just a stupid servant girl, too taken with fairy tales and daydreams to see that he was using me. My grandmother tried to warn me and later . . . the old hag came to me in my dreams."

"The Dream Teller?"

"Yes, but I didn't listen to her or my grandmother. I thought Roberto loved me and, blindly, I allowed him to use me. All he wanted from me was what his wife could not give him—a son. Once Rialto was weaned, he stole him from me, and when I tried to fight for him, Roberto beat me and threw me off the cliff in front of his castle."

Aria gasped in horror. "How did you survive?"

"I went over the cliff and landed in the arms of a vampire who was sent for me. The Dream Teller, one of the oldest witches known, had told him to be there and to give me the option of living or dying."

"He changed you over?"

"Yes. I was so severely beaten I would have died before morning had he not, and I couldn't accept death then. I had to make sure my son was all right."

"But you didn't take him from the castle."

"No. He was a mortal child and needed to be raised by mortals. I couldn't go out in the sun, and during the day sleep there are periods where vampires can't move as our bodies heal and replenish themselves. I couldn't raise a mortal child. And my mortal family were all servants to Roberto's family. They couldn't raise him, and I couldn't risk them knowing I was alive. They would have thought I traded my soul to the devil."

"You never left him though, did you?"

"No. I watched over him for twenty-eight years, only speaking with him on rare occasions when I knew we wouldn't be bothered. I didn't tell him who I was until the right time presented itself."

Aria smiled to herself, knowing her mother would have done the same, putting her child's needs before her own and at her own emotional expense. A sharp stab of sorrow sliced through her chest. With all the confusion and excitement of the past few days, she had managed to step away from the constant mourning she'd been drowning in, but with just one simple thought of her mother, the pain came back tenfold. Before she could blink it back a tear fell from her eye.

"Aria, child, what is it?" Seta's eyes were full of concern as she wiped the errant tear away with her fingers. Aria couldn't help laughing, however weak the sound was.

"I'm sorry. It's kind of weird hearing you call me child when you look so much younger than me."

"You'll get used to it as you meet more of our kind," Seta said with a compassionate smile. "It just takes a little adjusting."

"More of you are coming?"

"You'll meet more after you're . . ." Seta trailed off, looking at Christian, silently conferring, before turning back to look at Aria with a seriousness that wiped away any trace of a smile. "What Christian and I were talking about earlier, Rialto's fate, involves you."

"The Dream Teller said he was dying. Can I prevent that?" Aria searched Seta's eyes for the answer she craved. She nearly cried out in elation when Seta nodded. "What's wrong with him now? Why is he so weak and pale?"

"He tasted your blood and now he is addicted to it. He has tried to feed from other mortals since he tasted you, but their blood was sour. In desperation, we even tried giving him the blood of his sire." Seta looked at her wrist, rubbing a thumb over the pulse point. "He can't even stomach my blood, which is virtually the same as his own."

"So that's why we were both sick. But I'm better now. Why?"

"The mortal blood in you cured your ailment. Rialto doesn't have that advantage. He will steadily grow weaker and weaker until he is utterly defenseless. Just tonight he passed out and I had to carry him here. The day sleep will replenish some of his energy, but as far as his strength, it will wane through the next night and the next night and so on. I don't know how long he can survive if he keeps losing his strength so rapidly."

"But if he drinks my blood he'll be fine, right?"

"It's not that simple. He will become more dependent on your blood the more he tastes it, unless he does what fate intends."

"Which is?"

"You were meant to be one of us, Aria. Rialto was meant to be your partner and your sire."

Aria gulped, despite the fact her throat was bone dry. "You mean he has to change me over like he did Antonia?"

"No!" Seta rose from the floor, her eyes wide. "It won't be like that!"

"Aria, you are not Antonia," Christian interjected as he placed his glass on the coffee table before him and leaned forward, his elbows resting on his knees. "There are certain signs that can't be ignored, signs coming from you. Seta is a powerful witch, and there are things she sees that no one else can see."

"Like what?"

"Your auras." Seta bent down and took Aria's hands in her own. "When we first met at the hotel, I barged right in because I didn't know anyone else was in the room with Rialto. All I could feel was him. When I walked in, I saw the two of you entwined in the exact same aura. That doesn't happen, Aria, not unless you are two halves of the same soul."

"Two halves of the same . . ." Aria shook her head. A dull throb pounded in the center of her forehead. This was too much.

"I know of the dreams, Aria. Rialto had visions of you as a baby. Fate was telling him his soul mate had arrived. Fate led him to you."

"Fate killed my mother?"

"No, not exactly. We are helping you find her killer, but that isn't what brought Rialto to you. The dreams did; the passion he felt in them."

Aria could feel her skin heating up, imagined it reddening, as she averted her eyes, focusing on the wooden boards beneath her feet.

"It's all right, Aria. There is no need to be embarrassed. The dreams are only natural, seeing as how you two were meant to be joined."

"You mean like married?"

"Well . . . not exactly." Seta turned to Christian for help.

"Aria, Seta is trying to explain that the two of you were predestined to become one in blood and soul. There is a story older than she and I put together about vampires fated to mate and produce children. Under normal circumstances, children are not born to our kind, but these vampires fated to be together are special, chosen. Their children will grow to be great warriors, defenders of mankind. And one of them will save the world from eternal darkness."

Aria shook her head again, trying to clear the confusion settling there. Seta and Christian looked at her intently, their full belief in this story evident in the hopeful gleam in their eyes. Could it be true? It all sounded so cultish to her, so surreal. "Why would I be chosen? It doesn't make any sense."

"Those who are predestined to mate have special abilities which are to be passed down to their children, certain traits which will make the children powerful warriors."

"I have no special traits or abilities. I'm just a normal human woman."

"A born witch is created every other generation."

Aria frowned, wondering what that meant. "Okay, so if Rialto has a child the kid will be a witch. What's that got to do with me?"

"Rialto actually took some of my abilities when I turned him, so he can not pass on any magic to his child. You, however, definitely will give birth to a witch."

Aria shook her head. "But that would mean my mother was a witch."

"How do you think she knew when the two of you needed to leave that dreadful little town? You'd barely driven a few miles before your house was raided."

"How do you know that?"

"I'm a witch, as was she. We have a tendency to see certain things."

"No," Aria said, shaking her head against the memories starting to surface. All the dreams her mother had which turned out to be true, her warning not to get involved romantically with anyone in Pickahoe, the way she'd come to her in a dream to warn her about Rialto. The way she'd looked at her so sadly and hugged her so tightly and often during the last few weeks of her life . . .

"My mother knew she was going to die, didn't she? Why didn't she do something to prevent it? It doesn't make any sense!"

"A lot of things seem to not make sense, Aria. It doesn't mean they don't. If your mother did see her death coming and didn't take precautions, there was a reason, just as there was a reason she didn't let you know she was a witch. Maybe you weren't supposed to know. " Seta again grabbed her hands. "There were several times I heard the story of the predestined mates and thought it was all rubbish, but the moment I saw you, I knew who you were. Rialto needs you."

Aria glanced over to Rialto. He lay so still, so lifeless. She couldn't explain why she felt such a deep connection with him, or why she'd dreamed of him before they first met. Maybe there was something to this story that Seta and Christian obviously believed in, but she couldn't stop the fear slithering through her, the fear of "what-if." What if she turned out like Antonia? Would she kill innocents? Would Rialto have to kill her?

Was the risk worth it?

"What happened to Rialto after that night? What did he do after he killed Antonia?"

Seta's gaze fell to the floor as she released her hold on Aria's hands. Christian suggested Seta sit on the couch as he rose from it to pace. He stopped before the chaise and looked down at Rialto's resting body.

"He was deeply distraught after the incident. He took care of the mother and child first, giving the woman some of his blood so she could heal through the next day, and making sure they were left with someone who could care for them. Then he went to the cliffs."

Aria felt the sensation of being pulled away again, but fought against it, keeping her eyes open and fixed on Christian. She had a feeling she didn't want to see what Rialto had done.

"He lowered himself to the ground, stretched out and waited for daylight."

"Daylight would kill him," Aria said, horrified.

"Yes, but first it would make him suffer. The direct rays of the sun are cruel to our kind. They rip away at our flesh, slowly peeling away layer upon layer until there is no longer any barrier of protection. But first it heats our blood, bringing it to a scalding boil, cooking our internal organs. The pain is excruciating as we fry beneath the rays, waiting for our skin to peel away so the boiling hot juices inside can seep out, evaporating under the intense heat."

"Enough, Christian!" Seta was shaking where she sat, streams of tears running down her cheeks. "She gets the point."

Christian nodded solemnly. "Aria, he allowed that torture to happen to him. He would have allowed it to kill him, if Seta hadn't arrived and carried him out of danger."

"And you expect me to put him through that again?" Aria rose from her seat, punishing the floorboards beneath her feet as she paced the room, fuming with anger that Rialto would do such a thing to himself. "You're both crazy if you think I will allow it! Fate or not, I won't put that kind of guilt over his head."

"Aria, it won't be that way," Seta cried. "It is destiny. Antonia was not meant to be one of us. You are!"

"How do you know that? How can you be one hundred percent sure I'm one of these chosen few? Have you ever thought that this story you speak of is just that? A story? Something old vampires tell little ones to get them to sleep?"

"Don't be ridiculous, Aria!"

"Ridiculous? I'm the one being ridiculous while you two are spouting off old stories about predestined vampires who can have babies? Why me? Why in the world would I be chosen to give Rialto a child when everyone I've ever loved has suffered because of me? Believe me, Seta, I'm the last person who should be involved with your son. You said it yourself; my blood is poisoning him."

"But, Aria . . ."

"Enough!" She raised her hand for silence. "I don't want to be a vampire. I've had more than my share of guilt already, and I don't need anymore. And after seeing images of my childhood, Seta, how in hell do you expect me to agree to bring a child into this world who would have an even harder time trying to be accepted? I'm sorry, but I'm not the woman you think I am. I'm not the mother of Rialto's future child."

"Then you must be the angel of death," Seta said through clenched teeth, "because that is exactly what you will bring to him if he doesn't change you over."

# Chapter Twelve

"SETA."

Seta bristled at Christian's warning tone while she watched Aria leave the room in tears. It took every bit of restraint she possessed to keep from running after her. Instead, she turned her heated glare toward Christian's angelic face. So calm and peaceful looking, he made the blood flowing through her veins burn like molten lava. "What am I supposed to do, Christian? My son is dying."

"Maybe not."

"Of course he is. You know the story."

"I know a few versions of the Blood Revelation, as do most of our kind. The story has been passed down for centuries, and it has changed several times, depending on the age and origin of the vampire telling it."

"There are some consistencies."

"Yes, there are, but my point is we don't know the whole truth to the story. Maybe Rialto is supposed to fall ill and Aria is supposed to refuse him."

"Why would that be?"

"I don't know." Christian ran a hand through his short, dark hair and joined her on the couch. "But fate is fate. Everything happens for a reason. You were meant to go over the cliff that night. Rialto was meant to be left on that same cliff . . ."

"Do you really believe that?"

"Think about it. Ridding the world of evil is what we do. You changed Rialto over and he was able to rid the world of Roberto Garibaldi, an act that made the lives of several people much better."

"And everything that happened back then has led us to this night."

"Exactly, and everything happening right now is for a reason. I believe in your instincts, Seta. I believe those two are meant to be together. I felt the passion between them myself the first time I met Aria."

"But Rialto said he'll never change her over, and she says she doesn't want to be changed."

"Does she have to be changed?"

"Yes. For the prophecy to be fulfilled she has to be immortal."

"Can you turn her?"

"Believe me, if only it were that simple. The Dream Teller told me long ago that Rialto would eventually find his true love and that I absolutely could not turn her. Rialto still blames himself for what happened to Antonia. He needs to turn Aria, to see that he didn't taint her, that there was already something dark inside her." She looked at her son, once more feeling the rage which engulfed her each time she thought of the woman he'd been forced to kill. Why hadn't she predicted what was to happen? Why hadn't she been able to stop it? "I'm scared that once again I'm not going to be able to stop him from doing something to hurt himself. I can't *make* him turn her."

"Their feelings right now may change. Circumstances may change."

The fine hairs along the back of Seta's neck stood on end. "I didn't like your tone just then, Christian. Your last statement sounded a little ominous."

"Things are happening, Seta. Things have been happening for centuries. You're a witch. Don't tell me you don't feel it."

"If you're referring to the panic and sense of impending doom, yes, I feel it."

Christian's eyebrows furrowed. "Doom? I'm not sure I would call it that. It's more like a pull. I started feeling it the last morning I woke as a mortal. It's steadily grown stronger since. It's kind of like being on a train and not knowing the destination."

"Yes." Seta shook her head before resting it on the back of the couch, tired of this conversation and tired of trying to figure out whatever it was that Christian was trying to say. The only train she felt was the one that had gone off course and was speeding toward a major catastrophe. Something was *wrong*. Rialto was sick and that never happened to their kind. Eron was missing, and there was someone or some *thing* out there preying on innocent women and making it look as if vampires were to blame.

And she couldn't shake the feeling that it was all tied together.

Where was Eron? She would feel so much better if he were near. And he would be near if he could feel the fear racing through her veins. Eron would never leave her alone when she was in this much turmoil unless . . . something had happened to him. Again she tried to think of a way that could even be possible, but her head ached with the effort. Eron was extremely old and extremely powerful. He could fight off anyone.

"What are you thinking about over there?"

She looked at Christian, caught the concern in his eyes, although he was trying to appear nonchalant. "I can't feel Eron."

A spark of something flared in his eyes, but he quickly closed them and erased whatever emotion had momentarily escaped him. "He's dead?"

"No. He's not dead. I don't feel that, but I don't feel anything else either. I've called to him, but he hasn't responded. It's been like this for months now, and for some reason I've started getting images of him."

"What kind of images?"

"I saw him when I read the body we found in Leakin Park, and I've seen him in these flashes I've been getting, warning flashes of danger."

"So Eron is somehow tied up with this situation?"

"Yes, but I don't know how. He can't be the killer."

"Of course not, but he can't be a victim, surely. Who would have the power to overtake him?"

"I don't know. It would have to be someone very powerful themselves or extremely smart."

"It would take a maniacal genius, Seta. Eron's no fool."

No, Eron was no fool but someone had managed to fool him nonetheless. Seta glanced at her son, felt her pulse quicken. "There's more, Christian."

"Hmm?"

"The scent of vampire we found on the body; it was Eron's scent."

"What?" Christian's eyes darkened as he leaned in. "How is that possible?"

"I don't know. It was so faint that Rialto didn't notice. At least, I don't think he did. The scent was diluted somehow."

"Eron couldn't have killed those women."

"I believe we've already established that."

"Then how? I mean, if his scent was there, he had to have had some access to them."

"Or maybe the killer just had access to him."

Christian let out a slow breath. "You really think he's been captured? Eron, the most powerful vampire we've ever known?"

"It seems crazy, I know, but . . ."

"You believe it anyway."

"Yes." Seta gulped, her gaze once more zeroing in on her son. "And if there's someone out there powerful enough to capture Eron, how are we supposed to stop him from killing more women, stop him from fulfilling my vision and killing Aria?"

*WAKE UP . . . WAKE UP . . .*

Rialto squeezed his eyes shut so hard his head ached, willing himself to come out of this slumber, but it was no use. He could still hear her laughter. The maniacal sound of it seemed to echo off the mountains, intensifying his torture. He could smell the blood on the ground as it seeped out of whatever fragments of flesh were left on the bodies. There were so many dead. The heat of the bonfire warmed his skin, but the warmth didn't reach his heart. It felt like a block of solid ice in his chest, ready to shatter at the slightest touch.

"Why do you do this to yourself, Rialto?"

He stiffened as the old witch approached him from behind, always seeming to know exactly where to go, even though her eyes were useless. "What do you want?"

"I want you to stop this," she rasped in her old, tired voice, stopping beside him. His eyes still closed, he couldn't see her mouth, but knew it was pulled into a frown.

"Then help me to wake up, Dream Teller. Are you what's keeping me here?"

"No, I didn't bring you here, and I can't get you out of here with magic, either. This is your doing, Rialto, and yours alone."

He opened his eyes, carefully avoiding the scene before him as he turned to stare the old witch in the face, not quite sure if looking her in the eye mattered. "Let me out of here."

"I can't release you from your own torment, child, not when you're trapped in your own nightmare. Anyway, you denied my help back when it actually would have done you some good."

"Don't remind me."

The last thing he needed right now was the memory of the mistake he'd made over a century and a half ago. She'd come to him in a dream, advising him not to reveal himself to anyone, but the very next night he'd done just that. He'd revealed his true self to Antonia, ignoring her obvious horror at his revelation, and forced her into his world, a world she clearly hadn't been meant for. "Why didn't you just tell me not to change her over?"

"Would you have listened?"

No. There was no need to answer aloud; she already knew the truth. She knew everything, even more than his mother who was a powerful witch herself. "Why are you here now?"

"You need to end this torture. Stop wallowing in blame and guilt, Rialto, before you drown. You will be useless to her then."

"Useless to whom?"

"The one you were actually meant to be with."

He looked at her, noticing the wrinkles at the corners of her mouth turning upward as she faded. Alone again, he felt the chill night air more clearly as he realized what he needed to do to fade out of this dream world. He needed to look his nightmare in the eye, literally, and say goodbye. He squeezed his eyes shut and expelled a deep, calming breath, gathering his defenses. He didn't want to look into Antonia's blue eyes, didn't want to see them electrified by her murderous passion. It had been bad enough the first time.

Still, he wanted out of this hellish place.

"Antonia, it's time for me to let your memory go," he said as he turned in the direction of her dancing footsteps and opened his eyes, horrified when they clashed with emerald green instead of electric blue. "No! Aria?"

She stood before the bonfire, the same bloodstained dress Antonia had worn swirling around her body, the pale whiteness contrasting sharply with her light mocha skin. It was dark again, meaning she had been changed. *He* had changed her. "No, this can't be! You're supposed to be Antonia!"

Her grin was slow to spread, bringing out the menacing leer in her eyes. "I am Antonia. You did the same thing to me that you did to her. You took away my innocent soul and cursed me with evil."

"No!" Rialto shook his head feverishly. "I haven't changed you over. I only tasted you. I backed off before it went too far."

"You backed off on that night," she said slyly, her grin spreading into a full smile. Rialto's stomach churned when he saw the caked blood between her teeth—the blood of innocents. "You see, Rialto, this isn't a memory dream. This is a premonition."

She threw her head back and laughed before she stalked over to the baby carriage where the innocent child cried, not knowing it was being hunted.


"ARIA, NO!"

Rialto jerked straight up into a sitting position, cold sweat chilling his skin. Where was he? A brief glance around the wood paneled room, furnished with a sofa, chair, small kitchen area, and the chaise he was on provided the answer. He was in Christian's underground living quarters. How did he get here?

The last thing he remembered was walking alongside Seta. He'd been hungry and tired, his strength quickly leaving him and unable to hold down any blood, not even Seta's. He must have passed out.

"Great. Mommy carries her baby to safety again," he muttered to himself as he realized Seta must have carried him to Christian's. What had Aria thought about that?

*Aria.*

The beads of sweat rolling down the center of his back felt like ice shavings as he recalled the nightmare he'd just escaped. It had seemed so real, the evil burning in her eyes, the heartless way she'd stalked toward the baby carriage. He'd caused that. He had turned her into a brutal, soulless monster just like he'd done to Antonia. But he hadn't. He hadn't done anything. Yet.

Rialto muttered a foul oath as he rose from the chaise, a wave of dizziness nearly toppling him back down. His internal clock told him it was around eleven in the morning, much too early for him to be up and about, but the dream had knocked him for a loop. The last thing he could think about was sleep, not until he saw for himself that Aria was safe.

The dream was a wake-up call. He needed to protect her not only from her mother's killer, but from himself. He had promised to help find the killer and he would, but he needed to treat her like any other client, even though he wasn't being paid for his services.

He opened his senses and listened for her. He felt Christian's presence as well as Seta's. They were both sleeping, Christian having reached the mending stage, but Seta wasn't quite there yet. Her worry for him was evident.

*Rest, Rialto. You are much too weak.*

*Yes, Mother.*

He waited until he sensed Seta disappearing into the deep sleep, their mental link weakening, and then he made his way through the narrow tunnel which ran between the rooms. He passed the rooms where Seta and Christian slept, following Aria's scent.

He found her in the bedroom directly beneath the church. He stood in the entrance and stared at her, his hands in his pockets so they wouldn't reach out for her like they wanted to. She lay on her back in the bed, one hand resting over her abdomen, the other curled beside her head. He knew how uncomfortable she must be, fully clothed in that tight little T-shirt and equally snug jeans, breathing what little fresh air reached Christian's dwelling. He hadn't meant for her to spend the night here. She should be in her own bed, resting comfortably in her nightclothes. An image of her naked body resting against his under thin cotton sheets flashed through his mind, instantly heating his groin until it throbbed painfully. Dammit. Could he not even look at her fully clothed without his mind going there?

Muttering a curse under his breath, he fought to remind himself why he couldn't indulge in fantasy. The nightmare he woke from moments ago was too horrible to allow. It wasn't worth it. Not a million kisses, a million nights inside her, nothing. Nothing was worth the eternal hell he would suffer through if he lost control and turned her into something evil.

He had to find her mother's killer and he had to do it now. Then he could let her go. He knew full well he might die if he continued to thirst after her blood, but at least she would be safe.

He walked toward the bed almost hypnotically and stood beside it, staring down at her. Her chest rose and fell rhythmically as she slept, her stomach emitting a soft growl. Had they not seen to it that she had been fed? Rialto shook his head in frustration. She had to be worn out to be sleeping so late and hungry on top of that. If he was supposed to be taking care of her, he wasn't doing a great job.

"I'm going to find your mother's killer," he whispered earnestly, regretting the mistake once her eyes fluttered open.

"Rialto?" A crooked, drowsy grin emerged as she stretched, causing her breasts to jut forward, not a good move considering the current state of Rialto's body.

"Go back to sleep," he said gruffly, struggling to tamp down his urge to ravish her. Why had he stepped into the room? He should have known what would happen if she awakened all dewy eyed, soft, warm and inviting. He clenched his jaw tight as he saw the longing smoldering in her eyes.

Her eyes turned into narrowed slits as they inspected him. He'd forgotten she couldn't see as well as he could in the dark. "You look good, from what I can tell," she said sleepily. "It really gave me a scare when I saw you lying on the chaise so . . . still." *Deathlike* was what he heard her say in her mind. A pang of guilt hit him hard. He never should have allowed her to feel so much for him.

"How do you feel?" she asked.

"Tired," he answered honestly, averting his eyes. She was propped up on her elbows now, her T-shirt stretched taut over her chest, bringing attention to the two perfectly shaped mounds begging for his touch. She didn't seem aware of the invitation she was giving, but the action was wreaking havoc with his hormones.

"You should be sleeping. It's daytime."

"You should be awake."

"I didn't sleep much last night, and when I did it wasn't really relaxing."

Rialto quirked an eyebrow, sensing she was holding something back that might prove important. "Why didn't you sleep?"

"I sort of had a nightmare."

The way her gaze fell away from his tripped his inner alarm system. It had been a long time since he had seen the old witch in his dreams. Was it actually possible the hag had visited Aria as well? Knowing she was infamous for making vampires relive their darkest moments, he gulped back both anger and dread, his libido momentarily forgotten.

"What exactly did you dream about, Aria?" His voice may have been rough, his eyes dark and cold, but the degree to which she winced revealed that something other than his demeanor had scared her. "The Dream Teller?"

She nodded slowly as she rose to a sitting position, wrapping her arms around herself as though warding off a chill.

"Must have been some dream." He sat on the edge of the bed, his back to her. "What did she show you?"

"I saw Antonia," she said cautiously, seeming to hesitate before mentioning his former love's name. "I was there when those men . . . hurt her that night."

Hurt didn't begin to describe what they'd done to her, Rialto thought, as he swallowed hard, his jaw clenched tight enough to break a tooth. She had been innocent before he changed her over, and even if she hadn't been, nobody deserved to go through what she had that night.

"I'm sorry you saw that," he said. "Was that all you saw?"

"No."

He waited for the rest, but when a few minutes passed in silence, he accepted the fact that he would have to broach the subject himself. "You saw me change her over, didn't you?"

"Yes." Her tone was full of apology, which told him all he needed to know. She was horrified by what he'd done. He couldn't blame her, and it was probably for the best.

"I'm sorry, Aria. I never meant to turn her into a monster, and I never intended for you to know any of this."

"Why are you apologizing to me?"

"Because Antonia was the one I destroyed, but I can't apologize to her because she's not here."

He tensed when he felt her hand grip his shoulder, turning him to face her as she rose to her knees. "Who apologizes to you?"

"What?" He searched her eyes, baffled by the emotion he saw in them. Anger and disgust he could deal with, but the sympathy he saw was completely unexpected. He found himself at a loss for words.

Aria shook her head and let out a deep sigh. "In that dream, I saw what you did, Rialto, and yes, it was wrong. You didn't know that though, not in the state of mind you were in. You thought you were saving her."

"And what do you know of my state of mind?"

"I didn't just see what happened that night, Rialto. I felt it. I felt what was going through Antonia when she was attacked, how badly she wanted revenge afterward, and when you found her . . . I felt both of you."

"You felt both my emotions and hers? At the same time?"

"Yes. Antonia didn't want to be a vampire, but you loved her and you didn't want her to die. It was a mistake, Rialto, just a horrible mistake."

He didn't hear her words, too caught up in the fact that she'd felt Antonia's emotions as well as his own. Why hadn't he? Was it one of the old witch's tricks? Had she made Aria feel Antonia's emotions? He'd lived that night and not once had he felt what was going through her.

"Rialto? What is it?"

He jerked when she touched his shoulder, silently cursing himself when he felt her recoil. "I'm sorry, Aria. It's not you. You need to go back to sleep, and so do I." He stood to leave, and the room went black. He immediately fell back onto the bed in a half-sitting, half-lying position.

"Rialto! Lay down. You're not well."

"I'm fine. I just got a little dizzy."

"No, you are not fine." She was standing on the floor now, trying to lift his legs so she could position him on the bed. "Dammit, Rialto. Get yourself in this bed and rest."

"If I sleep here, where are you going to sleep?"

"There was a sofa and a chaise . . ."

"No. You need plenty of air and this is the best room for that. It's why you chose it in the first place. Just let me rest a few minutes, and then I'll go."

"You're sick because of me."

"That's nonsense."

"Your mother already told me, Rialto. You can't deny it. You need my blood to survive."

"Possibly."

"Possibly? *Possibly?* Is that all you're going to say? You could die!"

"Well, seeing as how I should have died over a hundred years ago, I'd say I'm overdue for it, wouldn't you?"

"Don't talk like that. It's not the least bit funny."

There was something in her tone that unsettled him. He turned to look at her, noting the deep concern in her wide, damp eyes and the hard set of her jaw. She was either terrified or pissed. "Relax, Aria. I'm not going to go jump off a building in an attempt to end my life. Even if I did I would land on my feet." He smiled, trying to ease her mind, but she didn't soften.

"You wouldn't jump off of a building, but would you lie in the sun? Would you do something so selfish and stupid?" Her voice rose with each word until she was nearly shouting. A stray tear escaped from her eye, trickling down her cheek.

Rialto felt his chest tighten, memories best left forgotten creeping back into the center of his mind. He'd tried to kill himself by sunlight many, many years ago. He'd punished himself for the murder of Antonia, but how would she possibly know that? "What all did you see in your dream, Aria?"

"I told you, and you're not going to get away with changing the subject."

"And just what is the subject? You're suddenly very angry with me and I haven't a clue as to why." Hell, maybe he shouldn't look a gift horse in the mouth. If she was angry with him she'd be less likely to put him in a position to lose control and change her over. But it still hit a nerve. He didn't want her angry with him, at least not without a good reason.

"Your life has value, Rialto."

"Ohh-kay." He stared at her, trying to read her face, figure out what was going on in her mind, but to his surprise, couldn't read her thoughts. It was as though she had thrown up a wall, a mental block to keep him from intruding.

"I'm going to sleep on the sofa," Aria snapped and then turned to leave, muttering a slew of colorful curses under her breath.

"Aria, wait."

"No. You need to rest. Look at you!"

Rialto groaned. The last thing he wanted was to see how pathetic and weak he must look. He felt like he had been put through the wringer at least twice. "Thanks. You really do know how to perk up a guy's ego." He was relieved when he saw her lips quirk, almost giving in to a smile. "I wanted to tell you that I'm going to find your mother's killer."

"You've already told me that."

"No, I mean it. I meant it then too, but . . ." He swallowed hard when he saw the exasperation on her face and what looked like a trace of sympathy. That irked him. "What I'm trying to say is that I'm going to do a better job of it starting the moment I wake tonight. We've let our attraction interfere, Aria. We have to stop that right now if we want to find the monster that took your mother away from you."

Aria nodded, meekly dropping her gaze to the floor, but she hadn't looked away quickly enough. He'd seen the guilt in the depths of her eyes. "You're a good daughter, Aria."

She looked at him, her eyes shimmering with restrained tears, and he felt an ache in his chest that almost made him forget men weren't supposed to cry. He felt her pain as if it were his own. If he didn't die from refusing her blood, he would die from caring for her. What brewed between them was just too intense.

She gave a miserable shake of her head. "A good daughter would never stray from the goal. I've been so worried about you . . ."

"That's my fault," he quickly interrupted. "I allowed things to happen that never should have taken place. You *are* a good daughter. What you have been subjected to these last few days . . . It's bigger than you. You just got swept away in the tide. We both did, but I won't allow it to happen again."

She nodded again, firmer this time. "So we stay strictly business, until we get this guy."

"We stay strictly business, period. For both our sakes."

Her eyes widened as if she'd been slapped, but only for a second. She quickly composed herself and nodded in agreement. "You're right. It's for the best."

Rialto should have been relieved, happy even, that she agreed with him so easily, but something inside his chest ached. It was a good thing he didn't need air in his lungs to live because he couldn't quite breathe.

"Okay." He found himself standing by the bed, looking at her, waiting. But what was he waiting for? Did he expect her to cry, to declare her undying love for him? Beg him to make love to her again? That was exactly what they both needed to avoid so why couldn't he just let go of the passion he felt for her? Passion be damned, he had a job to do.

"All right then. I'll see you at twilight. Christian will see to it that you're fed and taken care of when he wakes for his afternoon prayer session." He walked past her, pushing through the dizziness that was increasing with every step he took. He stopped in the doorway and looked back at her, watching her in profile as she fluffed the bed pillows, readying herself for sleep, and wondered why he felt as though he had just lost something very, very important.


ERON GROANED AS consciousness crept back in. He strained to focus his eyes but all he got for his effort was one big blur. Closing his eyes, he relied on his other senses, not that his telepathic abilities were working, but he still had hypersensitive hearing and sense of smell. Smelling could backfire, he had already discovered, as he was in some type of laboratory filled with odors that made his sensitive eyes burn as though they were filled with the fires of hell. Still, he knew if he ever got out of here he would have to know what was in the fluid his captor kept injecting into his system. You couldn't destroy something if you didn't know what it was. He couldn't put a name to all of the chemicals he smelled, but he could run tests, matching smell to chemical name.

*If* he got out of here.

He growled, the sound soft and impotent, failing to release his frustration. Instead, it made him angrier. He was Eron, a king amongst his kind. He hadn't run across a vampire older than himself in centuries. They were around, but not so many that their paths would cross. Most of the older vampires were the Elders, the most powerful and respected of their kind. They were rumored to live above the rest of the world in the Ancient Palace, a mountain region settled in the clouds where they were invisible to man and vampire-kind. They sat there on their thrones and watched the world beneath them, judging the entire vampire race.

Eron chose not to believe the rumors, instead believing they had gone underground, burying themselves deep in the earth where they could live mummified for an indefinite amount of time, a feat only the oldest and most powerful could do. But either way, they were probably laughing at him right now.

How had he been captured?

He struggled to find the answer to the question that had been looming over him during his entire imprisonment. How long had it been? He had tried keeping track of the days in his mind, but after the first month the blood loss reached a level that made him virtually incapable of tracking anything. His internal clock had failed him, along with many of his other vampiric abilities. The lab he was confined in was windowless, and if he was correct, underground.

He slowly opened his eyes, allowing them time to adjust to the harsh glare of the overhead lights. Bright light was painful to a vampire's sensitive eyes, a fact which Eron suspected his captor knew well. Indeed, his captor seemed to know a lot about vampires, as if he had studied them extensively for several years. He wondered if he was the first guinea pig manacled in this lab, or if others had hung from the same wall, eventually dying from the pain and blood loss.

Eron wouldn't die easily. He was confident in that. Even though he was drained repeatedly of his life preserving blood, it would take far more than that to kill him. As long as he still had some blood in him, any amount at all, he would survive. He was nearing the stage of his life where he could go underground and live in the earth as a mummy for centuries. He might do just that if he ever managed to escape.

Seta would dig him up and kill him for being so stupid.

He struggled to call out for her, but he couldn't. Their mental link was completely destroyed. The repeated blood loss was too great. If he weren't so old, he'd have been dead weeks ago. He wondered if Seta could feel him at all. Surely she would come for him, but then again, she had been furious with him the last time they'd parted ways.

He should have given her what she wanted. Hell, it was what he wanted too. When he was sent to save the little witch's life he hadn't a clue that she would enthrall him so. From the first moment she'd opened her eyes as a vampiress, he was infatuated. The brightest of diamonds paled in comparison to her unmatched beauty. She was fire and ice, attitude and cold aloofness. She got what she wanted by using both magic and feminine charm.

But she was never cold with him. He had trained her, taught her the ways of a vampire. Through him she had learned their history, their code, their purpose. He taught her how to use her vampiric abilities along with her inherent magical powers to protect herself and mankind. She was a powerful protector, and the best friend he'd ever had. Eventually she became his best lover as well, and that was when things had gone wrong.

The sound of footsteps outside the lab drew Eron's attention, temporarily taking it away from the pain in his heart. His captor was returning. He could smell the man's scent over the other smells permeating the laboratory. It was his own scent. How was that possible?

The door across the room from him opened, his captor bustling in with a wide-eyed look that clearly indicated something was wrong. Eron remained silent, long ago giving up the idea that the man might give him some useful information—or at least tell him why he felt so much animosity toward him personally.

The man opened up desk drawers, rifling through papers and files in a disorganized, erratic manner, slamming the drawers shut when he apparently didn't find what he was looking for. He did the same with the drawers and storage boxes under the lab tables, then ransacked the book shelves lining the left wall of the room.

"Where is it?" The man's eyes were wild, and his shock of red hair was a mess, as though he had been running his hands through it at length. "Where the *hell* is it?" His voice elevated a few decibels as his shaking hands clenched. Then he turned his gaze toward Eron, his eyes emblazoned with hatred and distrust. "You."

He walked like a predator, his head lowered but eyes still connected to where Eron hung from the wall. "Where is it? How did you move it?"

Eron couldn't stop the small chuckle from escaping. "First, I don't know what it is you're looking for, and second, I'm kind of at a disadvantage here. If I could move anything it would be my ass out of these manacles."

"You're talking much better today, like you've got some of your strength back. Maybe you have other powers back."

"Trust me," Eron said low and levelly, "the first thing I would have done if my powers had returned was turn your ass into barbecue when you first set foot in this room."

"Hmm . . ." The man seemed to ponder that information before retrieving a tined instrument from one of the lab tables. He walked to Eron and held the object in front of his face. "Bend it."

"Pardon me?"

"Bend it!" The man grinned devilishly as he shook the instrument for emphasis. "Bend it or I will ram it straight through your stomach."

Shit. Eron focused on the fork-like instrument, hoping like hell that a small amount of his telekinetic ability was still functioning. He was able to complete sentences without running out of breath since the man had eased off the amount of bloodletting sessions he had been subjected to for the past few months. Maybe . . . just maybe . . .

Nothing.

Eron screamed as the instrument was shoved into his midsection, the pain unbearable in his condition. "I should let you die," the man said between clenched teeth, "but the master won't allow it yet."

The instrument was retracted, allowing air to hit the fresh wound, burning Eron to such degree he couldn't blink back the tears. He was *crying*. The man would pay for this, even if he had to come back from death to destroy him, the man would pay for weakening him to this level.

"I will kill you and the demon that controls you," Eron managed to get out between teeth gritted against the pain searing through his body.

"Not if I find my journal first," the man said before turning and exiting the laboratory, not stopping to bandage Eron's wound.

Eron let his head fall forward so he could inspect the damage. When he saw the blood oozing out of the open hole, vampire or not, he would have vomited had he anything in his stomach. He needed to sleep right now, reach the mending stage before he bled out completely.

He closed his eyes and summoned sleep, thinking all the while that he might never wake again.

# Chapter Thirteen

"ARE YOU HUNGRY?"

Aria jumped as Christian's voice cut into her thoughts. She'd been awake for hours. After staring at Rialto's sleeping form for as long as she could bear without touching him, all that was left to do to pass the time was think.

"A penny for your thoughts," Christian said as he entered the room and sat at the end of the bed she was currently reclined on. "Looks like I interrupted some pretty deep thinking. What's up?"

"I'm starved, actually."

Christian grinned, looking even more handsome than usual. "And the other question I asked?"

Aria studied his face, amazed at the amount of compassion she saw in his dark blue eyes. "You really care about Rialto, don't you?"

"He's like a brother to me," Christian answered without a moment's hesitation. "Why? What are you planning to do?"

"Can you read my mind too?" Aria shifted, a feeling of paranoia washing over her.

"No," Christian answered with a smile. "Your feelings are written all over your face. You're clearly worried about Rialto and rightfully so. But I also see guilt. Guilt makes people try to fix things."

"I bet you're really good in the confessional."

Christian laughed. "It's not a sport one competes at, but I have learned how to see people quite well over the centuries. I pick up little things in their eyes, the tone of their voice, selected words. I know you have an idea how to help Rialto, and I feel compelled to make sure you're not making any decisions in haste."

"Why?"

"We protect our own."

"I'm not a vampire."

"You are Rialto's soul mate. That makes you one of us. Now, what are you thinking of doing?"

"Nothing, just . . . there has to be a way to stop this thing that's happening."

"Which thing would that be?"

"The sickness. There has to be a way for Rialto to live without changing me over."

Christian's eyes clouded over for a second before he blinked and looked away. "Sometimes acceptance of one's fate is the only means for survival."

Aria watched in surprise as he stood and walked toward the doorway, turning when he reached it. "What is it, Aria?"

She shook her head. "You're supposed to be a man of God. Why can't you believe that not everything is up to fate? Why can't you just *believe?*"

His grin was slow and sympathetic, never reaching his eyes which were dull and blank. "God granted us common sense and the ability to use it. I believe, Aria, more than I can describe. But I also believe we must do, and that we must figure out some things ourselves."

"So you're saying I can't beat this thing?" She rose from the bed and followed Christian through the narrow passageway, waiting for him to unlock the door which would allow them entrance to the church.

"You can't change what you are, Aria, what you were meant to be. All you can control is the effect it has on you when the change takes over."

Aria still pondered Christian's remark a few minutes later as they stood in a small room toward the back of the church. The room was barely large enough to hold the table and chairs sitting in the center, let alone the small refrigerator which Christian searched for food.

"Here we go," he said as he pulled out a plastic container and removed the lid, sniffing the contents. "Still good."

Aria watched curiously while he put the container in the microwave and nuked the food. "That's not anything with blood in it, is it?"

His answer was a chuckle.

"Seriously, what is it?"

"Chili. Some of the kids in this neighborhood don't always get enough to eat at home. I make sure I've always got something here for them."

"Do you eat?"

"I can. We all can. It's just not a requirement."

"How do you not get caught drinking blood?"

The timer on the microwave sounded, indicating the chili was done. Christian removed the plastic container, grabbed a plastic spoon out of a tray next to the microwave and set the two items in front of her on the table. He took the seat across from her and steepled his long fingers beneath his chin. Looking at those fingers, she noticed how smooth and light his skin was. It wasn't Rialto's or Seta's deep bronzed tan or her own dark brown. "You're a little pale. I darkened when I tasted blood."

Christian lowered his hands to the table and studied his palms. "I haven't had living blood in a long time. That's partly how I manage not to give myself away. I stay in the church, help those who ask for it. I open the doors in the day as well as in the night, and I'm careful to keep my home a secret."

"You live off of bagged blood."

"I find it more humane. True, I'm not as strong as a vampire my age should be, but bagged blood is easier to acquire. I couldn't live here and risk being found drinking from a mortal in some alley."

"The others get by with it."

"They travel. I choose to stay in one spot until I have no choice but to leave."

"When people start noticing you don't age."

"Right." He nodded toward the chili in which she was circling her spoon. "Eat or Rialto will have my hide. I'm supposed to be taking care of you."

Aria ignored his order, intrigued with the lack of laugh lines around his eyes and only one crease at the curve of his smile. "How old were you when you were changed?"

He frowned. "I'm not sure."

Aria stared at him. "Why aren't you sure? Surely you'd remember your age."

Christian shrugged, his eyes registering unease. "It's a long story."

Aria pondered that. "How long have you been a vampire?"

"Hundreds of years have passed since the night I was changed over. If you're trying to evade my original question, Aria, it won't work."

"What question?"

He looked at her knowingly. "What are you planning?"

"Nothing." Aria tried to appear casual as she took a bite of the chili. It was a little hot, but tasted decent enough.

"I'm not allowing you to leave this building without one of us with you."

Aria sighed in frustration. "How did you even know I wanted to leave?"

"It's in your face. You're anxious to be gone from here."

She set the spoon down. "I'm not going to do anything dangerous. I just want to find some information."

"Absolutely not, Aria. Seta has seen your future, and in her vision you were lying on a metal slab, dying. You're not going anywhere by yourself."

"Well, I can't stand to just sit here and do nothing while Rialto wastes away."

"The day sleep is giving him back his energy. He's not dying, not yet anyway." Christian paused, looked at Aria and opened his mouth as though there was more he wanted to say, but with a shake of his head, he closed his mouth and pushed away from the table. "Eat, Aria. You need your strength, too. I'm going to open the doors for afternoon prayer. You're welcome to join us if you like."

Aria waited until Christian left the room before she pushed the chili away. She couldn't eat when her stomach was in knots. Rialto was lying in a room beneath the church, possibly dying, and she was sitting on her butt doing absolutely nothing to help him. Although she had some prayers which needed answering, she wasn't going to join Christian's prayer group. She needed to find a way out of the church while he was occupied.

The room she was in didn't have a window so that route of escape was out. She walked over to the only door and put her ear against it, listening for Christian. She waited several minutes, but didn't hear a sound. She was in the back of the church. Christian and his prayer group would be in front, in the chapel. So far she'd only seen one door leading to the outside, and it was in the front of the building.

She turned the knob slowly, careful not to make a sound in case Christian also possessed hypersensitive hearing, and stepped into the hall. The hallway was narrow, but fortunately, not too long. She hadn't seen any exits when she came up here with Christian so she turned left, toward the two rooms she hadn't inspected.

The first room was smaller than the one she had just been in and only contained a small cot and a nightstand with a lamp. Like the other room, it was windowless and escape proof.

The second door was locked. Lock-picking wasn't a skill she had ever acquired so she muttered a colorful string of curses and kicked at the door with the toe of her boot. Somehow, some way, she was getting out of here before nightfall.


ARIA SAT ON THE edge of the bed and slipped on her boots. She'd waited patiently for Christian's afternoon prayer session to end and watched as he unlocked the door leading to his underground home, carefully memorizing the order in which each lock was unbolted.

An hour after coming back down into the hidden residence, she felt safe enough to venture out. It was about three hours before nightfall. Surely all three of the vampires were asleep. She went straight for the door and slowly, carefully, unlocked it, praying all the while she remembered the correct sequence.

The door opened and she slipped through, carefully closing it behind her, her hands shaking with the fear that one of her protectors would wake up before she left the church. She succeeded and hurried upstairs, stopping at the alarm panel beside the church's front door. She'd memorized the code she saw Christian punch in after his last parishioner left. She felt guilty as she unarmed the system, then reset it so the church and the vampires resting beneath it would remain protected, but she couldn't let precious time escape her when every moment brought Rialto closer to death. She didn't care what Christian said about Rialto regaining his strength. He was going to die unless they figured out a way to save him. Knowing him, Rialto would be too busy searching for the killer to worry about his own survival. That left the job up to her, and she wasn't going to give up on him, not without a fight.

Summer was drawing near, but the air was cool as Aria walked away from the church, wishing she had swiped Rialto's car keys before escaping. This was not the type of neighborhood she preferred to walk in alone. Aria picked up the pace, anxious to get out of the neighborhood before she was mistaken for a hooker.

Almost as if on cue, a car horn blared behind her. Aria kept her head down and picked up speed, almost coming to a jog. She looked at the buildings she passed, but none looked like the type of place to seek shelter. Another blast of the horn caused her to jump. Why hadn't she stayed at the church?

"Ms. Michaels!"

Aria halted at the sound of her name and turned toward the street to see a Crown Victoria roll to a stop beside her. The driver's side window was lowered to reveal the detective who'd been in her apartment just two days before. "I thought it was you," he said, angling his head out the window. "What are you doing here?"

"I was on my way to Enoch Pratt."

"And you chose to go there by way of the most dangerous street in Maryland?" He nodded toward the passenger seat. "Get in. I'll drive you."

"Oh, that's all right, I'll . . ."

"I'm not asking, Ms. Michaels. I have some questions for you. Get in the car."

Aria's mouth went dry as she looked into Detective Porter's eyes. They were compassionate but stern, the eyes of a man who was not going to take no for an answer. She exhaled a breath and walked around the front of the car, noticing the detective's stare never left her.

"Am I under investigation?" Aria asked as she slid into the passenger seat and closed the door, praying this wasn't a mistake.

"For what?"

"You tell me. You're the one with the questions and the not so friendly face."

"I'm concerned, Aria. There are too many bodies, er, victims, I should say. Sorry." He glanced at her before putting the car into drive and pulling out onto the street. "Too many victims and not enough clues. It doesn't make me a friendly, happy guy when I'm the man who's supposed to catch this freak and I have no idea who he is."

"Are you sure it's a man?"

"Are we back to your theory that the killer is a vampire?"

Aria rolled her eyes. "If you're going to insult me, I'd rather walk."

"What are you doing in this neighborhood?"

"What are you doing here?"

"Hel-lo. Homicide detective. I practically live here which explains why you shouldn't be in this area. You're not unfortunate enough to live here. Why pass through? Definitely not to get to the library, which is in the other direction from your apartment."

Aria studied the detective's profile as he steered the car onto another road, leading in the direction of the library. His features were devoid of any emotion, his eyes focused on the road before him. "If you have something to say, Detective . . ."

"Jonah."

"Excuse me?"

"Jonah Porter. You can call me Jonah."

"Well, Jonah, what are you getting at? Why did you pick me up? What questions do you need answered, and where is your partner?"

"That's a lot of questions. Let's see. My partner's sister is having a baby, so she's at the hospital. I picked you up because there's a serial killer on the loose and this isn't a good neighborhood for a woman to walk alone in, serial killer or not. I also need to know about your friends."

Aria's heart skipped a beat. "My friends?"

"Yeah, particularly the two I saw walking around late last night. You want to explain to me how a teenage girl can pick up a six-foot plus man and disappear within the blink of an eye?"

Aria's breath caught in her throat, sending a sharp pain through her middle. How could she possibly explain what he had seen? And why hadn't Seta and Rialto been more careful? Hell, Rialto probably hadn't been in any condition to cover his tracks, and Seta's concern for him could have clouded her judgment. "I don't know what you're talking about."

"That might have sounded believable, if not for the shaking in your voice."

"Look, whoever you saw—"

"I saw the man who calls himself Rialto Renaldi, your fiancé, as I recall. I saw him fall down and I saw a girl no more than eighteen, nineteen tops, pick him up, throw him over her shoulder and then *poof,* she was gone."

"Obviously you're not fit for this job if you imagine things like that! And to think you scoffed at me when I said a vampire killed my mother. At least there were holes in her neck to support my theory."

"Are they people, Aria? Who the hell moves like that?"

Unsure how to respond, she opted for treating the detective the way she'd been treated when she'd given the homicide department the theory that a vampire had killed her mother. "Were you by chance drinking when you saw them, detective?"

"Don't be cute, Ms. Michaels. I'm trying to help you."

"Then find the monster who killed my mother."

"I'm trying to. Tell me about Renaldi."

Aria grinned. "He's tall, good looking. Great in bed . . ."

"That's real cute. Do I need to show you the pictures of your mother after she was found?"

Aria's mouth gaped as she stared at him in enraged horror. "How dare you."

"I'm glad to see that you agree this isn't a matter to be joked about." He pulled over in front of the library and turned to face Aria head on. "Something sick and twisted is going down in this city. Your mother and others like her were left abandoned, their bodies completely drained of blood, and the only wounds were two small holes in their necks. Evil is in the air, and last night I saw something that defies rational explanation. I ask you again, Ms. Michaels. Who is this man you call your fiancé, and what the hell is he?"

Aria swallowed hard and forced herself to hold the detective's stare. "Why, Jonah Porter, I almost believe you think vampires really do exist."

"Yeah, I almost believe I do."

His gaze was hard and serious. Looking into his eyes, Aria found she couldn't breathe. "I saw you leave that church while I was passing by, Aria. It wasn't any coincidence I was there. We're investigating the guy who runs that church."

*They were investigating Christian?* "The police are investigating the pastor? Why?"

Porter shook his head. "The department, my partner for that matter, isn't investigating him. My brother is and I'm helping."

"Who's your brother?"

"Jake's a different kind of detective. He investigates people of . . . *questionable* origin."

"Am I supposed to know what that means?"

"It means the guy is dangerous. My brother captures people, and I use that term loosely, who are far crazier than the psychos I apprehend. If he's interested in this guy, you don't need to be around him." He gave her a hard once-over. "What's the connection?"

"What connection?"

"I meet a guy in your apartment who immediately gets my suspicions up just by looking at him. Later I see the same guy disappear into thin air, and today I catch you leaving a church where my brother swears the pastor isn't what he seems."

"Is anyone really what they seem?" She opened the car door and put one foot on the curb. "Thanks for the ride, Jonah. Now I'm going to help you by giving you a little advice. You're finding bad in the wrong guys. Rialto is a detective of sorts too, and he's helping me look for my mother's killer, a job that, quite frankly, you've done pitifully. Don't get in his way. You have no idea what you're up against."

She noticed Porter's eyes widen in surprise at her remark before she slammed the door shut and left him sitting at the curb.


HOT, SEARING PAIN ripped through Eron's abdomen, awakening him from dreamless slumber. He opened his eyes and saw a head full of red hair. He looked down to see his captor putting some type of lotion over his wound. The lotion burned like hell as it seeped into his skin. "What are you doing now?" He managed to get the words out between teeth clenched in pain.

"Trying to heal you. You should rest."

"Ah, I see. You can't let me die until you find my replacement."

His captor looked up, concern deeply embedded in his eyes. A series of bruises and a deep cut down one cheek marred his face, which was free of the usual evil smirk that adorned it. Eron felt strangely unsettled, as though this was the first time he'd spoken to the man. The only other time he'd seen that look in his captor's eyes was the day he'd come into the lab to retrieve a book, darting looks over his shoulder as though he feared being caught in the act.

"There are two of you!"

The man gulped and looked over his shoulder toward the laboratory door before stepping back from Eron. "Don't tell him I was here. He'll kill me."

"You're twins."

"Something like that," the man answered with a foul expression. It seemed the words he spoke left a bad taste in his mouth. "For what it's worth, I'm sorry. I would stop him if I could."

"Let me go."

"I can't."

"Why the hell not?" Eron tried to keep down his anger, knowing he didn't have the energy to remain conscious for long. He had to get through to the man. "If you fear him, I can offer protection."

The man smirked. "Says the vampire chained to the wall."

Fueled by rage, Eron tried to reach out for the man, but the manacles didn't allow him much movement. The hard metal cut into his already damaged skin, making him yelp in pain.

"Don't, Eron. You'll only make it worse. You can't protect me. Nobody can. He's grown stronger and smarter. Nobody can stop him now."

"Who is he? What does he want with me?"

The man opened his mouth to speak, then snapped it shut with a shake of his head. "If I tell you, might tell him and he'll know I was here." He placed the bottle of lotion in his pants pocket and shrugged. "I can't release you, but I'll help you as much as possible."

Eron struggled through the tug of unconsciousness trying to pull him away, having to know one more thing. "Why? Why help at all?"

"Because you were right."

Eron started to ask him what he meant, but unconsciousness finally succeeded in pulling him under.


ARIA NERVOUSLY glanced at the clock across the room. It would be dark soon, and she knew without a doubt Rialto, Seta and Christian were going to be pissed when they discovered she was gone.

Shaking off the fear of Rialto's reaction, she lowered her head over one of the many books she'd brought back to the table and continued to read. She'd grabbed every book referencing black magic, the occult, and witches she could gather into one armload. She didn't know what, exactly, she was looking for, but there had to be a cure for Rialto's sickness.

The book she was currently looking over sent tremors down her spine. It was filled with satanic rituals, spells for evil doing, ways to contact the devil and exchange your soul for personal gain. She almost felt like a devil worshiper for reading it, but there in the midst of all that evil she discovered something called The Blood Revelation.

The Blood Revelation was a way to defeat the devil. According to the book, the vampire race was born in evil, but when three innocents refused to allow the evil into their hearts, they started a chain of vampires whose sole purpose was to defend the innocent against acts of evil. According to the book, these three vampires judged the remainder of the vampire race, deeming who was good enough to fight for their side. It also mentioned vampires preselected to bring into the world mighty weapons which would save the world during a war between good and evil. Weapons in the form of children.

Aria dropped the book as Seta's words ran through her mind. Could it be true that she and Rialto were predestined to mate and give birth to a warrior? She picked the book back up and quickly thumbed through the pages until she found where she'd left off.

*These special preselected vampires will be known by their strength in conscience and beauty, but most of all their blood. Their blood will strengthen like none other. To drink from a preselected vampire who has not been transformed into his or her vampire self will cause an instant addiction to the blood, to which there is no cure. They must be transformed or whomever has drunk from them will die.*

*Those who are mated share the same soul, are part of one another from birth, and shall have no other mates. If they do not come together, demons will have free reign to walk the earth without fear of destruction.*

*These preselected vampires must be destroyed before given the chance to produce offspring. If they are allowed to produce a child then the child must be hunted and killed before it comes of age and harnesses its full power.*

"Aria."

Aria jumped, her body trembling in fear as Curtis sat beside her. "Hey, Curtis, I . . ." Her voice trailed off as she noticed the deep blue and purple bruises covering a large area of his face and the stitches which closed the gash running from his eye to the middle of his cheek. "What happened to you?"

"I was mugged," he answered with a shrug. "Just another day in Baltimore." His eyes lowered to the book before her, and for a moment she thought she caught real fear in them. But when he looked back at her all she saw was sorrow. "I read in the newspaper that your mother was one of the victims, Aria. I'm so sorry."

Aria closed the book and put her hand on his shoulder. "It's not like it was your fault, Curtis." The look of guilt that creased his face caused Aria's heart to skip a beat, but surely it was all in her mind. Curtis looked about as dangerous as a newborn kitten.

She cleared her throat, removing her hand from his shoulder and placing it in her lap. "It's bad enough reporters have been hovering around my apartment, trying to get a statement from me but I see they've put my name in their stories too. So much for respecting the privacy of the victims' loved ones."

"I'm so, so sorry."

Aria again looked into Curtis's eyes, her breath catching in her throat as she saw raw anguish glistening there. He seemed distraught, torn apart, almost as though he felt some personal responsibility for her loss.

"It's all right, Curtis." She felt compelled to reassure him, yet scared at the same time. But what was she afraid of? She didn't know, but something inside her was crying out that something was wrong here. Something was very, very wrong. She needed to get back to Rialto. "I, uh, I gotta go now, Curtis."

Curtis's hand clamped onto her wrist as she started to gather up the books strewn across the table. "Wait, Aria. I need to get the journal back from you." His eyes lowered to the cover of the book she'd been reading, narrowed, and then studied the others. "What are you up to?" His hand tightened around her wrist as his lip curled into an angry scowl.

"What do you mean?" She glanced around, dismayed to see there would be no witnesses if his sudden anger got out of control.

He gestured toward the books with his hand. "Kind of dark stuff, huh? More research?"

"Yeah. I like to be thorough."

His eyes darkened as they bored into hers. "How much research does one need for erotica? The characters screw each other, end of story. Am I correct?"

Aria's mouth fell open as she remembered how awkward he'd seemed after she'd brought up the topic of erotica only days ago. "Curtis, this isn't like you."

He blinked and the darkness in his eyes started to fade. "I'm sorry, Aria. I'm not feeling well right now."

"Maybe you should see a doctor. Those bruises look pretty bad. You might need more medical attention."

"Are you implying that I need to have my head examined? I'm not a psycho, Aria. I'm trying to be a good friend to you. Why must you make it so hard?"

"I'm sorry," Aria sputtered as Curtis's hand tightened around her wrist even more. His tight grip hurt. "I know you're a good friend, Curtis. I just think you're hurt and not quite yourself. That's all."

He stared at her, seeming to look through her, study her very thoughts. His eye color changed, grew darker, but Aria knew that was impossible. Yet, she couldn't shake the feeling she was being examined, and possibly not by Curtis. Finally, he blinked and released his grip on her, revealing a dark red band circling her wrist. "I'm sorry. You're right. I'm not myself today. I'm not Curtis Dunn."

Aria pondered over his last remark, finding it odd he would refer to himself in the third person. "Who are you today?" She didn't know what made her ask that, but the cold look she got in return made her wonder if doing so was a bad move.

"The journal, Aria. I need it."

"Sure. Can I ask why?"

"Because it's not mine and I need it back."

"Oh." Aria straightened the books on the table until they formed two neat stacks, the black book filled with dark rituals and information about The Blood Revelation was perched on top of one of the stacks. "I'm sorry. When you said I could borrow it, I wasn't aware there it was only for a short time. If I had, I wouldn't have kept it so long, and—"

He shushed her with an impatient wave of his hand. "It's all right. I just need it back. I didn't ask before I took it, and now my brother is upset because he needs it."

"He needs it?" A sense of impending doom swept over Aria, causing her stomach to churn. "What would he need it for if it's just fiction?"

"That's not your concern, Aria. I just need the damn book!"

"Okay, fine." Aria put her hands up, palms out in surrender. "I'll have to bring it back to you tomorrow night. It's at my apartment."

"I need it now."

"Well, I don't have it on me now, Curtis. You'll have to wait."

"Not until tomorrow. I can't."

"Curtis . . ."

"I'll take you home and you can get it for me."

Aria felt her blood turn icy at the thought of him taking her home, knowing where she lived . . . where she slept at night. But why should she be afraid? This was Curtis, the awkward, shy, geeky librarian's aide. What could he possibly do to her? But, looking into his eyes now, peeking out from his marred face, she got the strangest feeling there was another being altogether inside of Curtis Dunn.

"Is there a problem, Aria?"

"No, no. Not at all." She shook her head vigorously, nervously, and wondered if he could tell. What was going on? "Just, uh, help me put these books back and we can go, or do you have to wait until your shift is over?"

"I'm not working today. Let's get a move on, Aria. I want to be home before sundown." He grabbed the black book off the top of one of the piles and dropped it onto the table. "Where did you get that book, anyway?"

"Here, of course," she answered as she grabbed the other stack of books and followed him to replace them on the shelves. He hesitated and peered back at her.

"We don't carry books that dark. Who gave it to you? You can tell me."

"I did tell you. I found it right here on this shelf with the others." She replaced the other books and returned to the table.

"That's not a library book." Curtis followed behind her and picked up the book, checking the back cover. "See. No bar code."

Confused, Aria grabbed the book and flipped through its pages, inspecting the cover as well. He was right. There wasn't a bar code and no stamp or stickers anywhere identifying it as a library book. "But it was right there on the shelf."

"Maybe someone else left it by mistake or returned it to us, thinking it was another book."

"But why would the librarian place it on the shelf, knowing it's not a library book?"

Curtis shrugged impatiently. "Put it back where you got it. Maybe the owner will come back for it. You don't want a book like that to get into the wrong hands."

"How do you know so much about it?"

"Do you think they just let anyone work for the library? I know a lot about books, all kinds of books, and that is not a very nice book. Now put it back."

"Yeah, sure." Aria walked back over to the shelves and hid the book behind a group of others, hoping nobody else found it before she could come back to retrieve it. She wanted to take it with her, to see if there was anything else to be learned about The Blood Revelation, but something in Curtis's tone when he'd ordered her to leave it there scared her all the way down to her bones. Especially when his command to leave it there totally went against his concern that it could fall into the wrong hands. He seemed to just want her away from it.

She couldn't give the journal back to Curtis tonight. There was obviously something in it she'd missed. She needed to give him the slip, but how could she manage to do that? As adamant as he was that he was escorting her home to retrieve it, she needed a miracle to get out of this corner she'd backed herself into. She turned around and saw her miracle approaching.

"Detective Porter!" The relief she felt slipped into her voice, and judging by the way the detective's eyes subtly squinted for a second, she knew some of her fear had as well. When Curtis turned his head to see the man approaching from behind him, she nodded toward him and sent the detective a look she hoped said, *Get me away from this nut job now!*

"I'm glad I caught you before you left, Ms. Michaels," Jonah said, stepping past Curtis without pausing to acknowledge the other man's presence. "I have to speak with you. Allow me to escort you home." He took her elbow in his hand and started to move past Curtis.

"Wait a second!" Curtis's cheeks turned an angry shade of red, but Aria could see in his eyes that he felt threatened by the detective. "I'm giving her a ride home so she can return something of mine."

"Police business," Jonah said as he flashed his badge and quickly ushered Aria out of the library and into his car.

"Want to explain what that was about?" Jonah asked when he slid into the driver's seat and started the car, checking for traffic before pulling out onto the road. "You looked trapped."

"I thought I was," Aria answered honestly. "Curtis, that guy in there, is usually a really sweet, completely safe kind of guy. Tonight he was kind of crazy."

Jonah spared her a concerned glance before returning his focus to the road. "What did he do?"

"Nothing really. He just kind of weirded out. He let me borrow a book earlier, and then tonight he comes into the library on his day off to tell me he needs it back and got kind of threatening when I told him it was at my apartment."

"Did he actually threaten you?"

"No, no, it was just something in his voice and in his eyes." Aria shivered. "He gave me the creeps. Maybe I'm just on edge."

"Well, I can't do anything to him if he didn't verbally threaten you, but be on guard. If your gut tells you there is something wrong with a person, then there probably is. What's up with his face?"

"He said he got mugged."

"Maybe," Jonah said in a way that made Aria feel he didn't really believe Curtis's story. "Keep your distance from the guy. He's not so bad, feel kinda sorry for him to tell the truth, but his brother is a real wacko. I've dealt with him before. Crazy bastard thinks he's the son of the devil."

"Are you serious?"

"Extremely. According to his file, the twins were the result of a rape. Guess that's enough to make a person a little nuts."

Aria gasped. "Curtis's biological father was a rapist?"

"Yep. Mother kept both kids despite their paternity. She died while they were teenagers. Suicide. Cut her own throat."

Aria shook her head in sympathy as they neared her apartment building. Trevaris was outside fixing the front railing. She was surprised to find he was the only person out there.

"Looks like the reporters decided to leave me alone," she commented as the car rolled to a stop.

"For a while, at least. There was another body found downtown, but it doesn't seem to be related. They don't know that though." He shifted in his seat so he could look her in the eye. The light from a nearby street lamp spilled into the car, highlighting the contours of his face. "Like I said, I came to the library so I could speak with you. I told my brother what I saw, and there's some real concern that this guy you're involved with isn't who you think he is."

"Who are you talking about? Rialto?" Aria tried her best to appear calm although she suddenly felt queasy inside.

"You know that's who I'm talking about. I ran a search on him and couldn't find anything. It's like he doesn't even exist."

"How much info can you find on a person going by their name alone, Detective?"

"I have my ways of finding people in the system, Aria."

"Too bad you don't seem to have any way to catch a killer," she snapped.

"Aria—"

"Shut up, Porter. If you want to help me, you need to lay off my friends and focus on the fact that there is a killer on the loose. Rialto doesn't have anything to do with my mother's murder so he shouldn't be of any concern to you."

"According to my brother, he just might have something to do with it."

"Your brother is a dumb ass." Aria stepped out of the car and slammed the door shut before the detective could make another comment. She looked through the window to see him shake his head before pulling away from the curb.

"Sweets, is that you?" Trevaris asked from behind her. "What's goin' on with your skin, girl? You look all pale again."

She turned to answer but stopped as she caught sight of the two very pissed off looking vampires walking toward her.

# Chapter Fourteen

"SWEETS? YOU KNOW these people?" Trevaris's voice was full of caution as Seta and Rialto drew closer, their faces twin masks of fury. Aria could almost see Trevaris jumping to her aid, if Rialto snatched her up, which looked like a definite possibility judging by the tight set of his mouth, and that would cause one huge problem.

"I'm all right, Trevaris," she answered before the two vamps could swoop down on her. "They're really close friends. I'm safe with them." She no more than made that statement before Rialto's hand clamped around her arm and pulled her none too gently toward the apartment building's front steps.

"Hey, just a minute, man!" Trevaris's angry voice boomed behind her. She turned her head in time to see Seta raise a hand, and then Trevaris went flying backward. Fortunately a pile of garbage bags cushioned his fall.

"Stay out of this, fool," Seta cautioned him. "She is safe with us."

"You didn't have to hurt him," Aria snapped as she was pulled toward her apartment.

"If I wanted to hurt him I would have ripped out an organ," Seta responded matter-of-factly.

Once inside the apartment, Rialto released his grip on Aria's arm and turned her to face him, the anger in his dark, penetrating eyes burning through her. "Don't you *ever* do that to me again. You can't begin to imagine all the horrible images that went through my mind when I woke and discovered you were gone." His voice was a thunderous boom, his body shaking with barely constrained anger. Aria could only look at him.

"He nearly ripped Christian's head off when he figured out how you escaped," Seta said from behind her. "You owe the poor man an apology."

Christian. He'd trusted her even when he knew she'd wanted out. The last thing she'd wanted to do was to get him into trouble or cause a rift between the two old friends. "I'm sorry."

"Sorry and stupid." Rialto glowered at her. "I told you of Mother's vision. Someone wants you *dead!*"

"We've got more immediate problems here," she said.

Rialto's eyes widened, full of incredulity. "Is that a joke or are you that unconcerned with that little thing called your life?"

"Just calm down and I'll explain."

"Calm down?" Rialto shook his head. "Do you realize my heartbeat has just now returned to normal? We raced straight here, and what do I find? You in a car with some man. I thought it was the killer, Aria. I thought he'd captured you."

"Rialto, you know it was the detective you met here a few days ago."

"I realized that when I got a good look at him, but I didn't know it when I first approached. I thought you were in danger. Scared the hell out of me. What were you doing in the detective's car anyway?"

"That's what I'm trying to tell you. He saw you—both you and Seta."

Seta's head snapped up from the painting she'd been studying. "Saw us? What are you talking about?"

"He saw the two of you last night when Rialto passed out. He saw you pick him up and vanish into thin air. He knows you're not regular people."

Seta and Rialto exchanged startled glances as Aria walked over to the sofa and sank down into the soft, inviting cushions. What she really needed was a warm, bubbly hot tub to ease away her tension, but the sofa would have to do.

"Should we fear this man?" Seta asked her son.

"He's a detective. I don't know much about him, but I sensed his immediate suspicion when we met. I remember he reached for his gun, then stopped mid-action when he realized what he was doing. He might be a hunt-now-ask-questions-later type."

"Oh, he's asking questions," Aria said on the tail of a yawn, suddenly exhausted. "He wants to know what you are and what you're doing here."

"What did you tell him?" Seta gave Aria a hard look which made her shiver with fear.

"Nothing, of course. But Christian needs to be warned. The guy's brother is investigating him, doesn't think he's what he appears to be."

"Who is this brother?"

"John or Jack, or . . . Jake maybe?" Aria tried to recall the name of the detective's brother as Seta's inquiring eyes bore into her. The witch didn't look pleased.

"Could it be Jake Porter?"

"Yes, that's it. Do you know him?"

Seta let out a string of curses that would redden the cheeks of a hardened criminal and turned toward her son. "Jake Porter is that demon-hunting pit bull who ran Christian out of his last church. He was just a kid then. Imagine the damage he can do now." She turned sharp eyes back to Aria. "Watch out for that detective. He can't be trusted."

"Well, he's working the serial killer case so I'm going to have the occasional run-in with him. And he's extremely curious about the two of you, for all the wrong reasons. He even suggested Rialto could be involved in the murders."

"What?" Aria cringed at Rialto's bellow. "What would give him that idea?"

"Probably the fang holes in the neck," Aria answered. "I think he's starting to believe in vampires, and with what he saw last night, his imagination has probably kicked into high gear. Then there's the brother. He's telling him things, giving him ideas."

"Well, that's just great. All we need while hunting a killer is a detective hunting us." Rialto sank into the cushions next to her, resting his head along the back of the sofa. His cheeks were red, his breathing heavier than normal. All of the anger inside him must have taken its toll.

"Rialto, you shouldn't work yourself up."

"I'm fine," he snapped, causing her to pull back her hand before it reached his shoulder.

"She's right," Seta interjected. "Your energy is being spent far too fast. Let's all calm down and try to figure this thing out." She paced the floor in front of them, then turned toward Aria with her hands fisted on her hips. "And just why, may I ask, did you even leave to begin with, Aria?"

Aria swallowed, feeling two feet tall under the witch's hardened glare. "I thought I might find something at the library, a way to help Rialto get over this sickness."

"Well, after the fear you inflicted upon my child, I hope you did find something useful after all."

"Actually, I did find something. A strange book, like a devil worship manual. It had something in there about The Blood Revelation. I understand the situation better now."

Seta's eyebrow arched in a sardonic gesture. "And you found a cure for Rialto's sickness?"

"You know I didn't. According to the book, he won't get better unless I'm changed over. But . . ." Aria let her voice trail off, unsure of what she was going to say.

"What? Spit it out, child."

Aria looked at Rialto, his intense eyes studied hers. There was something swirling inside them, something that gave him the appearance of a wounded animal. That look reached through Aria's chest and squeezed her heart. "There's still hope."

"Don't, Aria." Rialto's voice was a low rumble of distant thunder. "Don't ask me to change you just to save my life. This *gift* is an eternal curse—if you even survive it."

"Rialto!" Seta's harsh tone lashed out like a whip. "Don't be foolish! I've told you that Aria's one of us. If she's finally realized what needs to be done then, damn it to hell, let her do it!"

"Actually, Seta, that wasn't what I was referring to." Aria sank deeper into the sofa cushions as Seta glared at her, obviously infuriated. She couldn't fight the feeling that if the killer didn't get to her first, Seta would probably do her in. "I haven't told you about Curtis yet."

"Who the hell is Curtis?"

"He works at the library. He's this geeky, scrawny little guy who talks to me a lot. He has a crush on me, I think." Aria felt Rialto tense next to her and suppressed a grin. She liked the idea of him being a bit jealous. "He gave me his great-grandfather's journal a few days ago, said the guy was a vampire hunter."

"It was Alfred Dunn's journal," Rialto interjected. His voice sounded strange.

Seta's eyebrows shot up. "Alfred Dunn? The man who hunted for Eron? Why didn't you tell me this before?"

"I didn't think it mattered since I had every intention of destroying it once this situation was resolved. And I didn't know Aria had obtained the journal from the man's great-grandchild."

"What was in it?"

Aria answered Seta's question. "It started off like a story, detailing how Eron killed Alfred's son, Patrick, and how Alfred went looking for him but couldn't find him. Then he added in lists of vampires and places they could be found. Eventually his writing got kind of crazy and didn't make any sense. There were parts that were completely unreadable."

"Are you sure there wasn't anything important in it? It was the man's life mission to destroy Eron."

"Well, I didn't think there was anything in it that could prove harmful, but after the way Curtis acted tonight . . ."

"What did he do?" Rialto sat up and leaned toward Aria, his eyes wide and focused, his jaw locked. He looked like a wild animal ready to pounce. "Did he harm you?"

"No," Aria answered with a shiver, "but if Porter hadn't walked in when he did I'm scared to think what would have happened. He came into the library all banged up, said he'd been mugged. He was acting crazy."

"Crazy how?"

"Just weird. He said he needed the journal back, that it belonged to his brother and he hadn't asked permission to take it. When I asked why his brother needed it, he got hostile. He even demanded I allow him to drive me home so he could retrieve it tonight. Said he had to have it, couldn't wait."

"Seems like he was awfully eager to have it," Seta commented. "I wonder why the sudden need."

"Yeah, and that's not all." Aria shivered again as a cold chill snaked its way along her spinal column. "The book I told you about earlier wasn't a library book, but I found it on the shelves. He seemed disturbed by the fact that I was reading it, mad even. He told me to put it back on the shelf so the owner would come back and get it, said it shouldn't fall into the wrong hands. But it would have made more sense if I'd kept it or destroyed it instead of putting it back on the shelf where it very well might land in the wrong hands."

"He just didn't want you to have it." Seta's eyebrows drew together as she mulled over the new information. "Maybe the book was left there for you. Maybe you're being guided."

"By whom?"

"The Dream Teller?" Rialto suggested. "You dreamed of her earlier. So did I."

"That's possible but not likely," Seta commented as she paced the floor with her finger to her chin. "She's never stepped outside the dream realm."

"Are you saying she only exists in dreams?"

"No. She must have a physical form, but she's never appeared to anyone in it. She's never stepped outside the bounds of the dream world."

"Who else would be guiding me?" Aria asked, goosebumps rising on her flesh at the thought of someone watching over her, guiding her. It seemed so intrusive.

"Have you ever seen a spirit?"

"Are you seriously trying to say a ghost left that book in the library?"

Seta shrugged. "It was just a thought. Truth is, the Elders may be behind the book. What was in it?"

"A lot of demonic stuff. Spells and rituals. Really dark stuff involving sacrifices and altars. Who are the Elders? Are they the three mentioned in the book?"

"What three?"

"The three vampires who refused to let evil inside them when they were transformed."

Seta nodded slowly, her eyes widening. "That would probably be them. We don't know much about our origins. We've heard of the Elders though. They're like rulers, judging our fates. With you being predestined to become one of us, it's a definite possibility they're guiding you toward us."

"If that was the intention of whomever left the book, they were wrong. According to it, I will be hunted until I give birth, and if I make it that far my child will be hunted. Why in the world would I knowingly give birth to a child who would have to live its life in hiding?"

"The same reason why your mother gave birth to you in that hick town. Love."

Aria drew back as though she had been slapped. The witch looked at her with a smug twist to her lips, knowing she had made her point. And, as much as Aria hated to admit it, Seta was right. Aria's mother had known a biracial child would be unwelcome in Pickahoe and that her paternity would have to be hidden, but she'd had her anyway. Aria couldn't help feeling ashamed that she wasn't as courageous and loving as her mother. "Yeah, well, if I never have the child I'll never love it, will I?"

Seta rolled her eyes and muttered something under her breath that Aria suspected was unpleasant. "And here I thought you were smart. You'll get what I was referring to when the time is right. I hope." She looked pointedly at Aria and snapped her fingers impatiently. "Get me this journal. Maybe it has something to do with the visions I've been having about books with blood coming out of the pages."

Aria shuddered at the image, but dutifully retrieved the journal from the backpack she'd left on the floor next to the sofa. "There's a lot of research in there," she said as she handed the book over to Seta. "I was hoping maybe there's something about The Blood Revelation in there that I missed. Some way to help Rialto without me having to . . . you know."

Sparks of anger danced around Seta's pupils but soon dissolved, her eyes growing warm and compassionate. "If I find anything in here, I can guarantee it won't be that. Sometimes we have to accept our fate." She looked at her son. "Before it's too late and we end up living with guilt and regret."


HE WAS GOING to lose his mind. Rialto clenched his fists together and bit into his lower lip, trying to fight back the urge to kick down the door to Aria's bathroom and drag her out of the shower stall and into his arms. Making it to the bed wouldn't even be an option.

"I know what you're thinking," Seta sang from where she was sitting at the dinette table, poring over Alfred Dunn's journal. "Go on in there. She's already naked so that part's out of the way. I'll just pretend I don't hear all the noise."

"Stay out of my head, Mother."

"Don't call me Mother in that tone. You make me feel as though I gave birth to Norman Bates." She looked up from the journal and stared him down with a look of utter ruthlessness. "We are bonded as mother and child, and as sire and fledgling. I can't help knowing what goes through your mind when your emotions are this strong. I won't do you any favors by ignoring what's going on." She dropped her gaze back down to the book before her. "Your body is craving what it needs for survival. I'll be damned if I don't at least try to nudge your foolish ass in the right direction."

Rialto growled, wishing there was some way to turn off his mind link with his mother when she was determined to snoop. His body quivered as he heard another splash of water hit Aria's skin, imagined the tiny droplets of water drizzle over the curves of her naked flesh. Damn his overactive imagination and hypersensitive hearing! The smells of soap and rain scented shampoo wafted out and teased his nose, driving him closer to the breaking point.

He could see himself kneeling before her on the slippery tile, using his tongue to trace the drops of water from her ankle, working his way up slowly, making her tremble with desire, following the wet path, dipping into hollows here and there until he reached one dusky nipple, already pebbled in anticipation of his mouth. "Son of a bitch!"

Seta laughed, refusing to stop when Rialto tried to quell her with a hard glare. "I'm sorry, darling, but from here it's rather amusing. Just give in to it."

"I can't. Just stay out of my head."

"Fine." She raised her hands in mock surrender. "But I'm not the only woman in this apartment that can feel what's going through your system. You bonded with her."

"What?"

Seta smiled devilishly. "She feels you and everything you're thinking of over there is running through her mind too. Why do you think she's still in the shower? She's trying to cool off."

"You don't know what you're talking about."

"I'm a woman, Rialto. I know what I'm talking about. She's in there, hot, wet . . . in more ways than one . . . and waiting." She nodded in the direction of the bathroom. "You don't have to change her over tonight. Just take a little sip and get your strength back. You'll need it to protect her if we come across the killer. And for goodness sake, don't pass up the opportunity because I'm here. I'll sever our link."

"You would do that?"

Seta grimaced. "What do you take me for? It's one thing to know what you're doing, but to experience it with you from inside your own body . . . That's just sick."

Rialto looked down the hall, focusing on the bathroom door. It was such a thin barrier between him and pure carnal bliss. Yet, he couldn't raise his body from the sofa.

"You know you want to," Seta said in the same singsong teasing tone she had used earlier. "Go get her, cowboy." She erupted into chuckles as Rialto speared her with a look of annoyance and forced himself to stand.

Just a little sip of blood mingled in with great sex, he reminded himself, as he put one foot in front of the other. He could do this. He could keep things under control.

ARIA'S BREATH HITCHED as she heard the bathroom door open. She was braced with her hands against the shower's tiles, her head bent as the water rained over her, ineffective in its attempt to cool her heated skin. She felt everything running through Rialto's mind, saw the images as clearly as if they were actually doing those things, and it made her hungry to reenact them. Damn the consequences.

The shower curtain swished as it was pushed aside. Rialto's presence sucked the air out of the stall, and his musky male scent enveloped her, filling her head until there was only room for one thought, the thought of him. His smell, his taste, his touch. Everything that was definitively Rialto.

"Can you feel it?" He whispered in her ear, and she knew he wasn't talking about the hard, straining length of him pressed against her backside, but of the electric charge in the air, the pull of their two bodies toward each other.

Breathing too hard to answer, she laid her head back, resting it on his shoulder as he bent over her, licking along her collarbone. "I won't change you," he whispered huskily against her skin, his warm breath igniting small fires throughout her body. "I will need to take a little sip of your blood to take the edge off this fever." He turned her around in his arms. "Did you see what I had planned?"

She nodded languidly, drunk with raw desire.

"Do I have your permission?"

She smiled slowly, then placed her hands on his shoulders and pushed him to his knees.

SETA PEERED CLOSER at the handwritten words in Alfred Dunn's journal, something in the change of script bothering her. Alfred Dunn had a neat, precise penmanship through the majority of the journal's beginning. What came later could only be referred to as chicken scratch, some parts written in such haste they were barely legible. The messy writing dominated the last third of the journal, and some scrawls were placed in between lines and within margins of the beginning text as though he had decided to make notes at a later time. A much later time, judging by the difference in inks.

Seta studied the differences in writing on one of the pages where the erratic scrawl first showed up and it all clicked. The writing was so different because the journal was written by two different people. So who was carrying on Alfred Dunn's research, and why? The great-grandchild? But, no, it couldn't be. Why would he give the book to Aria? Seta closed her eyes and recalled all the images that had flooded her mind in the last few days. Books, blood pouring from the pages. Needle. Eron. Rows of books . . . like a library. Alfred Dunn's great-grandson worked at a library. He gave Aria the book. It had to mean something. What was she overlooking?

Seta closed the book and rested her hands on the cover. She cleared her mind of all thoughts, focusing only on the image of Eron. If she could find out what happened to him, she could find the killer. She was certain of it. She meditated with her hands on the journal and Eron's face in her mind's eye. She felt her energies transfer into the pages of the book before her, and when the vibrations of the energy built to a deafening roar in her ears she finally spoke. "Find Eron."

She opened her eyes and watched as the pages of the journal turned on their own. She waited for them to stop and looked down at the book that lay open before her. The page staring back at her was a list. There were several lists among the entries and she had skimmed over most, not considering them important. She could have slapped herself as she looked at the list her magic had found. "Of course," she whispered, glancing at the list of Keepers written in the erratic scrawl near the back of the journal, noting the one listed next to Eron's name. "Who better to know what happened, but I already asked her."

She placed her finger over the Keeper's name and was hit with a vision so horrific it left the taste of blood in her mouth. Fresh blood, blood she would take from Eron's Keeper as revenge for what she had done to him.

"NO, ARIA!" IT TOOK all of Rialto's willpower to force her away, but it had to be done. He cursed as he saw his own blood dripping from the corner of her mouth as she lunged for him.

"I said no!" He pushed her down on the floor of the shower stall, holding her hands tightly over her head while he straddled her thighs. He licked his bottom lip, allowing the healing properties in his saliva to repair the damage she'd done. "This has gone too far. You weren't supposed to drink from me." She continued to writhe beneath him, digging her talon-like fingers into his hands. "Dammit, Aria. You could change."

"I don't care," she cried, continuing to struggle beneath him, sputtering out water that had made its way into her mouth when she spoke.

Rialto gripped both of her wrists in one hand and reached up with the other to turn off the shower. "That's the bloodlust talking. It's not what you really want." He waited until he felt the worst of the fight drain out of her, and then pulled her into his arms, her back to his chest, on the shower floor. He held her as she trembled, knowing she wasn't quivering from cold but from hunger, longing. *Need.* "I know it feels awful, Aria. I'm sorry. I shouldn't have allowed it to go this far."

"At least you didn't run away."

Shame sliced into him, deep and hard. He couldn't deny he felt like running right now, but her safety was too important. He could leave her with Seta for a short while, just long enough for him to straighten his head out. Then again, Seta would probably brainwash her, manipulate her just as she had manipulated him. Anger slowly started to burn through him as he recalled her teasing. She knew how on edge he was, how hungry. She knew if he fooled himself into thinking he could control things . . . But he did control the situation. Not as well as he should have, but there was no real harm done.

Damn it, there could have been and Seta knew it. Yet, she had kept on pushing with her taunting and coaxing.

"Get yourself together, dry off, and meet me in the living room." Rialto said as he quickly exited the shower stall and wrapped a towel around his waist, not bothering to look back as he left Aria in the bathroom. Her naked flesh was too tempting.

He marched into the living area, fully prepared to give Seta an earful, but stopped short when he saw Alfred Dunn's journal abandoned at the dinette table.

Seta was gone.

# Chapter Fifteen

ARIA TIGHTENED THE sash on her bathrobe and entered the living area to find Rialto standing at the dinette table reading a piece of paper. "I put your clothes in the wash. What are you looking at?"

He glanced at her briefly, just long enough for her to catch the hint of male appreciation in his eyes before they grew worried and returned to the small piece of paper in his hand. "Seta left a note. She found a list of Keepers in the journal and thinks Eron was betrayed by his. She went to find her."

"She left a note? I thought you two had that telepathy thing going on."

"She severed our link so you and I could have some privacy."

"Oh." Heat rose in Aria's cheeks as she walked over to the dinette table and lowered herself into one of the chairs. She pulled the journal in front of her and glanced at the list of Keepers. "So, what is a Keeper? Does this have anything to do with the murders?"

"Possibly." Rialto took a seat opposite her, the action of sitting causing his towel to ride up higher on his thighs. Aria closed her eyes, swallowing hard to suppress a groan. Maybe if she kept her eyes closed, she could refrain from ogling him and stay focused. "Seta has been getting images of Eron this whole time. He would never partake of anything like this, so we've concluded that he was somehow abducted, especially since Seta can't feel him. He was her sire so she shouldn't be having any trouble locating him. Aria, are you listening?"

Aria opened her eyes to find Rialto staring at her. "Yes, go on."

He looked at her quizzically before continuing. "So, um, anyway, she found the list of Keepers and thinks the Keeper helped in Eron's abduction. Keepers are mortals trusted with the care of vampires."

"Kind of like a personal assistant?"

"Yes, something like that. Some vampires get a Keeper to use as cover. They put their properties in the name of the Keeper and let the Keeper take care of all their business that needs to be done in the daytime."

"Do you have a Keeper?"

"No. I set up my business completely through the Internet, any calls received are fielded through an answering service, and I do all my banking through the Internet and ATM machines. I've never really liked the concept of Keepers. When you acquire a Keeper, you're putting yourself at their mercy more than you realize, a fact I'm afraid Eron has learned the hard way."

"So . . . you think Eron was captured and is somehow involved without his consent?" She glanced back down to the journal, to the name printed next to Eron's.

"Yes. Seta and I smelled the diluted scent of vampire on the body she read in Leakin Park. According to her note, the scent was Eron's, which I didn't realize."

"What do you mean by a 'diluted' scent? Vampires have a specific scent?"

Rialto nodded. "I know it's a lot to take in. Vampires have a specific scent which sets us apart from non-vampires. What was left behind on the body wasn't what a normal vampire scent would be. It was like it was . . . well, diluted." He shrugged and pulled the journal in front of him. "Seta also realized there are two authors, someone other than Alfred Dunn made entries in this journal. She wants me to check it for anything strange she may have overlooked. While I do that, you should get some sleep."

She was no longer tired and wanted to help. "If you're going to get my mother's killer I feel I should help."

"No offense, sweetheart, but you don't know what to look for. Grab some sleep and hopefully I'll have good news for you when you wake up."

If he waited for her to wake up. Aria had the sneaking suspicion he'd run out and kill the murderer without bothering to wake her. As much as she wanted the killer dead, she wanted the opportunity to look him in the eye first. She wanted the opportunity to inflict pain on him, even if it was Rialto who actually delivered the death blow.

"I don't want to be left behind when you go after the killer. I want to go with you."

"Absolutely not." Rialto's gaze lifted from the journal and locked with hers. "It's too dangerous. Seta had a vision of your death."

"This beast killed my mother. It's *my* duty to defend her."

Rialto looked at her, the worry in his eyes so strong it made her heart lurch. "When you speak of your mother's murderer you have the eyes of a killer, Aria. I can't stand seeing such raw hunger for bloodletting there."

"What are you talking about?"

Rialto raked a hand through his damp hair and leaned back in the chair. "You're not a killer and you shouldn't let your rage make you become one."

"Someone *murdered* my mother. He has to pay."

"Then let me take care of it."

"So it's all right for you to kill this monster but not for me to do it?"

"That's right."

"Because you're a vampire?"

"Because I lost any shred of innocence I had left the night I killed my father." He looked away as Aria gasped in shock at his announcement. "I've been a killer ever since."

"Don't say that. If you were a killer, I wouldn't be breathing now. You don't kill just for the hell of it. What did your father do to make you kill him?"

"He killed Seta, or at least he thought he did, and passed his heartless, barren wife off as my mother. The two of them wanted a son, and didn't care how they got one. They didn't count on one of the servants telling me the truth of my maternity when they saw my mother's features in my face. I'd seen Seta before at the cliffs by our castle, but she'd never told me she was my mother. Shortly after my twenty-ninth birthday, I discovered the truth. When I did, I attacked him. I avenged her. Unfortunately, I wasn't as ruthless as he. He didn't fight fair, choosing to stab me in the back, and he ended up nearly killing me." His eyes darkened into shiny black orbs as he looked at Aria, rage emanating from deep within. "Finishing me off would have been too kind. I'd attacked him so he felt my punishment should have been a slow death. He took me to the same cliffs he'd thrown my mother over twenty-eight years before and left me there to bleed to death. He didn't count on my real mother still being around to save me."

"Seta turned you into a vampire that night." He nodded, and she asked, "What happened then?"

"When I rose the following night, I ripped Count Roberto Garibaldi limb from limb and dropped his head at his wife's feet. The only reason I didn't kill her too was because I'd promised Seta I'd let her have her. I felt it was only right I let her destroy the woman who'd stolen her child. I realize now that we were no better than my father."

"You are better than him. Your father was a murderer, Rialto. He tried to kill his own son and the mother of his child."

"He was my father and I killed him. How can you even suggest I'm better?"

"Because you feel guilty. I'd bet my life there wasn't a shred of guilt that went through that man's mind when he attempted to kill you . If he'd felt any remorse over what he'd done to Seta, he would have never harmed you, his son. Your conscience is what keeps you from being a killer."

Rialto smiled at her and reached his hand across the table to cover hers, an action that caused heat to pool between her thighs and small beads of sweat popped out on her forehead. His chest still glistened from the shower. His damp hair was long and unkempt, adding to his dangerous charm. Just the mere touch of his hand and she craved the rest of his body—her gaze moved to the pulse point at his throat—and what flowed within it.

She could still taste the spicy tang of his blood, could still feel its magnetic pull. If she was going to survive this night without ripping into him like a wild animal, he was going to have to at least put on some clothes. The thin barrier of a terry towel was not enough. "It's going to take a while until your clothes are ready, but Mom and I held on to some of my dad's clothes. He was about your size."

Rialto's eyes widened in what looked like genuine surprise. "You would allow me to wear them?"

Aria nodded, her hands clenched tight. She wanted to reach out and run her fingertips against every inch of his exposed flesh and find a delicate spot to scrape her nails across until tiny bubbles of blood rose to the surface. She shook her head, trying to shake out the image. "In the chest at the foot of my bed. Pick out whatever you want."

He rose, the raw sexiness of his sculpted body doing strange things to her ability to breathe. "Thank you, Aria. I know how deeply you care for your parents, and how greatly you must cherish their belongings. I'm honored you'd share them with me."

In order to keep from pouncing on him, she kept her eyes averted while he left the room, then pulled the journal in front of her. Was she really going to have to become a vampire in order to save Rialto's life? Could she handle the mixed emotions Rialto so obviously felt about being one? She thought back over the events of the past few days, surprised by how strong her affection for Rialto was considering they'd just met days before. Yet, if she counted those barely remembered—yet always there—dreams, she'd known him far longer. But it wasn't long enough. She couldn't allow him to leave her so soon. There had to be some other way to save his life.

She flipped through the journal, trying to make out some of the sloppier entries. Who was the second author? Curtis's brother? Jonah said he was crazy, and from the sound of it a devil worshiper. Maybe he'd found something in his great-grandfather's research that called to him. She thought about it. Powerful beings which lived off the blood of others sounded like something that might appeal to a person with such darkness in his heart, but only because he didn't know the goodness in a real vampire's heart.

She glanced up at the sound of Rialto's footsteps and nearly gasped. He was wearing a pair of black pants and a billowy white shirt. His hair, nearly dry, rested along his shoulders in a cascade of thick ebony waves. She caught an image of a dream, but it escaped her too quickly to bring it into focus.

"Aria? Are you all right?"

"Yes, I . . ." She shook her head in order to rid herself of the niggling feeling that she was forgetting something important. "I think I've dreamed of you wearing those clothes."

His brows drew together as he seemed to search his own memory, then they shot straight up. "You have. I mean, I have." He looked down at the shirt. "I didn't even realize . . ."

"Didn't realize what?"

"This is what I was wearing in the last dream I kept having over and over again but couldn't finish. We must have shared the same dream. Do you remember how it ended?"

Aria shook her head in frustration. "No. I remember you in those clothes. You came to me and . . . I don't know." She dropped her head into her hands, massaging her temples which now ached with her effort to remember.

"It's all right," Rialto said as he sat in the chair across from her, but she didn't miss the disappointment in his voice. He obviously needed to know how the dream had ended, and something inside her trembled with the thought of what type of dream would make a vampire wake up without finishing it. Silence ensued for a few minutes before she lifted her head to find Rialto studying her with a guilty expression.

"What is it?"

He raked a hand through his long, silky hair. "In the shower . . . You drank from me again."

A sharp stab of fear sliced through her chest. "Am I going to change? Is that how it happens?"

He shook his head. "Your skin is going to darken again."

"You sound like you're apologizing."

"I felt you after you woke from our last . . . encounter. You were terrified when you saw your skin had changed. Personally, I think you're absolutely flawless, especially when you are darker, but I know it frightens you."

Aria looked down at her pale hands, a blush warming her cheeks. "I used to be. You and Seta have opened my eyes, Rialto. This isn't Pickahoe, and I'm not a scared, insecure little girl anymore. I loved my father, still do, and I have no problem wearing his skin."

A smile spread across Rialto's face, lending a sparkle to his dark eyes. "I'm glad to hear that. You are much too beautiful a creature to run from your true self." He reached across the table for the journal. "Did you by chance find anything odd in here?"

Aria shrugged. "Not really. Some of the chicken scratch is in another language, and I don't speak it, much less read it."

"I might," Rialto said as he looked down at the pages of the journal. "Irish. I happen to know a little."

Aria took the opportunity to study him while he read a cluster of pages near the back of the journal, admiring his full bottom lip, his perfectly straight nose, the way his eyebrows arched subtly. She was admiring those perfectly constructed eyebrows when they drew together, creating a series of worry lines across his forehead.

"What is it?"

"Son of a . . ." Rialto looked closer at the journal, as though rereading the text, making sure he'd read it correctly the first time. Slowly, he shook his head from side to side, seeming to have an internal argument.

"Rialto? What did you find?" Fear's powerful grip squeezed Aria's heart until a few beats were lost. "What does it say?"

Grave eyes connected with hers. "If I translated this correctly it means we've seriously underestimated who we've been dealing with."

TOO FURIOUS TO concentrate on teleportation, Seta had raced to Eron's West Virginia home in under two hours. She stood on the outskirts of his property, camouflaged by the many trees surrounding the large manor house, opening her senses to determine the degree of danger which lay before her. Satisfied the sole inhabitant of the property was Culla Wasser, Eron's Keeper who held no magical powers or immortal strengths, she marched toward the house with her head lowered, fists clenched, nails ready to rip away at human flesh.

With a wave of her hand, the massive front doors flew open, allowing her access to the foyer. She heard shuffling to her left and turned in that direction, entering a large den outfitted with white leather couches and chaises, shelves of books, medieval statues and an impressive stone fireplace.

Culla Wasser was before the fireplace, frozen as though she'd just risen from the nearby chaise in an attempt to run. Her eyes were large and round, her mouth agape. Seta looked straight into the woman's eyes and knew the bitch felt her own impending death. It put a smile on Seta's face.

"No point in running, Culla." She leered at the woman, watching her body shake with fear under her silky bronze-colored nightgown. "You've already been captured. Now I want to know exactly what happened, detail by tiny detail."

"I don't know what you're talking about." Culla smoothed her mane of auburn waves with a quivering hand and stood at her full height of five-feet-ten inches. "Eron isn't here. You should come back—"

"Eron isn't here because you handed him over to a killer!" Seta swung a hand and a burst of energy shot out from it, plowing into the woman. She flew backward, hitting her head against the mantel jutting from above the lifeless fireplace before crashing to her knees. "I saw you. I saw you putting poison in his drink, taking blood from him as he slept." Seta shook with the rage flowing through her veins as she recalled the vision that had sent her racing here.

Culla whimpered while she remained doubled over on the floor, wrapping one arm protectively around her middle and holding the back of her head with the other. Seta felt no compassion. "You knew his patterns, knew when he reached the deepest stage of sleep, knew just how to get to him. I know the how. What I want to know now is the who and the why."

Culla's head snapped up, a devilish smirk on her face. "Screw you, Seta. You and Eron thought you were so powerful, that no mortal was a match for your strength and wit, but I beat you. I outsmarted Eron, a king among his kind."

"Why? Why would you turn on the man who provided you with a life of luxury?" Eron's house was huge and richly decorated. He had money pouring in from several different sources and provided for the horrid woman as though she were his family. All she had to do was take care of a few daily business tasks for him. It was a dream job for a mortal.

"Because he wouldn't give me the gift."

It suddenly all made sense to Seta. "You want to be a vampire?"

"I want eternal life. I don't care how I get it. Or when."

"And what did you accomplish by hurting Eron?"

"Exactly what I wanted. There's a way to become a vampire without having the vampire's permission, and now I won't grow old or die."

"Are you sure that's true?"

"Yes." Culla smiled so that her face beamed. "Eron's blood is being drained daily. Once the formula has been perfected he will be my donor."

Seta fisted her hands tighter, aching to kill the woman now and be done with her, but she needed to know who Culla was working with. "And who is creating this formula?"

"Like I would tell you." Culla laughed haughtily, crossing her arms beneath her ample breasts. "You can't win, Seta. If you kill me you'll never get the name of Eron's captor, so why don't you be a good little vampire-witch and fly out of here."

"You have underestimated me," Seta said coolly as she stepped toward the woman, gaining strength from the fear she saw in the traitor's once mocking eyes. Her smile grew as Culla's faded away on trembling lips. "I don't need you to *say* a word."

Seta reached out and grabbed Eron's enemy by the neck, sinking her long nails into Culla's flesh. With a simple command, the fireplace roared to life. Culla started to whimper as Seta spoke the words which would give her the answer she needed. "Blood and flesh and all wickedness therein, give me the name of the abductor of Eron."

"And to think you sold out such a fine man for a formula you'll never get to see developed," Seta said to her victim before effortlessly ripping off her head and throwing it into the fireplace, letting the body drop to the ground.

Seta kneeled before the fireplace and watched as Culla's ashes drifted out of the fire and formed a name on the hearthstone.

"Who is Carter Dunn?"

Seta whirled around to see Rialto standing behind her, deathly pale and out of breath, studying the name provided by Culla Wasser's flesh and blood.

ARIA PACED THE aisles of Christian's church, where Rialto had dumped her before running out into the night to find Seta.

"Aria, would you please sit? You're making me dizzy."

She cringed at the sound of Christian's voice although it wasn't the least bit harsh. She'd done her very best to avoid any and all eye contact with him since Rialto had dropped her off an hour and a half before. She couldn't shake the guilt of knowing she'd gotten him into trouble with Rialto.

"I know you feel bad about me getting my hide chewed off earlier. I forgive you."

Aria stopped mid-stride and turned to face Christian, who was busy lighting candles at the front of the church. "Are you sure you can't read my mind?"

He looked at her and smiled. "I'm sure, and I wouldn't have to. You wear your emotions."

"Oh, really?"

He nodded, his growing smile adding a twinkle to his eyes. "You could never be a good poker player, Aria. You feel things too strongly to cover up. That might be what drew Rialto to you, why you were mated to him."

Aria sat in one of the pews, her curiosity piqued. "What do you mean?"

Christian lit the last candle, laid down the lighter, and sat on the back of a pew a couple rows before her. He held her gaze for a moment before speaking. "Rialto shut himself off after Antonia. He didn't allow himself to feel anything for anyone. I think the dreams he started to receive upon your birth helped him to feel again."

"And now I'm killing him."

The glimmer in Christian's soft eyes faded. "He's been dead for many years. Decades came and passed, and he hadn't inhaled a single breath of life, but then you entered his dreams, and he awakened from death."

"He was not dead, Christian."

"In the physical sense, no. But he was like a zombie. No feeling, no emotions. He helped those who needed it, but it was a chore to him, something he simply did. He didn't care about the mortals he saved, until he met you. He doesn't want to catch your mother's killer so badly because it's the right thing to do for mankind or because he's trying to prevent drawing the attention of mortals to our kind. He wants to do this for you, to please you. He doesn't want your pain prolonged."

"And to pay him back for that I'm doing nothing while he slowly dies."

Christian said nothing. He didn't have to. The sadness in his eyes spoke volumes within the few seconds that passed before he shuttered them. Then the front doors opened and a group of parishioners entered, silencing them from any further conversation.

After Christian left her to greet the newcomers, Aria leaned her head back against the pew and thought about Rialto. She was tormented by the thought of what it would be like living without him, knowing he died because of her, but she was torn over what to do. It had taken her over two decades to come to terms with her own ancestry. Could she stand the secrecy of being part of the vampire world when all she wanted to do was break free of her own self-imposed prison?

She looked at her hands, noticed the subtle darkening already starting to take over her skin, and smiled. She was white and she was black, and she was finally comfortable with that fact. Pickahoe and its small-minded inhabitants couldn't hurt her anymore. She could claim more than her father's last name now. She could claim his heritage. Her heritage. She was free to be herself.

But, if she became a vampire, the secrets and lies would be reborn. The shame of knowing she was different, misunderstood, even hated, would burn through her once more. How long would it take to accept herself then? The world had changed during her twenty-six years in it. Biracial people were widely accepted now. Would vampires ever be?

She squeezed her eyes shut to fight back the tears welling there. If she became a vampire then Rialto would live. If she stayed in her mortal form he would die, along with the only part of her that had felt alive in years. Brad had been a silly, stupid high school crush, and the few men who'd come after him weren't much more. She never knew love before Rialto, never enjoyed lovemaking on any level deeper than the mere physical one, and even that had been unworthy of comparison to him.

Rialto was a great man. He helped mankind, knowing full well they would not accept him if they knew his identity. He destroyed the evil among them, saving their lives and those of their children, protecting their innocence despite the fact he and his kind were blamed of the opposite. But still he did it. Because he was that kind of man.

What kind of woman was she? She'd lived her life in fear, starting from the earliest days of her childhood. She hadn't even acknowledged her father publicly until he was dead and she was forced to leave town. Was it brave of her to take his name after she fled the only little town that knew him? No. It had been a weak tribute at the most. And she'd failed to protect her mother. If she was going to be truthful, she knew the killer would never be punished if it weren't for Rialto. She'd thought herself brave for one brief moment in time, all the way up until Rialto rescued her from two street thugs. If she hadn't met him that night, she knew she would have given up by now. She would have done what she always did—hide behind a canvas and an easel, her only weapons a paintbrush and a palette, and she would have continued to paint the thoughts and feelings she was too damn scared to express in any other way.

That's what she would do after letting Rialto die. She would hide away and paint, pouring her worthless heart and soul into her artwork. Then she would sell it to the first bidder, because she lacked the backbone to do anything else.

"I suck as a human being," she murmured as she opened her eyes and absently gazed around her, glancing about the different paintings and sculptures adorning the room. None of the pieces appeared to be expensive which made perfect sense given the neighborhood surrounding the church, but even to her biased artist's eye, they were beautiful.

Her gaze fell on a painting of the adult Jesus and Mary in the far corner of the room. The artist hadn't portrayed them as being pale or smooth haired as most artists over the centuries had done. They were darker, with hair of coarse curls like the people in that time and place really were. But that wasn't what she'd noticed. She noticed the look of pure love on Mary's face.

Mary Ayers had worn that same look several times during her life. Aria smiled, remembering the few times her family was together in Pickahoe. Her father would come by with his tools, making sure to park his truck with the big MICHAELS HANDYWORK sticker on the side in clear view out front. To anyone who passed by, it appeared as though he were only doing his job. But inside the house they were laughing, playing, reading . . . being a family.

Aria clearly recalled a day when she and her father had danced in circles while her mother sang, her beautiful soprano voice filling the small shotgun house with its beauty. They'd danced until her seven-year-old legs could dance no more, and then they all sat together on the couch in the living room, listening to her father tell stories. She'd laid her head in her father's lap and closed her eyes, listening to the rich baritone of his voice until she grew tired.

"I had the dream again," her mother whispered to her father, obviously thinking Aria was asleep. "She is destined for greatness. Just wait and see."

Aria had peeked through barely open lids to see Mary Ayers looking at her with all the warmth and awe that the artist had created in his portrait of Jesus and his mother Mary.

The memory suddenly changed. Aria was twenty-six again, lying in her bed, feeling the wind from the open balcony doors caress her skin. She realized she was no longer remembering but dreaming, having dozed off in the church pew.

*She could no longer feel the hard wood beneath her, only the soft comfort of her own bed and the aching need in her body. Her eyes were closed, but she sensed another presence, a presence that could soothe the ache engulfing her body, fill the empty void in her heart. He was there with her.*

*Rialto.*

*She opened her eyes to see him standing at the foot of her bed, clothed in a billowy white dress shirt and black pants. Beneath those clothes she knew his body was rock hard, especially the part that bulged in the front of his pants.*

*She was on top of him in a second, making passionate love to him as he lay beneath her on the bed. Words were said, actions taken, but they happened so fast she was barely aware that she was sipping his blood before she was rammed into the wall, their bodies still joined. He reared his head back, roared, and sank his long, pearly fangs into her throat.*

*Instantly, she froze in fear. He was a vampire. She had intended to kill them all, and now he was going to make her one of them. He was going to force her to endure another life of fear, another existence where she simply did not belong. "No!" She screamed as she used all the new power in her body, fueled by the blood she had already sipped from him, and pushed him away.*

*Rialto stared back at her, the pain in his eyes unbearable to look at, but she fought to hold his gaze while her eyes watered. "I'm sorry. I can't do this."*

*He backed away, nodded, and fell to his knees.*

*"Rialto?" She dropped to her knees before him, but he pulled back at the feel of her touch, as though her hands burned him now. "Rialto! What's wrong?"*

*He folded over into a ball, his body racked with tremors.*

*"You've killed him," a familiar voice said from the balcony. Aria looked up and nearly choked on emotion.*

*"Mom?" Mary Ayers stood on the balcony, a vision of beauty and serenity in a long, flowing white dress. Her father stood next to her, and Aria felt her overjoyed heart drop as both their mouths turned down into disapproving frowns.*

*"You were supposed to save him, and in doing that, save the world," her mother said with a tone that shamed Aria to her core. "You were the first step in the plan and you failed."*

*"What plan? I don't understand."*

*"The Blood Revelation." Mary shook her head in disappointment, and the world outside Aria's bedroom suddenly filled with screams.*

*Aria ran to the balcony and nearly vomited at what she saw. Beneath her, bodies littered the streets, and blood ran along the sides of the roads like red rivers branching out from an ocean of blood. The shrieks that sent goosebumps crawling across her flesh came from all directions, filling the night air with their agony. "What has happened?"*

*"Your descendant was supposed to destroy the beast. This is what will happen decades from this moment, Aria, because you were too scared to fulfill your destiny. You had only one job—to provide life for a special child."*

*"And I didn't do it."*

*"No, and you let the one man who loved you more than any other die."*

*"No!" Aria turned and ran back into the room to Rialto, but all she found was a pile of ash.*

Aria jerked to a sitting position as a scream cut through the air, pulling her out of sleep. She blinked, bringing the church's interior into focus while her heart struggled to return to its normal beat. The dream seemed so real, her heart was still beating wildly in her chest. She couldn't get the image of Rialto's ashes out of her mind, but she tried to push it aside as she noticed frantic parishioners running out of the church. Another scream rang out from somewhere outside, bringing her fully alert.

"Aria, I have to help! Stay here!" Christian was bent over her, talking into her ear. By the time she opened her mouth to respond, he was already running out the door. Alarm bells clanged in Aria's mind, but she couldn't place what was setting them off. Something wasn't right, a subtle change in the air, something . . . off.

She glanced around, noting only a few people remained in the building with her, huddled together in fear of what was outside, yet she had a strange feeling the real terror was inside. *Where is Rialto? Why did he leave me here?* She shivered, fear taking over her body. Christian was a vampire, but he hadn't drunk fresh blood in ages. He wouldn't be powerful enough to go against anything stronger than a mortal man, and Jonah Porter was her only other source of protection until Rialto and Seta returned. She knew the police detective was parked somewhere outside watching her. Rialto had sensed him when he brought her to the church, unless the screaming from outside had diverted his attention.

Aria stiffened as she felt something behind her, something close enough to raise the hairs on the back of her neck. She started to turn her head, but two hands came from behind her and a rag soaked in something with a sweet, slightly chemical smell was pressed over her nose and mouth.

She didn't have a chance to see her attacker before the world faded to black.

# Chapter Sixteen

CHRISTIAN RAN DOWN the dark alley in search of the woman in distress. The terror he heard in the scream indicated she was in grave danger. He continued on until the screaming stopped abruptly, then turned into howling laughter. A group had formed in the spot where the sound seemed to bounce off the buildings like a reverberating echo, but there was no source for the sound.

"What the hell?" One of the men in the small group scratched his head, looking up and around, searching the fire escapes and dark shadows for the woman they all heard but couldn't see.

Christian's heart slammed against his chest as realization punched him in the gut. "It's a trick."

"Eh?" The man turned toward him. "What's that?"

"It's a trick. An illusion." He didn't wait for a response before turning on his heel and racing back to the church. Like an idiot he'd been lured away from Aria, leaving her behind to face who knew what. Since he wasn't drinking living human blood, he wasn't at his full vampiric strength, but he could still run faster than a mortal. He counted on his speed to save Aria, but his hopes were dashed when he entered the church and found her gone.

He let out a roar of rage so powerful the few parishioners who had started to file back through the door fled in the opposite direction. He searched the remainder of the church, hoping Aria had hidden somewhere. He called her name until his voice grew hoarse, never getting a response. She wouldn't have hidden beneath the church, not with people inside who could see the hidden door. She was gone.

Christian focused all his attention and energies on Rialto and Seta, trying to call to them, but it was no use. Lack of living blood limited his range of telepathic communication and they were too far away. Neither carried a cell phone. With the situation out of his hands and the weight of Aria's possible death on his shoulders, he fell to his knees and prayed to the only one he knew who could help.

"Well, look at that. A perfect display of sacrilege. I always knew church was the place to go when looking for hypocrites, but this takes the prize."

Christian didn't have to open his eyes to know who his new visitor was, but he did anyway, taking in the tall, slender but powerfully built man's angular features, light brown hair flecked with gold, and intense, narrowed green eyes which were burning with hatred. He was dressed in his usual attire of dark T-shirt and jeans, his uniform for night stalking and demon hunting.

Christian groaned in disbelief of what a bad day he was having. "I do not have time to deal with you tonight, Jacob."

"My enemies call me Jake, and I suggest you make time. My brother is missing."

"I have a missing person of my own to locate, and I really don't wish to be your enemy. I don't wish to be anyone's enemy."

"Too late for that. Your kind killed my best friend."

"I'm sorry that happened, however, your kind has killed several of my close friends and I'm not holding it against you. Now, please, I need to find an abducted woman."

"Aria Michaels?"

"How do you know her name?"

"Her mother was killed by someone who left fang marks. My brother is investigating the case. He was following her after he caught sight of your other two vampire friends. Tell me, Christian, what is Aria to you?"

"None of your concern, Jacob."

"It's Jake and it is my concern when my brother is involved. He was following her and now his car is sitting out on the street, abandoned. The woman's mother was murdered by what appeared to be a vampire, and now she's involved with one. What's going on?"

"If you've truly researched my kind, you know a vampire wouldn't have left marks."

"I know. That's why I'm here. What is it that's killing these women, and how are all of you involved?"

Christian clenched his fist, frustrated by being delayed. "I'm going to have to ask you to leave now, Jake."

"I don't think so." Porter quickly reached behind him and pulled a gun from his waistband, leveling it at Christian's chest. "You're helping me find my brother. Wherever the girl is, he's bound to be there too."

Christian laughed as he glanced at the gun's barrel. "I thought you were a pro, Jake. You know that thing won't kill me."

"It wouldn't if it were full of regular bullets. These UV bullets are nasty little bitches though."

Christian gulped. "UV bullets?"

Jake nodded, an arrogant smirk spreading across his lips. "Each bullet is full of pure UV, designed to enter your bloodstream and burn you alive from the inside out. It's quick, but I promise you it's painful."

Christian studied the man's face and determined he wasn't bluffing.

"What do you want of me, Porter?"

"Who took the girl?"

"I don't know. They believe they've found out who the killer is, but I wasn't told anything except they suspect demon involvement."

"This *they* that you refer to are the other two vampires?"

"Yes."

Jake's eyebrows furrowed together. "So the killer knows he's been discovered and has taken the woman for revenge."

"Possibly."

"So ask your friends who it is. For that matter, why the hell aren't they here? Have they already gone after the thing?"

Christian shrugged in frustration. "A friend of ours, Eron, was taken a couple months back. His diluted scent was found on the body of one of the victims. We think a mortal has been experimenting with him, stealing his essence."

"What the hell are you talking about?"

"I don't know!" Christian yelled in anger. "It sounds insane, but we found a journal written by a man who used to hunt Eron, and we think it has something to do with what's happening. Seta, the female vampire your brother saw, went to Eron's home to find out what she could from his Keeper. We think his Keeper aided in his capture."

"So why are we standing here? Use your telepathy and see what's going on."

"I can't. I haven't drunk living blood in nearly a year. I'm too weak to reach them. I've already tried."

Porter's mouth dropped open, and then he snapped it shut and said, "Are you shitting me?"

"I'm afraid not. Most of my vampiric abilities are not at full strength. I can't reach Seta and Rialto, and I'm no match for a demon unless, of course, I drink living blood and refuel my immortal strength."

"Oh, hell no," Jake said as Christian studied him, licking his lips as the scent of his blood seemed to intensify. He hadn't craved living blood so strongly in a long time, but his body was preparing for battle and knew what it needed. "Do you think I'm stupid?"

"No," Christian answered as he noted that Jake had unconsciously lowered the gun, a move the slayer normally would have never been foolish enough to do. "But I do think I'm faster than you."

He twisted the arm holding the weapon behind Jake's back and plunged his fangs deep into the struggling man's neck while he had the chance.

PAIN EXPLODED through Aria's body as she struggled to regain consciousness. At first her eyes only produced a useless blur, but her nose was more helpful, picking up on a mixture of chemical smells. She tried to rub her eyes, but her wrists were bound to something, as were her ankles. Her back ached from the hard metal beneath her, and she felt something sharp in her neck, like a pair of needles.

"Finally coming around?" a deep, male voice asked from above her. She blinked her eyes, trying to bring the fuzzy face hovering above her into focus. After her vision cleared, she looked into the face of someone who was so familiar and yet a stranger.

"I take it you're Curtis's twin?" The man was identical to Curtis except for the absence of bruises on his face and the harsh cruelty in his soulless eyes.

"And you're part of The Blood Revelation."

Aria's eyes widened in fear. "What are you talking about?"

"Don't act stupid, woman. I followed Curtis after I figured out he'd stolen my journal. I saw you leave the library as a tanned white woman. Now you're much too dark to be purely white, but I tested your DNA and you're not a vampire. The only way that could happen is if you're mated to the male vamp I saw at your apartment and you've drunk enough of his blood to bring out the full strength of your physical attributes, something that doesn't normally occur in mortals. So don't play coy with me. I know what you are and so do you."

"You were watching us all the time?" *Why hadn't Rialto sensed him?*

"I can follow people without ever leaving my home, a gift from the dark master. I would have grabbed you at your apartment, but your vampire sensed me. After the vampire left you at the church, I went to fetch you and got the man who was following you as an added bonus." He nodded his head to the left and Aria's eyes followed until she saw Jonah Porter, beaten, bloody, and bruised, shackled on the wall before her.

"Jonah!" She started to cry, horrified by what she saw, and enraged by the laughter erupting from the vile man who stood beside the table she was strapped to.

"His torture will be over soon," the evil twin said. "He will be lunch for a very hungry vampire."

Aria once again followed the man's gaze, angling her head to look behind her where she was able to just barely see another man imprisoned on one of the stone walls. His head of dark reddish-blond hair fell forward, and his body hung limply from the manacles clamped around his wrists and ankles. His body was built of corded muscle, but she could tell that there was no longer any strength in his limbs.

"Eron." Aria spoke the name impulsively, and the pale man looked up, only able to hold his head upright long enough for her to see the pain and hunger burning in his eyes. Huddled on the floor close to him, staring at her with wide, frightened eyes was Curtis.

"How long have you been starving him?" she asked.

"It was his own choice," the man said. "I brought him live girls, but he wouldn't take their blood. Hell, I even brought him a man in case that was his preference, and he wouldn't take that either. Defiant little twit. But he's been smelling yours and your friend's for a while now, and I know it's getting to him. He won't be able to resist much longer."

The sharp twin pains Aria felt in her neck seemed to intensify, but she couldn't move her head enough to see what was causing it. "What have you done to me?"

Her abductor laughed. "I'm killing you the same way I killed your mother and the other women. This little gizmo of mine makes what looks like fang holes in your neck and drains out the blood. I developed a blood thinner which makes the blood pour out like water, but I've decided not to use it on you. I want your blood pure. It's going to be a slow process compared to what your mother went through, but it will be nearly as effective. Once your blood stops dripping, I'll burn your body. I have to make sure you never have the chance to bear a child."

Aria tried to lunge forward, but the manacles around her wrists and ankles, combined with the sharp pain inflicted by the tubes in her neck, made the act impossible. "Who the hell are you? Why are you doing this? Why did you kill my mother?"

"My current birth name is Carter Dunn, and I'm doing this as a promise to my father, Lucifer."

"The devil is your daddy?"

"Yes."

Aria decided to let that one go. "So what's with the vendetta against vampires? Why are you killing women and making it look like vampires did it? Why *my* mother?"

He shrugged. "I pick the women at random, but she seemed to call to me. Ironic she'd be the mother of a Blood Revelation mate, huh? As for making it look like a vampire's work, I do that for revenge. Eventually, word will leak out about the fang marks. Soon people everywhere will be hunting vampires."

"Revenge for what?"

"Trying to kill off my kind."


*RIALTO! SETA! ARIA has been abducted! I'm sorry, but I have failed you.*

Rialto's heart jumped into his throat and its beat roared in his ears as his mouth went bone dry.

*Christian? What happened?*

*It distracted me, tricked me so that I left her unattended for just a minute. That was all the time needed for her to be taken. I'm so sorry, Rialto.*

Rialto closed his eyes as an overwhelming sense of anger and fear rolled through him. He started to will it away so he could remain focused, but realized it was not his own emotion he was feeling. It was Aria's. He felt a mental tug, as though she were pulling him toward her.

*I can feel her. She's calling for me mentally. Can you tap into the link?*

*No.*

*Then keep your senses open. We're on our way back to Baltimore. When we get closer, you should feel us. Follow us. The killer is Carter Dunn. Find out what you can about him.*

*I will. Hurry.*

*You know we will.*

Rialto severed the link and looked at his mother. Seta gazed back at him with unmasked fury in her eyes. "Let's go get this demon," she growled. She waved an arm, spoke an incantation, and Culla Wasser's body disappeared, along with the blood that had pooled around it, leaving no evidence of her execution.

They had barely left the manor when Rialto's legs buckled, his energy spent from the run across two states. "Dammit, this can't be happening now! I just drank from Aria a few hours ago."

"Your body is growing more dependent on her blood, Rialto, forcing you into changing her over. I'll have to carry you if you want to make it to Baltimore."

Rialto glared at his mother, backing away when she reached for him. "You are not carrying me around like a baby."

She sighed. "Come on, Rialto. We don't have time for this. Oh, to hell with it, I'll teleport us. It'll take some of my strength away, but obviously Christian has drunk living blood or he couldn't have contacted us. He'll help us fight."

Rialto stepped into her embrace and leaned against her for support as she closed her eyes and said the words that would zap them back to Baltimore within a fraction of the time running would take.

Once they arrived, Rialto led the way, following the pull of Aria's emotions, sensing her location from signals she probably wasn't even aware of sending, but they were weakening. "I think the killer is draining her, Mother. Her signal is getting weaker."

"Then let's hurry or both of you will die."

Suddenly, Christian's voice was in his head. *216 Rouge Road. The home of Carter Dunn, great-grandson of Alfred Dunn. That seems to be where you're heading.*

*Good work, Christian. Are you prepared?*

*I have lived this long without killing. I hope to continue, but I will do whatever it takes to save Aria and defend my friends.*

*We'll see you there.*

Rialto and Seta broke the link to preserve their energies, knowing they wouldn't have time to replenish any by feeding. Besides, feeding wouldn't help Rialto. They trekked on, faster now that they had a destination. Rialto tried to hold it together as he felt Aria weakening, fearing he wouldn't get to her in time.

They reached the house, a white-brick single story, and quickly crossed the large yard to peer inside the windows. The house looked empty, but there was no denying Aria was inside. Rialto could feel her.

"Oh, what have they done to you, Eron?"

"What?" Rialto looked at his mother. She seemed to wither against the side of the house.

"I can feel him in there, what's left of him. He's nearly been destroyed."

"We'll save them both."

"Look!" Seta pointed to boarded-up basement windows which could barely be seen above ground. "That's where they are. I can feel it."

"Let's go."

"No!" Seta grabbed Rialto's arm before he made a dash for the front door. "You're not strong enough, and with what we're going up against, I can't fight this battle alone. We have to wait for Christian."

"Somebody say my name?" Christian appeared behind them with a struggling man hog-tied over his shoulders. "Give it a rest, Porter," he said, dropping the tawny-headed man's body to the ground with a thump and keeping him in place with his foot when he tried to stand.

"Damn you, you bloodsucking leeches. I'll kill you all!"

"Oh, great," Seta muttered. "As if we weren't going up against enough, you decided to bring your own archenemy."

"I thought it was better we knew where he was," Christian said with a shrug before turning back to the man who Rialto deduced was Jonah Porter's brother. "Now, Jake, if you want to get your brother out of here alive, I suggest you shut up and forget about all of your pent up anger against my kind, seeing as how we're the only ones who are going to help you."

"Well, pardon me for being pissed, but when someone decides to suck on my neck I'd prefer they have tits!" Jake spat as he tried to undo the ropes around his wrists.

"Hey, you were the only thing available or I'd have been choosier," Christian responded, kneeling down to unbind Porter's ankles. "So, Rialto, what are we dealing with here?"

"A man named Carter Dunn," Rialto answered.

"A man?" Jake laughed. "I can handle this myself."

"A man who has been reborn, fathered by a demon that was possessed by the devil himself!" Seta snapped, looking down at Jake Porter in disdain. "If you want to survive this night, you will do well to follow commands, mortal. This man has already managed to capture one of the oldest vampires around, and is skilled enough in the dark arts to have blocked his trace from the victims' bodies, even from me, a vampire-witch."

"A witch and a vampire, huh? Killing you will be a twofer."

Rialto issued a warning growl. "We're not your enemy, fool. If Carter has taken your brother, you'll need to be on our side if you want him back. We can't focus on destroying Carter Dunn if we have to be watching for you over our shoulders."

"Okay, I got it," Jake grumbled. "We're dealing with a souped-up demonic bastard. I'll side with you this once, but if my brother doesn't make it out alive, neither do any of you."

"We're getting everyone out," Seta promised.

Jake nodded. "So what's the story? What exactly are we up against?"

Seta answered. "Alfred Dunn's son, Patrick, was a child molester. Eron killed him and Alfred hunted him from that day on until he died from old age. Apparently, Alfred learned of some dark magic which allowed him to plan his reincarnation. He made a pact with the devil and was reborn as one of his granddaughter's twins."

"That's sick."

"Vengefulness tends to make people crazy." Seta gave Jake a pointed look before looking at Rialto. "Are we ready?"

"We have to be," Rialto answered, staring at the house intently. "She's slipping away." He looked at Christian, who had untied Jake and was helping him to his feet. "Are we all together on this?"

"Yes," Christian answered. "What's the plan?"

ARIA STRUGGLED TO see behind her while Carter taunted Eron with a fork-like tool. "Leave him alone! Haven't you hurt him enough?"

"Not nearly enough," Carter said and gave Eron one more poke with the tined instrument in his hand before coming back to the table. He stopped and threw his head back, sniffing the air. "Ah, they've arrived."

"What are you talking about?"

He looked down at Aria, mouth curved into an evil grin. "Didn't you realize you were bait? I can't have vampires knowing my secrets, hunting me down while I try to perfect my serum. I must kill all of you, thanks to

Curtis and his idiotic notion that he should let you view my journal."

Aria glared at Curtis, who had yet to utter a word or look her in the eye. "Why do you hate vampires so much?"

"Because that one killed me." Carter pointed to where Eron hung from the wall. "Once I reached Hell I became a member of Lucifer's special army. It's my job to stop the vampires and preselected bitches like you from destroying our kind."

The man was completely insane, Aria decided. "You're really psychotic."

"Psychos only think they've seen the devil," Carter said with a wicked smile. "He flows through me." Carter turned for the door which would allow him to exit the basement laboratory. "Watch them, Curtis, and if you help them in any way you will be a ball-less traitor, more so than you are now." He laughed as he left the lab.

Aria glared at Curtis with all the strength left in her. "I'm dying, Curtis, and the only man I've ever loved will die too, and it's all your fault."

"I'm sorry," Curtis cried, finally raising his head to look at her. "I didn't mean for this to happen. I was trying to help when I gave you the journal."

"Why didn't you just tell me your brother was insane?"

"Because there are two souls in me, Aria, and they battle each other every day."

"What the hell is he talking about?" Jonah asked, his words laced in pain. "He's as crazy as the other one."

"He's Alfred Dunn," Eron rasped, his voice barely audible. "I finally figured it out."

Aria started to ask Curtis if that was true, but a wave of dizziness washed over her and she blacked out. But not before realizing the drops of her blood spilling into the bucket beneath the table were coming much slower.

"YOU KNOW, IT would've been really great if you'd let me bring some of my weapons," Jake said angrily as the four crawled through the living room window, staying vigilant as they entered the house.

"Shut up, Porter," the three vampires said in unison while they studied the room. Besides a large heap of books, some ratty old furniture, and statues of demons and humans in various sexual poses, the room was bare.

"Porter and Christian, find the basement and get everyone out. Seta and I will handle Carter. He probably already knows we're here."

"Score one point for the vampires," Carter said, stepping into the room. "Now excuse me while I kill you."

He threw his hands up and chanted something that sounded dark and menacing before fire sprang to life in his palms. He hurled the flames toward them, but Seta quickly stood in front of the group and threw up her hands, redirecting the flames back at Carter.

Christian and Jake ran to the left, leaving the room in search of the basement as Rialto and Seta stayed behind to battle.

"A witch, eh?" Carter asked after shielding himself from the fire. "You'll be fun to kill."

"You'll die trying, anyway," Seta retorted and threw a ball of energy at Carter, ramming him against the wall and pinning him there with an invisible weight.

"She's fading!" Rialto cried, feeling Aria slip deeper away.

"Go to her!" Seta shouted over the roar of energies spiraling around her. "You're of no use to us if you're both dead. Save her and save yourself!"

"Will you be all right?"

"Yes! I can hold him off by myself for a little while."

Rialto ran out of the room, following Aria's scent to the basement below. He entered the subterranean room to find Christian removing Eron from where he hung on a wall. Jake Porter stepped over the body of Carter Dunn's beaten twin and started to remove his brother's manacles.

Aria lay on a metal table in the middle of the room, two tubes in the side of her neck leading to a bucket below the table. She was bleeding to death. "Aria!" Rialto ran to her and stared down at her in horror. Her skin had begun to darken when he'd left her earlier, but due to the blood loss it was now a deathly pale. Her lips were dry and cracked, and dark rings had formed beneath her eyes.

"She had already lost too much by the time we arrived," Christian said apologetically as he approached them. "I don't think putting her blood back into her will help. Her organs have most likely started to shut down. There's only one way to save her now."

Rialto nodded, understanding he had a choice to make. He either saved Aria, or he died with her. "My mother needs help."

"Of course." Christian gestured for Jake to follow him, and together they left the lab, Jake helping his brother to walk.

"What are you waiting for?" Eron asked from where he lay on the floor. "Save her."

"It's not my choice. It's hers," Rialto answered as he removed the tubes from her neck and covered the holes with his hand, feeling her barely throbbing pulse.

"She's nearly gone," Eron rasped.

"I know," Rialto said, feeling tears well into his eyes. He held Aria's hand in his much larger one and spoke her name. Her eyelids fluttered open, widening when she saw him standing over her.

"Rialto." She tried to smile, her green eyes sparkling with a hint of tears as they met his somber brown ones. "I knew you'd save me," she said weakly.

Rialto swallowed past the ball of emotion lodged in his throat and shook his head. "You've lost a lot of blood. We were too late."

"But you're here now." Her forehead wrinkled in confusion. "You can save me now."

Rialto's head and heart ached with the choice being forced upon him. He'd only sired one other vampire, and she went mad. Antonia hadn't deserved what happened to her, and the thought of the same thing happening to Aria clawed at his insides.

"I'm not Antonia," Aria said, seeming to read his mind. "I want the gift."

"It's not a gift, Aria. It's a curse."

"Rialto—"

"Listen to me." He bit his lip, knowing he didn't have much time to search for the right words. Instead, he looked into her trusting eyes and spoke from his heart. "I love you, Aria. In the two centuries I have walked this earth, I've never felt a love so pure and strong. I don't want to let you die, but whether or not you stay with me isn't my choice."

"Rialto—"

"No, wait." He placed a finger over her parched lips and prayed for the time he needed. He could feel her fading away quickly. "I can save you if I share my blood with you, but by doing so I'll turn you into what I am. You'll be a predator, Aria. You will have to drink human blood to survive, and you may eventually be forced to kill. If you can handle the knowledge of that, then I will save you right now. Can you handle the loneliness of outliving everyone around you? The thought of being a monster, an outcast? Can you live in my darkness?"

Aria smiled so weakly it ripped away a part of Rialto's heart. "I—" She swallowed, although her throat was undoubtedly dry, trying to finish her sentence. "I finished the dream, and I figured out what Seta meant too, about my mother giving birth to me out of love. She loved my father, and she had his baby despite the risks. I love you, Rialto, and I want to have your baby despite the danger, despite whatever we will go through to protect her. And you're not a monster. I would be honored to be what you are."

Rialto smiled, blinking back tears. "Are you sure?"

"Yes, now save me, Rialto. Save us both and save our future child. I want to spend forever walking beside you in the twilight."

Rialto nodded and lowered his mouth to the holes in her neck, suckling what was left of her blood, praying there was enough left for the transition.

He sipped from her until she hovered just over death, and then he quickly brought his wrist to his mouth, cutting a narrow gash across the skin. He lowered his wrist to her lips and fed her from it, allowing her to drink the nectar from him that would give her exactly what she'd asked for. The promise of forever with him by her side.

He started to feel dizzy as she greedily devoured his blood, but he didn't have the heart to pull away. She had lost so much. The more he could give her the better, he thought, as blackness engulfed him and he faded into darkness.


"LEAVE ME."

"Not a chance in hell," Jake muttered as he half-drug his brother toward the room where the vampires and the demon were fighting. "Kick your pansy ass into gear and let's get out of here."

"Leave me and help them. They have to get out before the police come, and I have to be here to explain this mess."

"You want me to help a bunch of bloodsuckers?"

"That vampire hanging on the opposite wall from me was so hungry he ached, but according to that son-of-a-bitch psycho, he wouldn't touch any victims that were brought to him. They're not the bad guys here."

Jake muttered a curse as he lowered his brother to the floor. "I can't just leave you."

"I'm the detective on this case, and there are vampires killing the murderer. Vampires, Jake. How am I supposed to explain that?" Jonah shook his head. "Look at me. I've been beaten to a pulp. I can't just waltz back in to work like nothing has happened. Just be a good little brother and do as I say. Leave me here. I saw gallons of blood and all kinds of satanic crap downstairs. The department will believe me when I say I don't remember a lot if they find me here like this, and with all the evidence they'll find in this place, I won't have to explain much of anything. I can let them draw their own conclusions."

"They're going to want to know how you happened to come across the killer in the first place. What are you going to say? A demon possessed man kidnapped you right out of your car?"

"Aside from the demon part, that'll work. The killer was on to me, and he got me before I got him which is pretty much true. It'll bruise my ego, but it's better than telling them about the vampires and spending a long vacation in the loony bin."

Jake cursed, knowing his brother was right. "You're banged up pretty bad, Joe."

"Then hurry the hell up and clear out of here so I can call myself an ambulance."

Jake nodded and made his way toward the room where the fighting was going on. There was a loud ear-splitting crack as he approached, and he threw his arms in front of his face to block out the blinding light. He heard a woman scream, followed by evil laughter, and knew the vampire-witch was losing the fight.

"I hate demons," he muttered as he looked at his defenseless hands. He didn't even have rock salt or holy water with him.

The light faded and he looked in the room to see Carter Dunn standing over the witch's fallen body. Christian was on his knees, spouting out Latin with his hands clasped together under his chin.

"What the hell?" Jake muttered, knowing Dunn could easily kill the vamp and then he'd be the only one left to defend the rest of them. And he didn't have any way of trapping the demon so he could perform an exorcism, either. He'd be dead before the first few words were out of his mouth.

But as he watched, he was surprised to see Dunn look toward Christian in fear as the vampire continued spewing out Latin. A halo of light formed around Christian, the witch and, more to his surprise, himself.

Roaring, the demon made a lunge for the vampire, but the halo of light burned through his skin and forced him backward.

Seta rose, renewed strength blazing brightly in her eyes as she raised her hands and used magic to pin Dunn against the wall.

Christian opened his eyes, stared straight ahead at Dunn and in English thanked the father, the son and the holy ghost.

With a high-pitched scream, Carter Dunn turned into flame and then fell to the floor as a pile of assorted charred limbs.

Jake looked at Christian and found the vampire smirking at him, amused by the shock he knew was etched on his face.

"What the hell was that?"

"The power of prayer," the vampire responded matter-of-factly. "If you wouldn't mind, Mr. Porter, we will need some help getting our friends out of here."

Jake could only gape at the vampires as they passed him to collect their friends.

# Chapter Seventeen

RIALTO BLINKED, the grogginess of the day sleep beginning to evaporate. He didn't recall making it back to the soft bed he was lying in. His last memory was of feeding Aria . . .

Aria!

He sat up, taking in his surroundings. He was in Christian's home beneath the church. "Aria!" He called as loudly as his voice would allow. The sound of running feet echoed in the hallway moments before Seta and Christian entered the room.

"You're awake!" Seta exclaimed, joy prominent in her voice.

"Yes, I'm awake. Where is Aria? Is she alive?" His heart constricted in his chest, threatening to cease beating if she hadn't survived.

"Yes!" Seta cried, kissing his cheeks and forehead. "I was so worried about you. You gave her too much blood and passed out. I had to feed you myself, and the both of you have been at rest since last night."

"Come on." She grabbed his hand and led him through the hall to the next bedroom where Aria lay sleeping on top of the bed, her skin browned by his blood, her lips a deep crimson.

"She has not awakened yet?"

"No. It's barely nightfall," Seta said as she pulled two chairs beside the bed and gestured for Rialto to sit next to her.

"What if she wakes like Antonia?"

"She won't," Christian assured him, approaching from behind to rest his hands on his shoulders. "It is not her fate."

Rialto breathed deeply, trying to soothe his nerves. The images of the night before assaulted him. "Oh my God, what happened? Did you kill Carter? Where's Eron?"

Seta looked sad for a moment, but quickly waved the emotion away. "Eron was so injured we had to put him in the earth."

"He died?" Rialto's heart plummeted to somewhere near the bottom of his stomach.

"No!" Seta quickly shook her head from side to side "He has reached the age where he can go underground for long periods of time. The earth will heal him and he will rise stronger."

Rialto released a breath of relief. "And Carter?"

"We destroyed him. He almost overpowered me, but Christian saved us all with his prayers. Between my powers and Christian's faith, we took him out." She looked over at Christian and smiled. "But, he wasn't Alfred Dunn, as we had believed."

"Then who was he?"

"Patrick Dunn. Alfred made a deal with the devil to bring back both he and his son so they could be together again."

"So Curtis was Alfred?"

"It appears so. That's what he told Eron, Aria, and Jonah before he escaped."

"Escaped?"

"He was unconscious before Christian and the Porters left the lab. Eron could barely move, and you had passed out. He got away before we destroyed his son, or brother, or whatever he was, and made it back to you."

"Is he a threat to us?"

"I don't know. He was sick enough to deal with the devil, requesting to be brought back to life through his own granddaughter's body. Jonah said he'd made a comment about being two souls. I believe the old soul, Alfred, is fighting against the new soul, Curtis."

"Well, let's hope the new soul wins the fight."

"Amen," Seta murmured. "On the bright side, I don't think Jake Porter is going to chase Christian out of his church again. We seem to have his gratitude."

"I guess he's pissed his brother got pinned to a wall."

"Apparently. It takes the heat off of us for a while, anyway." She patted Rialto's leg and stood. "She'll wake soon, darling."

Seta and Christian left him beside Aria's bed, waiting for her to rise. He felt beads of sweat pop out on his forehead and lowered his head into his hands, unable to bear the wait. "Please let her be all right," he prayed as he waited for the results of what he had done.

"Rialto?"

He looked up to see Aria sitting on the bed, glorious in her newly darkened skin which was offset by the long white gown Seta had dressed her in. Her eyes had deepened to a blinding shade of emerald.

"Aria?" Rialto sprang from the chair to stand at Aria's bedside and hugged her to his chest before pulling away to look her over. "How are you? How do you feel?"

"Better than ever." Her smile lit the room. "And terribly hungry."

Rialto felt panic start to set in as images of Antonia devouring a whole village ran through his mind.

"Relax, Rialto. I'm not that hungry."

He laughed at the look in Aria's eyes. "I forgot that you will be able to see inside my head so clearly now. And that part of the changing includes you waking hungry. I must take you to feed, and the cycle will be complete. You will be a vampire. You must drink from a living mortal, Aria. Can you do that?"

She seemed to think that over. "I guess, but can it be a really bad person?"

"Yes," Rialto said with a laugh, "but don't tell me you're ready to kill."

"Of course not!" The look of indignation on her face was priceless. "But I just can't rob the blood of somebody who doesn't deserve it."

"So, what's your pleasure? Mugger, child abuser, or pimp?"

Aria pressed her lips together, deep in thought. When she looked into Rialto's eyes, hers were sparkling. "The man who lives in the apartment below mine. He beats his wife and once took a crowbar to Trevaris when he tried to intervene. Let's go lunch on him!"

Rialto laughed at her enthusiasm, but quickly sobered, realizing he was going to have to take her away from her friend. "Aria, you know you'll have to move from the apartment and say goodbye to Trevaris and any other friends you might have. That goodbye will be forever. You can't have mortal friends. It's too dangerous."

"I know," she said, standing from the bed to wrap her arms around his waist. "I just wanted to do Trevaris a favor before I have to leave."

"Do you resent me for taking you away from everything you know?"

Aria laughed. "You worry too much. I love you, and if this Blood Revelation thing is true, we're going to have a baby. What more do I need to know?"

"Well, when you say it like that . . ." Rialto smiled, finally able to let go of all his doubts and believe things were going to work out. He dipped his head to kiss Aria's blood-red lips, and in the moment, when their hearts melded together, he saw the image of their unborn daughter.

"What just happened?" he asked in surprise as he pulled back to look into Aria's wet eyes.

"I think that was a gift from my mom, her way of letting me know I've done the right thing and that we're going to be fine. It turns out she was a witch, you know."

"So I've heard." He dipped his head once more, brushing a kiss over her full lips. "Our daughter is gorgeous."

"And destined for greatness," Aria murmured, pulling his mouth back down to hers. "Just wait and see."

*The End*

Printed in Great Britain
by Amazon

44123456R00108